OCT 1 5 2014

W9-BZV-187

The Edison Effect

Books by Bernadette Pajer

The Professor Bradshaw Mysteries
A Spark of Death
Fatal Induction
Capacity for Murder
The Edison Effect

The Edison Effect

A Professor Bradshaw Mystery

Bernadette Pajer

Poisoned Pen Press

Library of Congress Catalog Card Number: 2014938498

ISBN: 9781464202506   Hardcover
       9781464202520   Trade Paperback

Poisoned Pen Press
6962 E. First Ave., Ste. 103
Scottsdale, AZ 85251
www.poisonedpenpress.com
info@poisonedpenpress.com

Printed in the United States of America

To Bill Beaty, my go-to science guy, and George Myers,
who introduced me to his great-great grandfather,
Professor Joseph Marion Taylor.

Chapter One

"Bradshaw, it's Thomas Edison! He's here!"

Of all the interruptions, this one was so unexpected that Professor Benjamin Bradshaw wondered if he'd not yet fully recovered from his concussion.

It was a warm summer afternoon on the campus of the University of Washington. A box kite danced below billowy white clouds drifting in the blue sky, and a touch of color in the elm saplings hinted at the approach of fall.

Bradshaw stood on the lawn between Lewis and Clark Halls, arms outstretched to Missouri Fremont as she abandoned Colin Ingersoll and his kite. She approached Bradshaw with a smile that took his breath away. This was a moment he'd resisted for two years. A moment he wasn't sure was wise. The differences between him and Missouri might be insurmountable, and yet, here he was. His heart thundered. He doubted he'd ever been happier—or more frightened—in his entire life.

Little more than a week had passed since he'd been left for dead in a rotting cellar during an investigation of gruesome murders. He'd thought himself fully recovered, other than a dull ache in his shoulder where the weight of a cast iron frying pan had struck, until the shout about Thomas Edison pierced his overwhelmed emotions. For a terrifying second, he thought he might still be back in that cellar, hallucinating.

Certainly, such romantic moments were rare for him. As Missouri approached, he knew he would never forget this moment, the way her dark amber eyes gleamed with joy and affection, the way the golden highlights shimmered in her short mahogany hair. She moved in her summery gown with the grace of a queen and the bounce of a child.

Their fingertips had not yet touched when the shout carried to him again, its urgency penetrating his cocoon of fearful happiness.

"Bradshaw! It's Edison!"

As he continued to gaze into Missouri's eyes, he was aware that Colin Ingersoll had turned toward the shout. Colin, a lanky and likable engineering student, was Missouri's would-be suitor, and he was no doubt confused by Missouri's abandoning his side to welcome Bradshaw so warmly.

"Hurry!" Assistant Professor Hill came running toward them from the direction of the Administration Building, shouting, "It's Thomas Edison! Here to see you!"

Missouri's eyes flickered with delight. She asked, "Is it *the* Thomas Edison, do you suppose? The Wizard of Menlo Park?"

Bradshaw smiled. "He has been known to attempt to steal the great moments of other men's lives."

"Are you and I in the midst of a great moment?"

"Only if you consider me confiding my feelings for you a great moment."

She gave a little gasp.

And then Hill was upon them, panting and grinning and tipping his hat to Missouri. He grabbed Bradshaw's arm and pulled. "Come on!"

◇◇◇

It's disconcerting to enter a deeply familiar place and find a celebrity there, a man one had previously seen only in published photographs or artistic renderings. But here he was, Thomas Edison in the flesh, in Bradshaw's own office on the second floor of the Administration Building. In his mid-fifties, his hair thin and white, his complexion pale, he yet exuded strength. He wore an expensively tailored, crumpled suit, and his sagging posture revealed a lifetime at the workbench.

Bradshaw had grown up knowing the great inventor's name. He'd been twelve when Edison, eighteen years his senior, invented the phonograph, and fourteen when the first practical light bulb secured Edison a place in history. As Bradshaw's own curiosity and exploration into electrical matters became an obsession, he'd read everything he could get his hands on about the man. He knew that Edison had only three months of formal schooling before being labeled "addled" by his teacher, and so he'd been homeschooled by his mother, who had encouraged his curiosity. Edison had been flat broke and sleeping in office basements in New York when, by chance, he'd impressed a stock broker by fixing a stock ticker, winning the man's admiration and a high-paying job. Soon after, he invented an improved stock ticker, which he sold for a small fortune. He'd used those funds to build an electrical empire. Yes, there was much Bradshaw admired about Thomas Edison.

And much he disliked. There were far too many stories of greed for them all to be the mere fuming of jealous rivals. It was well known he'd cheated Nikola Tesla out of promised wages. And the War of the Currents a decade ago, pitting alternating current against direct current, had gotten downright ugly. It was still ugly. Rather than accept the scientific fact that each current had applications for which it was best suited, Edison continued to slander alternating current and those he considered his rivals. To protect the income from his many patented direct-current devices, he performed public stunts, such as electrocuting stray animals, in attempts to put fear of alternating current into the hearts of the general public. Just this past January, Edison had electrocuted an elephant in a bizarre display, which he captured on moving film.

Still, childhood impressions are deep-seated, and Bradshaw felt his palms dampen at the sight of Thomas Edison standing by his office window, looking at a copy of *American Electrician*. Edison didn't turn when he entered, even though Bradshaw had spoken to Hill at the door, telling him to wait in the hall and make sure they weren't disturbed by eager students who were already lining up to meet the famous inventor.

"They will have their chance once I've spoken to him."

Hill whispered eagerly, "But why is he here?"

"I have no idea," said Bradshaw, closing the door with an audible click, wondering if Edison had heard. It was said that the famous inventor of Menlo Park was nearly deaf.

Bradshaw began to move toward Edison's peripheral vision to announce his presence without startling him, but Edison's senses must have been heightened by his hearing loss because he spoke as if fully aware that Bradshaw had shut the door on adoring fans. "When they stop being eager to see me, that's when I'll worry."

Edison's voice was pitched higher than Bradshaw expected. It contrasted with his fierce reputation. "They are our future, Professor Bradshaw, and their excitement both inspires and depresses me. Think of all they will invent, and all we will miss, because of our mortality." He closed the magazine and returned it to the shelf, then he at last turned to Bradshaw, his wide mouth spread in a grin, his blue-green eyes warm with intelligence and humor.

Bradshaw quickly wiped his hand on his jacket before offering it. "It's a pleasure to meet you, Mr. Edison." He didn't shout, but he did enunciate carefully. He'd read that Edison could hear well enough in a quiet room to converse easily.

"Likewise, Professor Bradshaw."

They shook hands, and Bradshaw knew he was beaming. It wasn't every day that one met a childhood hero.

"Have a seat. Can I get you anything? Water? Coffee? I can send to the dorms for some lemonade."

Edison took the offered seat near the bookcase but refused refreshment. Bradshaw sat opposite him.

"I haven't got much time, so I'll get right to the point, Professor. I've been hearing for some time now about a former student of yours, the one who tried to assassinate President McKinley."

Bradshaw's enthusiasm dissolved into disappointment, then anger. He hadn't realized how flattered he'd felt that Edison had chosen to pay him a visit until this revelation that his visit had nothing to do with him.

"Oscar Daulton," Bradshaw said quietly.

"Eh?"

"Oscar Daulton," he said more distinctly.

"Yes, that's the name. I'm told he invented a device that could transform direct current, and I came to see if there was any truth to it, or if it's simply an electrical tall tale."

Bradshaw cleared his throat. "It's uncertain. He did display a device that appeared to do just that. And I believe he used that device to set a trap to assassinate McKinley, but the president's visit to Seattle was cancelled and the trap killed my colleague instead."

"You believe? You're not completely certain?"

"I can't be certain when I have no proof. I never saw the internal workings of the device, and my deductions over how Oglethorpe died were based on circumstantial evidence. Oscar Daulton confessed to the crime, but he would not explain how it was done nor verify my conclusions. And you likely heard that before his arrest he threw the device overboard into Elliott Bay."

"But you saw it? In operation? This device of his?"

"The one and only time I saw Daulton's device was during a student exhibition in the spring of '01."

Edison sat forward expectantly. Bradshaw struggled with conflicting emotions. Here was an opportunity to discuss with the famous inventor something potentially history-making. Yet here, too, was the danger of glorifying a device invented by a madman with the intent to kill. Edison abhorred weapons and was vocal about his intention never to invent them. Yet he was also a man irresistibly drawn to new ideas.

"Tell me," said Edison, his tone friendly, his eyes demanding.

Bradshaw came to the decision that there was no harm in stating what had already been made public. "The device was housed in a large cigar box," he began, "and the working components hidden within." He went on to describe the bank of glass jar batteries and a silent electric flame arcing between metal rods that protruded from the cigar box.

"Come now, Bradshaw. A silent air gap? That makes no sense. Surely there was some buzzing or such, you just didn't hear it. Was there a lot of background noise at this exhibition? Chatter and clanking and all manner of sounds?"

"There was some noise, but on the whole the event was subdued. I expected a loud buzz from the flame, but heard none."

Edison took no notes, but he gave Bradshaw the distinct impression he was memorizing every word and visualizing the device. The grooves between his eyes, developed, no doubt, from years of close scrutiny and study, deepened.

"Was there much heat from the cigar box?"

A tap at the door saved Bradshaw from an immediate reply. He excused himself and opened the door slightly to find a telegram delivery boy, a freckle-faced youth familiar to him. Behind him, a crowd of students and staff milled expectantly, a few craning their necks to see into Bradshaw's office.

The boy beamed with self-importance, tipping his cap. "Telegram, sir."

"Thank you very much." He signed the receipt and reached into his pocket for a coin, then exchanged the tip for the message. The boy turned and swaggered importantly through the crowd. Bradshaw tucked the wire in his pocket without reading it and heard whispers of, "Did you see him?" before he softly closed the door.

In that short time, Mr. Edison had seated himself at Bradshaw's desk and helped himself to the sketch pad and a pencil.

"What were the dimensions of the cigar box?"

Bradshaw stood beside Edison, estimating as best he could the size of the box, the number of batteries in the bank, the length of the rods, and the distance between them.

"Rather small for what it was purported to do. Was there much heat?" Edison asked again.

"When I placed my hand upon the box, I felt no heat."

Edison looked up at him. "Eh? No heat?"

"No heat at all. But then, it had only been on a minute or so before I touched it."

Edison studied his sketch again.

"You say it was powered only by this bank of batteries and yet displayed a steady arc across the rods? The current shouldn't have been sufficient to make the leap."

"No, it shouldn't have been."

Edison frowned over the diagram. The silence of the room became heavy with what they weren't saying, about the War of the Currents, about Edison's resentment over the triumph of alternating current. The proverbial elephant in the room had an all-too-real counterpart that had lost its life at Coney Island. If it truly worked as demonstrated, Daulton's invention could be Edison's greatest revenge against Nikola Tesla and Westinghouse and the backers of alternating current.

Bradshaw said carefully, "I questioned Daulton about it, and he refused to explain. He did say, however, that the device also worked with alternating current."

"That was reported in your city's paper, but I gave it no credit. Reporters know nothing of electricity."

"In this case, the report was accurate. He did say it."

"Are you sure it wasn't a trick of some sort?"

"No, I can't be sure."

"There must be evidence somewhere, someone the young man confided in, notes he took, materials he used."

Bradshaw moved around his desk to sit opposite Edison, feeling like a guest in his own office.

"Oscar Daulton was a troubled young man. He had no close friends, and his family disowned him after he was arrested. Only I visited him in jail, and he refused to confide in me. I inherited all his worldly possessions, which amounted to very little, including a personal journal in which he never wrote of his electrical experiments. I searched everywhere I could think of, from his dorm room to the hut by the lake where he was known to study, but found nothing. Although he was often unnerved by life, he displayed an impressive ability for memorization when calm. It could be that he devised his inventions in his mind and never recorded anything, as a way of ensuring secrecy."

Mr. Edison dropped the pencil and sat back. "Sneaky little

bastard. I can't abide a weak man, Professor. I don't understand them. Nothing I have was given to me, and nothing came easy."

Bradshaw resisted the urge to defend Oscar Daulton, who had been weak, it was true. His mental and emotional instability had been his undoing. But the boy had not been dealt a fair hand in life, and he hadn't been born with the resources to handle either the humiliation of his family's treatment of him or the horrors of war. His life might have turned out differently had he not been haunted by what he witnessed while serving in the Philippines.

"What's your theory, Professor? Surely you've come up with some ideas. You've got a patent or two, and a reputation for cleverness, I'm told, solving crimes for the police. What do you make of it? How did he do it?"

Bradshaw met Edison's gaze squarely. "I don't know."

Edison said nothing, but his jaw was set tight and he scrunched his mouth, either in disappointment or disbelief. Bradshaw hadn't spent enough time with him to know which, but Edison stood with a swiftness that shouted his time had been wasted.

He tore the sketch of the device from the pad, folded it precisely, and tucked it into an inner jacket pocket.

"Well, Professor, I appreciate your time."

Bradshaw resisted the impulse to apologize. "It was an honor to meet you, sir," he said instead.

Edison started for the door, then halted, pointing across the room to a table by the window. There sat a small wooden box painted to depict Santa Claus and a Christmas tree and smiling children holding festoons of colorful electric lights. "I brought you a sample. They'll be in department stores across the country by the holidays. We're the first to the market with pre-strung lamps."

The "we," Bradshaw knew, meant Edison and the General Electric Company.

"Congratulations. And thank you." Bradshaw had years ago devised his own festoons of colored electric lights that he placed on the Christmas tree each year, but he knew it was a luxury most Americans couldn't afford since it required a skilled electrician to wire them. Prewired lights would be a money-maker.

With a nod, Edison opened the door to his adoring fans. Bradshaw crossed to the window, his thoughts spinning. Even the sight of the dancing box kite and of Missouri once again at Ingersoll's side failed to pull him from the implications of Edison's inquiry.

He'd not told the whole truth, and he sensed Edison knew it. No inventor could resist exploring the mystery of Oscar Daulton's invention, not even Bradshaw. Despite his qualms, despite the moral conundrum surrounding the murderous use of Daulton's discovery, Bradshaw had been compelled by inventor's curiosity to follow clues. He was nearly certain that melted sulfur had been used as an insulator. And the components the sulfur insulated? He had ideas about those, too. Ideas that at times made his hands itch. But as yet the moral dilemma of what to do with the knowledge had held him back from exploring them, even from thinking too deeply about the possible flaws and feasibility of his guesses. If he was right about Daulton's invention, it was both genius and yet obvious, and ironically based on something Edison himself had discovered many years ago. If he was right, Daulton's invention followed a natural evolution in electrical engineering. The world of invention would grow in leaps and bounds, even faster than now, once it became known. And yet. And yet. The device had been used to kill.

Bradshaw couldn't come to terms with it.

Someone would discover it eventually. Someone else. Without his help.

A movement below caught his eye. He saw Edison descend the wide stone steps of the building and head down the path that led to Fifteenth Avenue, surrounded and trailed by admirers for whom he was granting autographs as he walked. Among the group was the messenger boy who'd delivered the telegram, reminding Bradshaw he hadn't yet read the message.

He pulled the telegram from his pocket and glanced at the sender's location: Shoreham, Long Island, New York. The message read simply: TELL EDISON NOTHING and was signed N. TESLA.

Chapter Two

December, 1903

On a cold, dark, wet morning, as Bradshaw entered the picket gate before his home at 1204 Gallagher on Capitol Hill in Seattle, the front door flew open and his son came running out in his stockinged feet.

Bradshaw knew Justin's exuberance had nothing to do with his father's early-morning return home from the scene of an electrical fire. From the dark, drizzly sky, a few white flakes fell.

"Snow!" Justin shouted, his face turned up to the precipitation. Bradshaw swallowed admonishments about wet socks, understanding that to Justin snow was a rare and magnificent event. His own childhood in Boston had been blanketed white for days at a time, and he'd spent countless hours digging tunnels and building forts.

He gently prodded his son up onto the covered porch and they stood together, watching for flakes between the cold raindrops.

"Will it last?" At ten and a half, Justin stood nearly five feet tall, but his voice was still little-boyish, and he was able to give hope more credence than the factual evidence before his eyes. A few hours earlier, when Bradshwa had been summoned to the Ballard Power Plant, the flakes had been huge and prolific, covering the wet streets and the fringes of the smoldering building in a thin white sheet. By the time he had determined the fire's origin to be a burned-out transformer, the whiteness had vanished. The temperature was nearly forty, he gauged, and not likely to drop.

"I'm afraid not, son. Best get your boots. I'll walk you to school."

Bradshaw believed the paving of Broadway, the main business street atop Capitol Hill, to be a vast improvement over the old dirt and gravel road, especially on miserably wet winter mornings. But his son and the neighbor boy, Paul, who accompanied them, bemoaned the lack of really good mud puddles and had to content themselves with small pools of rain that formed in the shallows of the concrete sidewalks and gleamed in the light of the arc street lamps. Justin was particularly expert at angling his rubber boot before stomping in such a way that he could aim the spray precisely on target. The target being Paul, who leaped out of the way just in time.

They arrived, damp but presentable, at the corner of Broadway and Madison where Justin and Paul were enrolled in the grammar school operated by the Jesuits of the Seattle College. Bradshaw watched them disappear inside, heard the final clang of the door as the last student arrived, sensed the noise of the waking city around and below him—streetcars, wagons, trains, pedestrians—but none of it concerned him. Nor did he move. He stood in the drizzle, chewing his lip, staring at the steps that led up into the church, knowing Father McGuinness was inside.

Since September, he'd postponed what must be done. He'd promised Missouri he would have a frank discussion with his priest while she was away. He now had less than a week until she returned home for Christmas. But his feet felt glued to the concrete.

A physician of homeopathy. That was her goal, and he had no doubt she would succeed. She'd passed with high marks the entrance exams to the Hahnemann Homeopathic College in Philadelphia without any sort of special preparation, demonstrating excellence in English, Latin, and algebra, and a respectable understanding of physics. One week. That's all they'd had together before she'd left to pursue her dream. One week of looking into her eyes without hiding his love. One week of feeling like a much younger man, full of hope and happiness. After a decade of emotional isolation from anyone save his son, and more than two years of loving Missouri Fremont from afar, he felt as if he'd been broken open. He didn't entirely like it. He felt vulnerable. Exposed. Foolish.

He'd come to the conclusion that romantic love, this sort of head-over-heels love, was for much younger men. While he was not yet forty, he was but a year and a half away from that milestone. If he were lucky and lived a long life, he was now middle-aged. He was a respected professor, private investigator, father. He'd established a solid, comfortable, secure life and he had no wish to do cartwheels down the street. Or cry like a child.

Yet he'd nearly done both. He'd been so choked up waiting with Missouri for her train at the station, he'd had trouble speaking, and he wondered at her ability to leave him. How could she? Did she not love him as much as he loved her?

"You could visit me," she'd said in reply to his brimming eyes as they stood surrounded by other waiting passengers.

He'd said past the lump in his throat, "What if we married?"

It was not a matter foreign to them, but one they had not decided conclusively. There were variables, obstacles. Barriers. She searched his eyes, and he could see she was wondering at his meaning, questioning his asking when nothing had yet been resolved. She said carefully, "Are you proposing?"

"It's a supposition. What if we married?"

She continued to look hard at him. "I have four years of schooling ahead of me."

"What if we married …instead?"

"You're asking me to give up homeopathy?"

"I'm not opposed to you being a doctor, I just can't fathom living without you for years."

"There are no homeopathic colleges here, you know that. And now that I know it's my calling in life …it's part of me. It's bigger than me. The homeopathic approach to healing is being threatened." She'd launched into a passionate speech about how the American Medical Association was determined to wipe out homeopathy, a topic now familiar to him, but he'd heard very little as he looked into her passionate amber eyes and silently begged her not to go. Her words penetrated his silent pleading when she said, "For me, it's more than a calling, it's matter of faith, of believing in something important and living in a way that supports that belief. Can you understand that?"

And there they were, at the crux of it. The reason why his question had been a supposition and not a proposal. He said quietly, "Indeed, I can." He did not need to mention Catholicism.

She took a step nearer him, and all the people and noise of the platform became an insulating blur around them. She said without accusation yet with piercing directness, "Do you feel it would be a sin to marry me?"

"We've been through this."

"No, we've discussed the laws of your church. I'm asking if you believe in those laws. Do you believe it would be a sin to marry me? Immoral? An act wrong in the eyes of what you call God?"

"Don't we believe in the same God?"

"What's in a name? That which we call a rose by any other name would smell as sweet."

"Missouri, the play you quote ends in tragedy."

"Making it even more appropriate. I have no idea why anyone considers *Romeo and Juliet* the least bit romantic. It infuriates me. Two lovers choose death rather than follow their hearts and cast off the artificial bonds of family name."

"You can't be comparing family loyalty to religious faith."

"Can't I? Both demand members adhere to strict manmade rules at the cost of natural harmony."

"You have no faith?"

"You know that's not true. I have faith in love and kindness and decency and passion and the beauty of nature and the miracle of life."

"You didn't mention God," he said.

"Didn't I? We're back to the rose again."

"Couldn't we deal with this issue simply? Without a complete reevaluation of the strictures of the Catholic Church?" Or, he thought, a complete upheaval of his understanding of the nature of God?

She said, "In other words, you want me to go through the motions and pretend to be Catholic to avoid the messiness of the two of us actually acting according to our true beliefs."

"Yes. Could you?"

"You wouldn't respect me if I did that."

"I'd be willing to make that sacrifice."

"I wouldn't. Now, Mr. Bradshaw—"

"Yesterday, you called me Ben."

"But today, I'm about to board a train and I can see from the look in your eyes and the direction of our conversation that you're having a difficult time letting me leave, and I fear such an intimacy would send you over the brink. I know how you hate a public spectacle."

He found himself once again unable to speak.

She said, "I know I am frustrating you, and I don't want you to feel completely hopeless. So I'll confess. I was baptized in the Catholic Church, my father insisted. It means nothing to me, but it means something to the Church, and it may prove helpful when you speak to your priest."

Only now, he had no faith her confession would help. What good was a baptism if she no longer considered herself a Catholic, if she didn't actively practice? Or believe?

And so he stood in the cold drizzle, stomach churning, feet planted, dreading the discussion he must have, a talk that could end in one of two ways. Either he would have to abandon the Church, or abandon Missouri. Food or water.

He was spared the dreaded conversation by Detective James O'Brien of the Seattle Police, who hopped off the streetcar and joined him on the sidewalk. In his usual garb, a long dark coat and Roosevelt hat, and with a friendly, freckled face and intelligent eyes, he always put Bradshaw in mind of a cowboy-priest.

He was neither, of course, being both a city man and a married father of four, but he was Catholic. Besides Henry Pratt, he was Bradshaw's closest friend. He knew about Bradshaw's dilemma and sided with the Church. He thought Bradshaw should find a nice Catholic girl, like he'd done. Bradshaw had never intended to look for a girl, Catholic or otherwise. He'd been content as a widower. Mrs. Prouty, his stout and stern but devoted housekeeper twenty years his senior had been the only woman in his life until that fateful evening a couple years ago when he opened his front door to find Missouri Fremont on his porch.

O'Brien said, "Mrs. Prouty reported your calendar shows a class at noon today. Can you cancel?"

"I can call in a substitute if necessary." Assistant Professor Hill was qualified to cover the class, but Bradshaw tried to not let his investigations interfere with his teaching. "What have you got?"

"You know Vernon Doyle?"

"Electrician at the Bon Marché?"

"He was found dead this morning in a show window, clutching a string of Edison's Christmas lights."

Chapter Three

The doors of the Bon Marché were supposed to open at eight a.m., but when Bradshaw and O'Brien arrived at the First Avenue entrance at half past, they had to elbow their way through a crowd of wet, disgruntled shoppers outside. With less than three weeks remaining before Christmas, shoppers had little patience for a police investigation that kept the doors of their favorite department store locked.

Bradshaw heard their grumbling only as a vague murmur. He'd begun his investigation the minute he'd heard Vernon Doyle's name, mentally cataloging what he knew of the man: a competent electrician, mid-forties, balding, short and stocky. He worked two years ago at the tent factory that had gone up in flames, killing the manager. The fire had been set by a part-time employee, an electrical engineering student named Oscar Daulton. The very same student whose mysterious lost invention had drawn Thomas Edison to Seattle. And that connection unsettled Bradshaw.

Coming down Pike Street, he'd eyed the many telephone lines running to the Bon and the absence of lines from any electric utility. With a basement and three floors covering a total of nearly eighty-four thousand square feet, it was the largest department store north of San Francisco and west of Minneapolis. Several dynamos on the premises powered the elevators, carrier system, and electric lighting, and provided current to the telephone batteries and the sewing machines in Alterations. It was a city unto itself. As they drew closer, he could see that all the windows of the building, the outside signs, and lamps were dark.

When a uniformed patrolman unbolted the entrance door for Bradshaw and O'Brien, several female customers tried to push their way in, insisting they had toys to buy before the sale ended.

"Their Santa promised my Johnny a new wagon!"

The patrolman rebuffed them and bellowed above the growing complaints, "This is police business, have some respect!"

As they entered the Men's and Boys' Department, the oil lamp in the patrolman's hand cast eerie shadows on the well-dressed mannequins. The air was rich with the scent of new fabric, and swags of holiday garland winked in the meager light. The overhead arc lamps and the incandescent lights in the glass cases were dark, but scattered oil lamps produced enough light for Bradshaw to read the enormous sign hanging from the ceiling: The Tunnel to Toyville. An arrow pointed into the depths of the store.

"Oh, you must be Professor Bradshaw! And Detective O'Brien? Thank you, thank you for coming!" Hurrying from the dark recesses was a tall gentleman in a crisp pinstripe suit and bow tie, an oil lamp swinging at his side. He spoke with perfect diction that nevertheless revealed his Swedish heritage.

"I am the store manager," he said extending a strong, cool hand, "Ivar Olafson. The owners are away but I have sent them a wire to return at once. It's a tragedy. A tragedy!"

"Is the lighting not working or has the power been turned off?"

"We, that is to say, our maintenance manager and chief electrician, Mr. Andrews, has turned off all the lighting. He left the power to the carrier system on, and the power to the elevators, as they are on entirely different circuits than the lights."

Bradshaw had never met Andrews, but he'd heard of him and knew he was well respected. "I'd like to speak to Mr. Andrews."

"Certainly! He is making an inspection of the wiring. Shall I send for him now?"

"Let him continue his inspection. I'll see him before I leave."

"Very well." Olafson had an expressive face with bushy arched brows that lifted and lowered and contorted in ways that bordered on comical. "Please, come examine our situation and assure me I may turn on the lights again and open the doors to the public. If we don't open soon, they will go to Leader's or McCarthy's or Frederick & Nelson!"

The show window was adjacent to the entrance. Because of the gathered crowd, Bradshaw had been unable to discern during his approach that oak-framed privacy screens of thick cream cloth had been placed to block the view into the window from the outside.

"Mr. Andrews said you may want to know some particulars about our window lighting system when you arrived, so I will tell you what I know. He, of course, will be able to explain in greater detail. All the windows have nearby electrical cabinets where fuses and switches can be accessed. Mr. Andrews lights the show windows at precisely seven each morning from a main switch box that is connected to the window circuits. Depending on the weather, the lights may be shut off again for a portion of the day, but they are always turned on again before dusk and left on until midnight. If it is Mr. Doyle's night to work, he is in charge of shutting them off from the main. After midnight, enough light enters the windows from nearby departments that he can see well enough to continue working. The window lights were on for a short time this morning before the accident was discovered. At that time, I thought it best to shut off all of them in the entire store until we could be assured the wiring is safe. We were trained to do so, of course, but I never imagined an emergency would arise in which I would need to give such a command!"

Mr. Olafson had prepared the window for inspection with a half dozen bright lanterns. The base of the show window was raised six inches above floor level, and a low ceiling split the space in two, horizontally, providing a platform on which more merchandise could be displayed to the street. The four male mannequins in the lower display depicted a Christmas morning scene. A kneeling youth mannequin presented a gift to one made to look like a small boy; both wore warm woolen robes over flannel pajamas. Father- and grandfather-styled mannequins wearing smoking jackets and morning trousers watched from armchairs. Only the boy mannequin had been posed standing, for the ceiling was too low for the adult figures.

A small fresh-cut Douglas fir stood in the center of the display, its tip nearly touching the low ceiling. It had been decorated in gold tinsel garland and red glass balls. Gaily wrapped gifts were piled under the tree along with several Edison GE Holiday electric outfit boxes.

The body of Vernon Doyle lay on its side amidst the artificial holiday happiness. Doyle's hands were near his chest gripping the green cloth-wrapped wire of a holiday festoon. Shards of glass winked where several of the small carbon lamps had shattered. Doyle's eyes were partially open, his features frozen in a mask of confusion, his lips parted, his brow furrowed. He hadn't expected what hit him. His skin was ruddy over his cheeks. A web of broken capillaries over his fleshy nose told not of his death but of a life of habitual drink.

For a moment, Bradshaw simply stood outside the display, taking in the details, while O'Brien jotted down notes. The festoon wire trailed from Doyle's hands to a clockwork mechanism mounted to the back wall of the show window. It was a type of automatic timing clock that Bradshaw was familiar with. Many businesses with regular lighting needs were beginning to use them.

He stepped aside to the cabinet located in the wall adjacent the window. The door of the asbestos-lined cabinet stood open, revealing the neatly labeled fuses and switches within. The panel controlled the power to two of the show windows and the lighting in the nearby entrance. All but one of the knife switches were up, in the "on" position, but no electricity flowed through them since they'd been cut off at a main terminal. The switch in the "off" position was labeled "special."

"Mr. Olafson? Does this 'special' switch operate the timer there on the wall?" He pointed to the clockwork mechanism where the festoon was attached.

"Yes, you are correct. Mr. Doyle installed that clock device especially for this holiday display. Mr. Andrews explained to me that it is on a separate circuit from the rest of the window lights. When the windows are switched on and off from the main box, anything attached to that circuit is not affected. It is used for special lighting and other electrical displays. That's why we chose this window in which to feature Edison's Christmas outfits, because it has a separate circuit that can be dedicated to them. Doyle intended to have Edison's lights cycle on and off every twenty minutes to prevent them from overheating."

"Did you throw this switch to the 'off' position?" The glass fuse looked dark, but he couldn't tell for certain if it had blown.

"No, I touched nothing," Olafson said, peering into the electrical box. "Neither did Mr. Andrews, although he did look inside. He turned the lights off from the main box, as I explained."

Bradshaw believed in redundancy when it came to electrical safety. Had he been the electrician given this task, he would have disconnected the holiday lights entirely from the circuit before exposing his fingers to bare wire. But he knew many electricians grew complacent. After years of working with electricity without incident, they felt safe in situations that placed their lives potentially in the hands of someone else. Doyle had trusted the position of the knife switch. He'd not foreseen anyone coming along and throwing it, sending a current into his body, from one hand across his chest to the other hand. The muscles of his heart would have been shocked from life-giving beats to unproductive quivering. The medical term was cardiac fibrillation. He taught it to his students as well as the technique of artificial respiration, which had the potential to prevent death in such cases. No steps had been taken to save Doyle. While gasping for breath, he would have been aware of his approaching death.

Bradshaw instinctively drew a deep breath.

The mood in the store was somber, but it was far from quiet. Warm air thrummed in the central air ducts, water gurgled in the pipes. No effort had been made to hide the mechanics of the store. The pipes and conduits were routed on the ceiling along with cables suspending arc lamps, and cables bearing wire baskets that whisked orders and payments to cash boys for delivery to bookkeepers on the third floor. Some of those baskets were in action now, sailing through the darkness with a metallic zing between stockrooms and floor displays as clerks took advantage of the delayed opening by stocking displays and filling mail and telephone orders for merchandise. A swooshing sound echoed from somewhere in the building. A spiral steel chute ran from the top floor to the basement, Bradshaw knew, and wrapped merchandise was sent sailing down to the Delivery Department.

"Mr. Olafson," Bradshaw said. "How many employees are here now? In all the various departments?"

"Oh, somewhere between two and three hundred, I'd say. There are usually around fifty here at night between midnight and six, when the day shifts begin to arrive. We have more than four hundred employees. This time of year, we run beyond full staff from opening until closing, with extra stockers at night."

Plenty of time, and plenty of people, Bradshaw thought, to remove or destroy clues to what had happened, whether intentionally or accidentally.

"Do you have a guard patrolling at night?"

"Of course! We have a man on duty seven days a week, from midnight until six in the morning. He's been sent for but hasn't yet returned. He reported nothing irregular upon leaving."

"Who handles security during the day?"

"Two lead detectives split the day, both female—they make the best store detectives, you know—and a dozen plainclothes men and women who mingle with shoppers. Our floorwalkers and managers are also trained to watch for theft from both customers and employees."

O'Brien asked for names, jotting them in his book, and Bradshaw stepped up into the window, ducking his head to keep from bumping the ceiling. "Who placed the screens?"

"I did that myself," said Olafson. "I let no one enter the window. My clerks brought them from Women's Furnishings, and I alone carried them in and disturbed as little as possible."

While still overcast, the day was brightening, and feeble sunshine filtered around the edges of the screens. Bradshaw peered behind one and was dismayed to find curious faces pressed against the glass trying to see in.

He turned to face the holiday display. A handwritten sign before Edison's holiday lights announced that a single outfit of eight lamps cost five dollars, and a triple outfit of twenty-four lamps cost twelve dollars. While Bradshaw had known the cost of the lights would be high due to the price of the fragile bulbs and the wiring labor, he hadn't anticipated they'd be out of range for the average family. Most men scarcely made twelve dollars a week.

He turned to the window lighting. Several incandescent lamps with silvered reflectors ran the length of the window at the top and bottom. The bottom row was now blocked by the screens. On the oval wool rug of the display floor, Bradshaw spied a linen handkerchief that showed severe scorching. It appeared brand new, and Bradshaw's first thought was to glance at the mannequins. A linen kerchief was tucked into the breast jacket pocket of the grandfather figure. The father figure had no kerchief, yet the handwritten sign at its feet listed a kerchief with the other articles on display.

He sniffed the linen. The acrid smell was strong and fresh.

O'Brien asked, "What is it, Ben?"

Olafson clapped his hands together. "I clean forgot! The handkerchief was on the floor by the footlights when I placed the screens. I kicked it aside and it went out of my mind. I saw that it looked burned. Is it, Professor? Has it been burned? Tell me it has not!"

"It is scorched. You found it beside the footlight? Was it touching the lamp?"

"No, not touching, but it was close enough that it alarmed me. We so worry about fire, you know! The sprinkler system does not extend into the windows. We keep a bucket of water handy at all times, of course, and one of sand for electrical fires. They are here," he said, pointing to a storage bin beside the window that served double-duty as a display stand.

Olafson began to wring his hands. "Oh, dear me. If it had caught fire! Careless! My window dresser thinks only of the aesthetic lines of his displays. It is not the first time he's nearly set the place ablaze. I may have to let him go, but he is the best window dresser on the west coast. Where will I find another half so good?"

It was a rhetorical question, but Bradshaw found it curious that Olafson immediately blamed the designer. The window was easily accessible; anyone could have entered. A designer would, before he left, step back and inspect his work and surely see a kerchief out of place.

"The window lights were turned on at seven?"

"Yes, at seven."

"What time was Mr. Doyle found?"

"At half past seven. I had Andrews turn off all the lights almost immediately, even before summoning the police. Is that important?"

Past experience had taught Bradshaw to add as little information as possible to a crime scene, and the scorched cloth proved to him that this was a crime scene. How severe the crime, he didn't yet know. The heat of an incandescent lamp would set a linen cloth ablaze within minutes. If the handkerchief had indeed been on the footlight when Mr. Andrews turned on the power, then someone must have entered the window display shortly after seven and moved it, deliberately leaving it behind. That someone could not have missed seeing Doyle lying dead.

"Who removed the cloth from the light?"

"Who? Oh, that I don't know. It was there nearby, as I said, when I placed the screens. It was Billy Creasle, the assistant window dresser, who found Mr. Doyle and reported to me, but he said nothing of preventing a fire. Of course he was so upset, it might have gone clean out of his mind, too."

"I'd like to speak to him."

"He was unnerved by his discovery, as you can imagine. He is young, just turned eighteen. One of my most promising workers, but still a boy. I sent him home."

O'Brien reached for the scorched cloth, but Bradshaw carefully tucked it inside the breast pocket of his jacket. "I'd like to keep it until I can perform some tests."

"Don't forget, it's evidence." O'Brien made note of it in his book. The Detective Department of the Seattle Police, and thus Detective O'Brien, had recently come under the command of Captain Tennant, who had established more rigorous procedures for recording and preserving evidence. O'Brien was ambivalent about some of the new requirements, such as regimented notetaking. While he'd always been careful with evidence, and he'd been championing for the routine use of modern methods such as fingerprinting and the Bertillon Anthropometric System, O'Brien had been investigating crime on the streets of Seattle long enough to have established his own system, which was based more on common sense than on strict adherence to procedural rules.

O'Brien snapped his notebook closed. "So what was Doyle doing?"

"Joining festoons." Bradshaw got down on all fours to peer closely at Doyle's hands. He then saw that the cord had been supplied with a junction plug to make joining easier. This plug was in Doyle's grip. The few inches of bare copper he'd exposed, and that he'd intended to join within the junction plug, was pinched between his fingers. The charge had left telltale evidence of its deadly passage. A slight swelling and blistering of the fingertips and palms that must have at first been red were now turning gray against bloodless white. The skin was not burned, indicating exposure had been of short duration.

Whoever had thrown that "special" knife switch must have almost immediately turned it off. But it had been too late.

Bradshaw got back on his feet to make an inspection of the automatic time switch.

O'Brien watched over his shoulder. He asked, "Is the clock to blame?"

"No," said Bradshaw. "Doyle hadn't yet wound the clock mechanism or set the time. The festoon is properly attached, however, completing a circuit to the special switch in the cabinet." He drew another deep breath. "I've seen all I need here. Let's speak to Mr. Andrews."

Bradshaw and O'Brien and Mr. Olafson met up with the chief electrician on the second floor, where he was inspecting an electrical panel situated in a hat stock room, lit by lamplight. Martin Andrews was a man of fifty-odd years, with sandy hair going to gray. He shook Bradshaw's hand firmly, and readily offered all he anticipated Bradshaw might ask.

"I arrived just before seven as usual, lit up the show windows from the main box, and at half past was summoned by Mr. Olafson to the Men's window. It looked just as you found it. I touched nothing, other than to cut off power to all the lighting from the mains. Vernon Doyle was our window man. His duty was to install and maintain all show window lighting, and the lighting in the department display cases. I have two other electrical men working for me. An apprentice, who changes out lamps, cleans the globes, and trims the arcs, and a skilled man, who troubleshoots and handles major repairs. Professor, from what I saw, I know you're looking for whoever threw that special switch in the cabinet and energized that wire when it was exposed in Doyle's hands. I know you'll be wanting to know pertinent facts. Doyle worked hard and was respected as an electrician. I was not his friend, nor were the others, but there was no dislike between us. I'd say it was a matter of having no common interests, other than electricity. I was home with my wife all last night. Her parents are visiting for the holidays, they can attest to that."

O'Brien jotted down names and addresses in his little notebook.

"My apprentice works from ten in the morning until eight at night, and he is staying at the YMCA. My skilled man has been in Portland since last Monday. His mother passed away. He's due back tomorrow."

More names and information went into O'Brien's notebook. He gave Bradshaw a look that said he wished everyone were so easily interviewed.

Bradshaw said, "Thank you, Mr. Andrews. If you think of anything else, let me know."

"I will." He closed the panel door and said, "If you're done examining the window downstairs, we're safe to turn the lights on."

"As soon as the scene has been cleared," said O'Brien, who took charge of removing Doyle's body to the morgue. A few minutes later, the store and show windows erupted in light. A cheer sounded outside, but the employees within, who were aware of the cause of the delay, simply hurried to their positions.

Bradshaw and O'Brien fought the tidal surge of incoming shoppers and finally gained the street, turning toward Yesler and police headquarters, hunched into their coats against the cold wet wind.

"Notebook's shut up in my pocket, Ben. What didn't you say back there?"

Bradshaw didn't answer immediately. In another half block, he stopped, facing the new brick home of the Seattle Tent Factory.

O'Brien shook his head and implored with a whine that would have done Justin proud, "Not with Christmas coming. Make it a simple accident, Ben. Or at least keep it inside the Bon. Lorraine will kill me if I miss another holiday."

"Vernon Doyle worked here in the spring of 1901 with Oscar Daulton. He was here the day the old factory burned to the ground."

"Well, that's just a coincidence, not a connection."

"I spoke with Mr. Doyle after Daulton's arrest and he told me all he knew about Daulton, which was very little."

"See there, you're worrying for nothing."

"After Thomas Edison paid me a visit, Doyle began saying he knew the secret to Daulton's invention. Not to me. I did not socialize with the man, but to others in the electrical trade. Gossip of that sort spreads."

"Son of a—is it true?"

"Does it matter?"

"Aah, Ben. The notebook's gotta come out of my pocket."

"I know, but it's not my fault. Blame the Wizard of Menlo Park."

Chapter Four

"We hanged Oscar Daulton two years ago," Chief Sullivan said after hearing Bradshaw explain the possible connection between the death of the Bon Marché's electrician and the young man convicted and executed for murder. "And you're telling me he's still causing trouble?"

"It's the search for his lost invention that may be to blame. As I said, it's only one theory, but one I feel must be explored."

"It's out in the bay, isn't it? Didn't you chase Daulton onto a ferry?"

"I did."

Sullivan scowled, but Bradshaw felt no need to defend himself. He might help the police, but he didn't play the games of power that at times crippled the department. His single-minded goal was to find the truth of the matter. His methods would not be swayed by police or city politics. Rumors were flying that Mayor Humes might soon give Sullivan's job to a new man, and an upcoming mayoral election had the names of potential chiefs and mayors flying. Sullivan's wasn't among them. Some of the men on the force had been quoted as saying a new chief would clean up the detective office, which rankled Sullivan and angered O'Brien. The city of Seattle had never seen such tight control over gambling and the Tenderloin District.

The realities of policing a modern city of over one hundred thousand citizens with a force of eighty-some men clashed daily with the idealists who wanted the city squeaky clean. Seattle was not the wide open city it had once been, yet it was true that below Jackson Street, in the section of town designated for such businesses, parlor houses and dance halls thrived and continually attempted to crawl back up toward Yesler.

Bradshaw knew that the public didn't cringe at news of a murdered gambler or drifter, but murder at the Bon Marché, the store that had become a beloved institution to Seattle residents, was different. Chief Sullivan would be facing intense scrutiny from all factions, from the mayor in city hall to the mothers who visited the Bon daily, taking advantage of the free child care provided to shoppers.

"I've seen the articles about the hunt for Daulton's contraption," the chief said. "And the ads." He thumbed through the newspaper on his desk then flipped the paper around for Bradshaw and O'Brien to see. They were both familiar with the quarter-page advertisement:

"Wanted: Information about the inventor assassin Oscar Daulton. $5,000 reward offered to those who provide information that leads to a patentable invention. See J. D. Maddock, the Globe Building."

The chief said, "You think someone killed Doyle over what he knew about the invention? Seems like a coincidence to me."

O'Brien said, "Our professor doesn't trust coincidences, assumptions, or presumptions."

Chief Sullivan snorted. "I'd never close a case if I had to work like that. But I want the truth here, and speed. Vernon Doyle was a respected electrician working in an establishment women and children frequent. I want them to feel safe. I want them to *be* safe."

Bradshaw said, "The chief electrician examined the lighting system throughout the store and found it sound. I examined the wiring in and around the show window, and there is no doubt that Vernon Doyle's death could not have been accidental. It was deliberate. Someone intentionally energized a wire in Doyle's hands, but the shoppers of the Bon Marché are safe. You can assure the press of that."

"You may be right, but there will be many who say otherwise until Doyle's killer is caught. O'Brien, Captain Tennant is in court today. Get back to the Bon, but report to Tennant first thing in the morning. And Professor, just so I can honestly say every single avenue is being explored, I'd appreciate you looking into the possibility of this being tied to Oscar Daulton. Usual terms, but the minute you decide there's no connection, you let me know."

"Agreed."

◇◇◇

When they were back on Third Avenue, the blustery morning stole hats and threatened umbrellas. Detective O'Brien jammed his Roosevelt hat low as Bradshaw clutched his own derby atop his head.

O'Brien said, "Do you want to talk to the boy, the assistant window dresser who found the body?"

"Yes, if you don't mind, but the chief made it clear what my role was to be in this investigation."

"How do we know the boy isn't a closet inventor or treasure hunter?"

Bradshaw grinned. "We don't. I have his address. Shall we meet up in an hour at the office of Edison's representative?"

"Present a unified front to the good attorney? Yes, indeed."

They discussed the case as they trekked to Pike Street. There they parted. O'Brien turned down to Second Avenue and the Bon Marché while Bradshaw headed up the newly regraded street to Sixth Avenue. The regrade had removed the steepest portions of Pike for several blocks, and most buildings had been preserved by jacking them up on stilts then constructing new stories beneath them. The row houses that were his destination now sat above businesses that had set up shop in the newly created spaces.

At Sixth, Bradshaw waited for the streetcar to pass, then dodged horse droppings on the fresh brick pavement to hike the stairs up to a wooden walk running the length of the row. He knocked on the front door of the third house.

The door was opened almost immediately by Mrs. Creasle, who replied to his request to see Billy, "Must you see him today? He's had such a shock." Mrs. Creasle was a slight woman of late middle age, with silvering fair hair, and a pretty but forgettable face. This feature had been passed on to a number of daughters who all came to the door at his arrival, one after the other, eyeing him curiously, and asking if he was the famous Professor Bradshaw they'd read about in the newspaper. He said he supposed he was.

"I won't keep Billy long," he said to Mrs. Creasle.

She sighed in resignation and led Bradshaw, not into the parlor as he expected, but to a room she called Billy's "storeroom," at the back of the house.

It turned out not to be a room for storage, but a small room dedicated to the past and future of the department store, its walls covered in posters of Macy's, Harrods, Woolworth's, and Bloomingdale's. On a round table backed by a dark curtain, miniature homemade mannequins in doll clothes were arranged like a store's show-window display, complete with descriptive signs. Billy, a young man, small and pale like his siblings, stood beside the table, turning a handle that made the tabletop slowly spin.

Mrs. Creasle departed after introducing Bradshaw to her son, but she left the door ajar and he suspected she was listening from the next room.

"How does it work?" Bradshaw asked, hoping to put the boy at ease for he seemed nervous, keeping his attention on his display and glancing often toward the open door.

"I, uh, built it like a giant butler's assistant." He rubbed his palms on his trousers. "Do you know the device? A large round tray that sits on ball bearings and spins around? I read a description of one in a newspaper. It's for serving meals. The writer called it a 'Lazy Susan.' Mine is for turning window displays and spins the same way, only with a hand crank, and the full-size model will have an electric motor. On my next design, the mannequins will stand on inset bases that spin separately."

"Like the figures in a music box?" Bradshaw was dismayed to learn that O'Brien's comment about the boy possibly being an inventor was true. He had no wish to discover another young man, who obviously had the potential for a successful future, to be guilty of murder.

"Yes, like a music box, only motor-driven, not spring. I'll be able to control them separately, and I'll install a clock mechanism, so all the products are fully rotated in about five minutes. You can't have it longer than that without losing a customer's attention and risking them crossing the street to the competitor."

"I dare say such a display would keep shoppers entertained. Where'd you learn to do this?"

"Oh, I picked it up here and there." Billy shrugged, but a grin revealed his pleasure at the compliment. "I think the novelty of it would at first draw a crowd, but people soon get used to things, you know, and you must keep presenting new attractions."

He was a fidgety young man, unable to keep still, moving about his display with a tape measure. He met Bradshaw's eye openly enough, though, when he spoke, and while eager to show off his display, he wasn't so self-absorbed as to be unaware of Bradshaw's reactions. Indeed, Billy seemed to adjust his presentation in response to Bradshaw's comments. Billy Creasle was a born pleaser, a showman, with a feel for his audience.

"Can you take a break for a minute? I need to ask you some questions about this morning."

Before sitting, Bradshaw quietly closed the door. Billy was eighteen, old enough that his mother could not demand a presence at his interview. With the door closed, Billy seemed to relax a bit, although he fidgeted with the tape, unspooling a short length, then reeling it back in. Up close, dark smudges were visible under his eyes, as if he needed sleep.

"What time did you arrive at the store this morning?"

"At six. I signed the register. We all do."

"Can you walk me through your morning, everything you can remember up until you found Mr. Doyle?"

"I did what I usually do when I arrive, which is to see to all the window displays, replace any merchandise that was sold from them, and change out any merchandise that we no longer have in stock. I didn't get to that window in the Men's Department until half past seven, and it was then I found Mr. Doyle and called for Mr. Olafson."

"Did you see anyone unusual in the store this morning? Anyone unexpected?"

"No, I can't say I did."

"Did you see anyone near that window before you entered it?"

"No, no I didn't. I passed through the department a couple times this morning, collecting things I needed for displays. There wasn't anyone on the sales floor near the window that I can remember. The stockroom was busy, and the clerks were at their counters doing inventory and cleaning fingerprints off the glass cases, but nobody was over by the window."

"Do you know anyone who didn't like Mr. Doyle? Or who had been arguing with him?"

"I didn't work much with him. His shifts usually began just as mine were ending. He was a bit full of himself, but I don't think anyone at the store had anything against him."

"Full of himself?"

"He was always saying, 'In the beginning, God said, "Let there be light," then He created the electrician to distribute it.'"

Bradshaw was familiar with the expression, except the standard version had God creating linemen, not electricians, to distribute light. Practical electrical work took intelligence, skill, and a certain amount of self-confidence that bordered on bravado, especially for the men who restored downed power lines after storms. It was an amusing quip coming from a swaggering lineman in climbing hooks who carried a fifty-pound crossarm up a pole with the ease of a mother carrying her child, but it could seem boastful from an electrician climbing a ladder in a department store to change out an incandescent lamp. Doyle's job had been far more complicated and potentially dangerous than changing bulbs and trimming arc lamps, but the environment of the Bon Marché, with its ferns and finery, did not lend itself to such statements of bravado.

"Do you know of anyone not employed at the Bon who had argued with Mr. Doyle?"

"Funny you ask because I'd never heard anyone arguing with Mr. Doyle until yesterday. A man named Maddock, that attorney in town that represents Thomas Edison and has all those advertisements in the papers offering a reward for information about that lost invention. He was in the store last night, arguing with Doyle."

"What time?"

"About nine, I'd say. No, more like half past. Mr. Doyle had just started his shift."

"You work long hours."

"They don't make me. I love my job. I plan to be a manager one day of a place even bigger than the Bon. Why, do you know that at Marshall Field in Chicago—a store ten times the size of the Bon—their manager, Mr. Henry Gordon Selfridge, began as a stock boy in the wholesale house? If he can do it, so can I. I'm on salary at the Bon, not hourly. It was my idea so I could work as much as I wanted without costing them overtime."

"What did Mr. Doyle and Mr. Maddock argue about?"

"I didn't hear enough to follow. They kept their voices low, but I could tell they were angry. When Mr. Maddock left, he said to Mr. Doyle, 'You know where to find me if you change your mind.' Then Mr. Doyle muttered some unrepeatable words and I told him the Bon Marché didn't condone such language, and he gave me a nasty look, but held his tongue. I get that a lot because of my age. No respect, even when I'm right."

"What time did you leave the store last evening?"

"About midnight, maybe a little after."

"You started at six in morning? Eighteen hours, Billy? And back again at six today?"

"Like I said, I enjoy my job. During the holidays, there's a lot to do and it's easier when the store isn't packed with customers. I came home at noon yesterday for a few hours then went back."

"You say Mr. Doyle was liked well enough. Do you know if he had particular friends among his coworkers? Anyone whom you feel it would be helpful for me to speak with?"

Billy blushed a bit, and spooled out a foot of tape. "I wouldn't want Mrs. Doyle to learn this, Professor, but I'm fairly certain there was something between Mr. Doyle and Mrs. Adkins. She's one of the store's seamstresses."

"Anything you tell me in confidence won't get back to Mrs. Doyle unless absolutely necessary."

"It's not a matter of knowing but seeing, seeing them together, I mean. At the store, he'd corner her somewhere while she was working, hemming a skirt on a mannequin or something, and I could tell he was flirting with her, and she was mad about it. I don't think she wanted anyone to know about them."

"Perhaps that's all it was, he flirted and she rebuffed him."

"Except I saw them together at the Washington Hotel. They stayed in the same room President Roosevelt stayed in last May."

Bradshaw lifted his brow.

"Silly to take a room like that and then not be able to tell your friends you slept in the president's bed."

"How do you know this?"

"I followed them. Followed him, actually."

"Because?"

"Because I overheard him tell one of the runners to stop by his house and tell his wife he had to work late, only I knew he didn't. When he left the store, I followed him to see what he was up to. I know it wasn't a very nice thing to do, but neither was it nice for him to lie to his wife or tease Mrs. Adkins. I followed him to the Washington. Did you hear they might put a tunnel underneath the hotel? Right through Denny Hill, instead of taking the hill down. Makes more sense to me."

The leveling of Seattle's streets was a sore subject with Bradshaw and one he didn't care to discuss with Billy, but he did agree a tunnel made more sense than tearing down a hill.

"You said you followed Doyle to the Washington?"

"That I did, and I saw Mrs. Adkins there, too."

"Why are you so sure they were together?"

"If they weren't, it seems awful strange they both went into the President's Suite."

"Did they see you?"

He shook his head. "When you work at a department store, you learn how to follow people without being noticed."

The boy had the makings of a detective, but Bradshaw refrained from saying so. He didn't want to encourage the boy's spying on coworkers simply to satisfy his own curiosity.

"It's best you don't share what you learned with anyone, other than the police if they ask."

"Oh, I wouldn't! I haven't told anyone but you."

Bradshaw highly doubted that. Would a boy of eighteen withhold such gossip from his friends? And why go to all the bother of tailing Doyle if not to somehow make use of what he learned?

"Describe for me, please, exactly how you found Mr. Doyle this morning."

"Like I said, I got to the Men's window late. I knew I didn't need to make any changes. I just needed to give it a quick look to see that all was as it should be."

"Were the window lights on when you entered?"

"Mr. Andrews turns them on at seven and it was half past."

"What did you notice?"

"What do you mean?"

"As you approached the window, did anything seem wrong? Anything alarm you? Anything look out of place? Did you see, hear, or smell anything unexpected?"

Billy studied the tape measure in his hands, turning the small crank to wind it in completely, all while his knees jiggled. "No, no, no, I just went to do my job. I saw Doyle lying there as soon as I stepped into the window. I shouted for help and Mr. Olafson came. He said Doyle was cold. That he was dead." Billy chewed his lip, and the tape unspooled and rewound.

Bradshaw didn't like his three consecutive denials. No, no, no.

"Professor, does that mean he'd been dead for a long while? Being cold? A very long while?"

"Possibly."

"You don't get cold right away when you die, do you? It takes time."

"It depends on the circumstances." Bradshaw knew well that factors such as the cause of death played into how quickly a dead body would feel cold to the touch. Once the life force was gone, the body became an object like any other and its temperature leveled to the surrounding temperature. But he didn't believe such facts would help this young man recover from the trauma of discovering a dead man.

"In this case, I estimate Mr. Doyle died before seven."

Billy's head snapped up and his jiggling momentarily ceased. "How much before?"

"I'm not yet sure."

The fidgeting began again. "I was afraid. Well, I was afraid that maybe if I'd gotten to the Men's window sooner, I might have found him before he died."

Bradshaw watched young Billy's face carefully as he said, "The coroner will determine the approximate time of death. He's often able to pinpoint very closely in circumstances such as this. You should not blame yourself for doing your job and arriving at the window when you did."

Billy nodded, but he kept his eyes on the tape measure as he chewed his lip.

Bradshaw did not say, for he did not know, if Vernon Doyle had been alive when Billy Creasle signed his timesheet at six that morning. Could the boy have saved Doyle if he'd arrived at the window sooner, preventing someone from throwing the switch that sent a lethal current through the electrician? Or had Billy been the one to throw the switch, returning at half past seven to pretend to find Doyle dead?

The house was quiet as Bradshaw continued to study Billy. The ticking of a clock in the room, and the muted sounds of traffic outside, were slowly drowned by the return of a steady, heavy rain.

"Billy, if you have something to tell me about Mr. Doyle's death, it would be best to do so now. The truth will be learned."

Billy looked up, his eyes wide and pleading. "I have nothing more to tell, Professor. Honest. He was lying there in the window when I got there. That's all I know."

Chapter Five

The Globe Building on First and Madison housed offices, retail shops, and hotel rooms for single men. John Maddock, Attorney at Law, had secured a room on the fourth floor, and Professor Bradshaw found the door extensively stenciled with Maddock's name and credentials, and the assertion that he was the "Seattle Representative of Thomas A. Edison, Specializing in Patent Purchasing, Pre-Patent Sales, Infringement Litigation, and the Sale of Genuine Edison Inventions and GE Products for Home and Office."

Bradshaw stepped into a small room that had been fashioned from a much larger one, subdivided by panels topped with privacy glass patterned like water droplets. Detective O'Brien was already there, examining shelves of products for sale. Electric coffee percolators, fans, phonographs, and related paraphernalia. Telegraph kits, small dynamos, meters, electric chandeliers, and storage batteries. There were incandescent bulbs in assorted shapes, sizes, and colors, and a large stack of the new colorful Christmas light festoons. From the next room, the clackety-clack of a typewriter came through to them, and the whir of a fan, and the deep tones of a male voice, the precise words obscured by the typing and whirring.

Under the same audible cover, Bradshaw quietly told O'Brien about his interview with Billy.

O'Brien said, "The boy could come in handy with his habit of snooping. He didn't mention the burnt handkerchief?"

"No, and I gave him the opportunity. He knows something, but he isn't eager to share."

"What he knows may implicate him in some way. He's certainly not shy about tattling on his fellow employees. Which reminds me, the senior window dresser, Troy Ruzauskas, swore he knows nothing of a misplaced handkerchief in his window, and he swore he was not to blame for any fire hazards, or electrocutions, not ever."

"The vehemence of innocence or protesting too much?"

"Too soon to say, but I don't think he's our man. A clerk in Men's Shoes, adjacent to Men's Wear, said the store manager, Ivar Olafson, is overly fond of the little boys working at the store and smitten with Billy. Gives the lad preferential treatment, promoting him out of turn."

"I don't like the implications."

"Neither do I." O'Brien eyed the percolator shaped like a miniature potbellied stove. "How well do those work? Do you think Lorraine would like one?"

"Your wife doesn't like coffee, you do."

"This would make it easier for her to make it for me, wouldn't it?"

"I advise you to think about that question, Jim."

O'Brien shrugged. "Mr. Andrews is in the clear. He was home all night. Four roommates verified the apprentice spent the entire night at the YMCA, and the Bon's other electrician is indeed on his way home from Portland."

"You had a profitable morning."

"The miracle of the modern telephone, my friend. Before coming here, I paid my respects to Doyle's wife. If I'm any judge, her shock was genuine, but she doesn't have an alibi. She was home alone, she claims."

"You think there's a chance she did it?"

"As a married man, you bet I do."

"You may be a selfish lout, but Lorraine loves you."

"And your point would be? Just promise we'll have this wrapped up by Christmas." O'Brien grinned, then his face went serious, and his voice lowered to a near whisper. "Why has he not paid you a call, Ben? This attorney. If he's searching Seattle for clues to Daulton's invention, I'd think he'd start with you."

"I have no doubt Mr. Edison informed him of our conversation a few months ago, and that I said I knew nothing more than what was already publicly known."

O'Brien tipped up the brim of his hat and narrowed his eyes. "There are times your nerve surprises me, Ben. Thomas Alva Edison brought light to the world. Every child in this country knows his name. Are you saying you lied to him?"

"A power greater than Edison brought light to the world, Jim. And Mr. Edison hired a team of men to devise a long-lasting filament to capture the light at a profit. I sell my soul to no man, and I certainly don't give it away. He tried the direct approach with me and failed. His representative—" Bradshaw silenced as the typewriter suddenly ceased its clattering, and the inner door opened with a squeak of its hinges.

A gaunt man emerged, looking more like an undertaker than an attorney, in a crisp black suit with a high white collar. His mouth was wide, his lips thin, and one of eyes drooped at the corner, giving him a perpetually sad countenance that was out of kilter with his jovial tone. "Gentlemen, I'm sorry I kept you waiting. What may I do for you today? An invention to sell? A patent to file? Or are you in search of a good bargain on the hit of the holidays, Mr. Edison's holiday lighting outfits?"

Bradshaw said they were interested in none of the above and introduced himself. Maddock's wide mouth fell open with a gasp. "Professor Bradshaw! It is a pleasure, sir. Well, now, I do understand why you're here, but I must say it is a pleasure, nay, an honor, sir." He extended his hand and shook Bradshaw's with firm enthusiasm. "An honor, sir," he repeated. "Truly. Your reputation for electrical forensics, as you coined the phrase, is legendary. My favorite case so far was the one you solved just this summer at the ocean, with the electrotherapeutic chair. I've been studying your patents, too, and I must tell you your inventions are brilliantly conceived. Simplicity of design, so streamlined yet incorporating the latest advances in electrical theory. Inspired! I'm John Davenport Maddock. My friends call me J.D., and I hope you will, too."

"Thank you, Mr. Maddock." Bradshaw trusted instant informality even less than exuberant praise. "This is Detective James O'Brien with the Seattle police. We'd like to ask you a few questions."

"Certainly, come through to my office." He led them through the door into a room so small it could be crossed with two generous strides. An overabundance of furniture, books, and files made it feel all the smaller. A candlestick telephone rose above the clutter of a rolltop desk that was situated within arm's reach of a stern-looking woman dressed entirely in black, who sat at a typewriter. She greeted them with a curt nod, and the tight bun on her head never wavered.

"Miss Finch," Maddock said, "complete your typing, then you may take your lunch break. I placed several letters in your outbox. Please be sure those go out today. I'll be in the next room. Could you bring me back a sandwich, egg salad on white? That's a good girl."

Miss Finch returned to her typewriting without a word, and the vigor with which she hit the keys gave Bradshaw cause to believe she resented being called a "good girl."

Maddock pulled a manila folder from the desktop stack then said, "This way, gentlemen," and led them to the next room, which proved to be the largest and included a window with a view of the adjacent brick building. The room had a parlor feel, with several chairs arranged about a round table, but it obviously did double-duty as Maddock's living quarters. A fold-up bed was secured to the wall, its rectangular undersurface inadequately disguised with a poster of the Edison film, *The Great Train Robbery*, on which a narrow-eyed cowboy with a fat mustache and a handkerchief at his throat leveled a pistol directly at anyone sitting in Maddock's guest chairs.

"Now, I'm certain we can take care of business quickly," Maddock began, opening the file to reveal a typed page that had the look of a legal document. "We'd love to avoid a long drawn-out case as much as you, and I'm sure we can find terms that are mutually agreeable."

Bradshaw said, "Excuse me?"

"I know, we aren't off to the best footing, Professor." He nodded toward O'Brien. "The good detective at your side speaks volumes. Usually, inventors arrive with their attorneys, but I'm no stranger to the other sort of law man, you know." He laughed. "In this business, competition is fierce, and the rules can get complicated. I assure you, it is a minor matter of the law and civil not criminal, yet I perfectly understand the instinct to bring a policeman to such a confrontation. I hold no hard feelings, I assure you, and please know this is simply business. My respect for you could not be greater nor more genuine. It's really with great regret that I was obligated to proceed."

With his tone now matching the sadness of his drooping eye, Maddock truly did appear regretful, but Bradshaw was still baffled. He said, "Mr. Maddock, I have no idea what you're talking about."

Maddock's surprised gaze shifted back and forth between them. "The lawsuit? For patent infringement? Oh, dear. You didn't get served this morning?"

"Only breakfast by my housekeeper, and since then I haven't been home."

"And you didn't teach your class today at the university, I'll wager. I gave that as your primary working address. I understand you also keep an office in town, but you are not regularly there."

"Are you telling me you're suing me for patent infringement?"

"I'm afraid I am, or rather, the Thomas Edison Company is."

"On what?"

"Your detective microphone."

Bradshaw clamped his jaw tight. It was all nonsense. Edison had no case against his microphone or anything that he had patented, he was sure of it. But it would take money to prove it, possibly a good deal of money, in a long drawn-out legal battle. He'd seen many such cases play out in the past few years.

"Well, Ben," O'Brien said, "this clears up why Maddock didn't come to see you. When the direct approach failed, Edison switched to extortion."

Maddock frowned as if faced with a child about to steal a cookie. "Detective O'Brien, that's a very serious accusation. Are you sure you want to make it?"

O'Brien stiffened. "Are you sure you want to sue Professor Bradshaw for infringement? I don't know how things operate back East, but out here in the Wild West, we don't take kindly to false accusations."

Bradshaw put a calming hand on O'Brien's arm, and for a moment they spoke not at all. The typing in the next room ceased, a chair scraped the wood floor, then the tap of a pair of women's heels (more delicate than Bradshaw thought Miss Finch capable of) receded, and a door closed.

Maddock sat back, his thin mouth smiling, his drooping eye gleaming. He appeared completely sure of himself, enjoying his role.

Bradshaw said to O'Brien, "Do you want to ask him, or shall I?"

"I'd like to, if you wouldn't mind."

"He's all yours."

While they said this, Maddock eyed them curiously, a single brow raised.

O'Brien made a show of pulling his notebook from his pocket, licking the tip of his pencil, and holding it poised before asking, "Mr. Maddock, where were you yesterday morning from nine a.m. until this morning at the same time?"

The joy slid off Maddock's face. "What?"

"You heard the question."

Maddock sat up, adjusting himself in his chair. "I did, but I don't understand why it's being asked."

"Are you refusing to answer?"

"Am I in some sort of trouble?"

"Did you do something the Seattle police would consider trouble?"

"Of course not."

"Then please answer the question."

"I was here, I went out to eat, I filed papers at the courthouse, I did some holiday shopping, I came back here."

"What time did you return here last evening?"

"Ten o'clock."

"And did you go out again?"

"No, I was here all night. Alone."

"You're sure?"

"There's nothing wrong with my memory, Detective."

"Where did you do your holiday shopping?"

"The Bon Marché."

"Did you speak to any employees of the Bon Marché while you were there?"

"Of course I did."

"Who?"

Maddock stared at O'Brien, then his eyes shifted to Bradshaw, his expression controlled. Bradshaw could see he was thinking, reviewing whom he spoke to, what was said, what he did, that might have been observed or overheard. His focus glazed for a moment, and then a smile crept onto his face. He shook his head, not in denial, but as if in disbelief.

O'Brien said, "Mr. Maddock, would you like to speak to your attorney before answering, or do you represent yourself?"

"Only a fool represents himself, Detective, but no, I have no need of an attorney. Is this about Doyle? Vernon Doyle?"

"It is."

"What did Mr. Doyle say occurred in our conversation? I have a right to know what I'm being accused of."

"Mr. Doyle hasn't accused you of anything, not directly."

"Then what has he said? We had a vigorous but gentlemanly discussion regarding a subject of mutual interest on which we disagreed. If he said otherwise, he's lying."

"He said nothing at all."

"Then why are you here asking about my visit to the Bon?"

"Mr. Maddock, tell me about your conversation with Mr. Doyle."

"It was a private conversation concerning business matters."

"Are you refusing to speak?"

"Yes, Detective. I am refusing to speak on matters of no concern to the police."

"But your conversation with Mr. Doyle does concern the police, Mr. Maddock."

"Why on Earth should it?"

"Because Vernon Doyle is dead."

Maddock's smile froze, but the joy had gone out of it. "Good God."

"He was found this morning in the Men's Wear display window, clutching a string of Edison GE Christmas festoons."

Maddock's mouth fell open with a small gasp and the hint of a smile. If Bradshaw was not mistaken, Maddock was greatly relieved by O'Brien's statement. His gasp slid into a controlled frown. "This is about the holiday festoons? The new Edison lamps?"

"It's about Vernon Doyle's death."

"Edison's product is certainly not to blame. I'm sure you will find after a thorough examination that the building's wiring or Doyle himself is to blame for the unfortunate accident, not Edison's festoons. Have you examined the scene yet, Professor?"

"I have."

"And?"

"The case is still under investigation. I'm not at liberty to reveal details."

Maddock extended his hands, palms up, in a gesture of innocence. "I'm sure you have found Mr. Edison's product to be completely blameless. I do appreciate your letting me know about the matter. As Mr. Edison's legal representative in Seattle, I can certainly handle any issues that arise from this unfortunate accident."

"It wasn't an accident."

Maddock blinked. "Not—you mean it was intentional? How does one intentionally kill oneself with a festoon of lights? Did he hang himself?"

"He was electrocuted."

"Intentionally? Perhaps Mr. Edison has a claim against Doyle's estate for misuse of product?"

O'Brien said, "Don't be daft, Mr. Maddock. It wasn't suicide."

"Someone else misused Mr. Edison's lights, bringing about the demise of Mr. Doyle? I will want to know who was at fault, of course, so that I can take appropriate legal action. Well, thank you for your consideration in coming here today. I know you will keep me informed of developments. Now, is there anything else—"

"Yes, you can tell me about your heated conversation with Vernon Doyle. You weren't exactly quiet in your discussion. There were witnesses."

"Then let your witnesses tell you what was said. I left the Bon before ten. My conversation with Mr. Doyle has no bearing on whatever occurred thereafter."

Chapter Six

The rat-a-tat of a tapping telegraph key greeted Bradshaw as he approached the door to his own office in the Bailey Building, a couple blocks from the Globe. He wondered what it would be like if all the various tapping and hammering, banging and clanging sounds of the city could be brought into harmony to form a symphony, rather than unnerving discord.

Seattle was a city in perpetual motion, with destruction and construction happening side-by-side, above and below, and all the while business continued uninterrupted at a feverish pace. Like ants detouring around a leaf dropped onto their path, the people of Seattle found ways around the messes and just kept going.

Bradshaw's door was stenciled more modestly than Maddock's with his name and "Electrical Forensics Investigator," and below, "Henry Pratt, Assistant." When he opened it, the tapping ceased, and a string of cuss words more suited to the Klondike than a place of business reverberated off the walls.

"Henry!"

"Oh. Sorry."

"I could have been a client entering."

"It's this dang-nabbit Morse code. Dots and dashes—they all blur in my brain. Look here, I just sent a wire and it came out gobbledygook." Henry tore the paper from the ticker of the practice telegraph device, crumpling it into a ball that then met its siblings in the wastebasket. Taller than Bradshaw, broader, gruffer, but no less intelligent, Henry Pratt had the physique of a logger, the speech of a miner, and the education of a scholar. He could, if he disciplined himself, fit in with the highest echelons of society, but he preferred the dives of the lower regions where, he said, it was easier to spot the liars and cheats.

He'd begun two projects recently. He was lifting weights in order to prevent a back injury from crippling him, and he was learning the art of the telegrapher. The exercise program was going exceedingly well, as was the academic portion of the telegraphy. But the dots and dashes were proving unexpectedly difficult for him.

"At our age," Bradshaw said, "it's more difficult to learn a new language, and that's what Morse is. Keep at it, and one day it will suddenly seem clear."

"You wanna bet? What are you doing here, anyway? Thought you had a class to teach this afternoon."

"We've got a new case."

"That fire in Ballard?"

"I'd almost forgotten about that. No, that was a burned-out transformer, no one hurt, though the building's a total loss. The new case is complicated, usual terms with the SPD, and I'll need both you and Squirrel." Squirrel was the nickname of the fact-finder they used to gather background information on persons of interest. "Do you know anyone who works at the Bon?"

"I know a few. Fellow in shipping, one of the drivers. I'm friendly with a gal in Notions, but I can't say as I know her. She knows me, though, and hides in the back room when I come in."

The grin on Henry's face told Bradshaw his friend enjoyed his game of cat and mouse with the Notions girl.

Bradshaw hung his damp coat on the rack. "See what you can find out from the gossip at the Bon, then we'll compare notes." He gave the facts of Vernon Doyle's death and what he'd learned from interviews thus far. Like O'Brien, Henry cringed at the shoe salesman's use of "overly fond" and "smitten" in regards to Mr. Olafson's feelings toward the boys and Billy Creasle.

A cursory knock came simultaneously with the door's opening. A smiling young man stepped in, looking windblown but congenial, and he handed Bradshaw a thick, plain, rain-spattered manila envelope. The young man spun on his heel and left, and the door clapped closed behind him.

Bradshaw had no need to look. Without opening it, he handed the envelope to Henry, who grunted his disgust and tossed it in the wastebasket. It struck with a *thunk* and the basket tipped over.

"My sentiments exactly, Henry. Now, fish it out and take it to my attorney."

Henry uprighted the can and kicked the envelope toward his desk, a workspace as clean and tidy as Maddock's had been cluttered. Henry was a minimalist, even with paperwork. The things he liked to collect were friends. Physical possessions mattered to him only in the moment, to use or enjoy, then dispose of or pass on to someone else. When he'd hunted gold in Alaska, it was the hunt that excited him. He'd never given much thought to what he'd do if he ever struck big, although he could tell a good tale of the life he truly didn't want to lead. "You really think this could be about Daulton's invention? Would Maddock have sent his man around with these papers if last night he offed Doyle at the Bon? Wouldn't he be trying to play nice instead?"

"The best defense is a strong offense. And if he's our man, he'd know it would look suspicious if he didn't follow through with the suit. No, we can't read anything into his proceeding. And as yet I have only the coincidence linking them. There are several other equally plausible explanations and therefore suspects, so keep an open mind when you ask around."

"You ought to put in a few hours in your basement tinkering, Ben. Figure out what Daulton did and put an end to it."

"It's not that simple, Henry."

"If it were simple, the Wizard would have hired someone to figure it out by now and not sent Maddock to town to harass you."

Bradshaw crossed to the window and looked down on the blustery bustling street, but his vision was turned inward. Even more than the puzzle of Oscar Daulton's invention was the moral dilemma tainting it. He didn't want to be the one responsible for bringing to the world an invention birthed through anger and stained with blood. Neither did he want Edison to profit from it.

He took a deep breath and turned away from the window. "Who else is searching for Daulton's invention, Henry? And which of them knew Vernon Doyle?"

"Good question. A visit to the docks and the diving outfits ought to give us something. They were all fishing for the thing when it first went overboard, and I know I read something about some recent dives."

"Who do we try first?"

"Oh, Jake Galloway of Galloway Diving. He's the best. No question about that. The man's got skill and nerve. Holds the record for deep diving, in these parts anyway."

Bradshaw didn't doubt Henry's assessment. With his gregarious manner and enjoyment of a good chat over coffee or anything stronger, he made friends wherever he went and gathered details of Seattle life that often proved useful in investigations.

"I'll begin at Galloway's tomorrow."

"You don't sound sure of yourself."

"Because I'm not. Doyle had a cocksure manner, and he bragged about knowing Daulton when it was to his advantage. That tendency to feel connected to something of perceived importance wasn't likely limited to lost inventions. He might have annoyed someone for an entirely different matter."

"Well, the chief hired you to look into this angle, right? And O'Brien is poking around the Bon and Doyle's private life. So with me and Squirrel digging, we're sure to catch a scent of the right trail soon. Don't worry, at least not yet. Say, maybe Jake Galloway will take you for a dive. Cheese and crackers, Ben, I've never seen a man turn green so fast. You want me to go?"

"I can handle the docks. If diving is necessary, I'll leave that to you."

"Nah, they weigh you down something fierce to get you to sink, and I don't think my back could take it. So when's my niece due home?"

"Five days."

"Ha! That brought your color back. That reminds me, I got her a present. Can't wait 'til Christmas. I'll show you." Bradshaw followed Henry into the small storage room where they kept records on closed cases and an array of handy tools of their trade, including several of Bradshaw's detective microphones. A cot against the wall was neatly made with a wool blanket and white-cased pillow. Henry often slept there when an investigation went late, or whenever he was in the mood for solitude. It had been a few days since Henry had slept at Bradshaw's house, in the bedroom that had been his ever since Bradshaw moved to Seattle. There were a few times over the years when Henry had gone off to find adventure, including the spring and summer of '01 when he'd been in Alaska and his niece, Missouri Fremont, had temporarily moved into his room.

Bradshaw thought back to that spring evening two years ago when he'd opened his front door to find her standing there, skinny and pale, her amber eyes warm and wise and looking deep into his soul. He'd known then that his life would never be the same, but he denied it. For a very long time, he denied it to everyone, even himself.

"It's full of homeopathic remedies." Henry interrupted Bradshaw's drifting thoughts. "Ain't it the prettiest box you've ever seen?"

It was indeed a fine wooden case of polished cherry. Inside, lift-out trays were divided into small felt-lined compartments, perfect for glass vials to travel safely. On the outside of the case, a blank copper tag awaited an inscription.

"I was gonna have her name engraved, but I didn't know what to put."

Henry caught Bradshaw's eye, and they both looked quickly away. Henry cleared his throat, and a dull ache squeezed Bradshaw's heart. Should the case say "Dr. Fremont" or "Dr. Bradshaw" or, heaven forbid, some other last name, should things turn out disastrously?

The tag was attached to the case by a leather sleeve. Bradshaw slid out the tag.

Henry snorted. "I'll put the bow there."

Chapter Seven

The smoke emitted by the handkerchief held a particular sharpness. The kerchief was made of a cotton and silk blend, dyed a deep indigo. Bradshaw thought it likely the dye was at fault for the smoke's potency, but Mrs. Prouty cared not for explanations. She threw open the door at the top of the stairs and shouted down to Bradshaw in the basement, wanting to know how much longer she was expected to endure the odor.

He'd burned worse. His sulfur experiments a couple years ago had driven her out of the house. "I'm done," he called out, and the door slammed shut.

He'd replicated the Bon Marché's incandescent show window lamp with a silver reflector, and using several of the same brand and color handkerchiefs as the one he'd found scorched, he'd replicated the window particulars. He recorded his findings in precise detail in case they were needed for a criminal trial. From the time the lamp was energized, it took one minute and ten seconds for the cloth to scorch, another two minutes to smolder, and another three minutes to fully ignite if the handkerchief was not removed. If the handkerchief was removed at the time of scorching, fire was prevented. If the handkerchief was removed at the time of smoldering, the sudden increase in oxygen burst the cloth into flames. What were the odds of someone entering the show window at precisely the right time, just before the removal of the cloth would lead to fire? And since it was an impossibility that whoever removed the cloth didn't see Vernon Doyle lying dead, why did they not report it?

Bradshaw's experiments brought him to the irrefutable conclusion that the handkerchief had been intentionally placed over the lamp and intentionally removed. The cloth could not have fallen accidentally into such a position to create such scorch marks. This placement must have occurred sometime between midnight—when the window lights were shut off—and seven, when they were turned on again.

Had it been placed, then, after Doyle was killed? By the killer, hoping that when the lights came on, a fire would ensue and destroy any evidence of what had happened in that window? Why else would anyone have placed the handkerchief over the lamp? Yet, if fire had been the goal, why had the cloth been anonymously removed? Had it been placed prior to Doyle's death, but after midnight, after the window lamps were turned off? For what purpose? Again, intentional fire-setting seemed the only logical answer. Motive? An angry employee? Anarchism? Personal vendetta? And why remove the cloth prior to setting fire? Had Doyle's death complicated an arson attempt and thus motivated the arsonist to abandon the attempt? Or were the two crimes even related?

He didn't have enough information to begin to form an opinion. He needed more facts. It was time to head to the waterfront.

A monster climbed out of the deep. Tethers of rope and hose ensnared the bulky dripping canvas body, and the otherworldly domed copper helmet with three round glass eyes winked in the sudden sun break. Two tenders sprung into action, aiding this creature onto the dock. One tender removed the lead-weighted belt from the monster, while another detached the helmet, revealing a man's head of thick black hair and a pale clean-shaven rugged face. The man stepped out of the weighted boots and stood with canvas-clad feet on the rain-darkened dock. The tenders peeled off the diver's dress, leaving the man in thick woolen underwear and barefoot. He reached down into the legs of the vacated suit and pulled out thick wool socks, but he didn't don them. He was given trousers and a flannel jacket, and then a tender pointed in Bradshaw's direction. The man nodded his chin in acknowledgement.

Bradshaw retreated into the office to wait. Located north of the modern new piers and warehouses that stretched from the Moran Brothers shipyard to Broad Street, Galloway Diving shared a weathered dock on an old wharf riddled with mismatched buildings. From the outside, Galloway's office could best be described as a shanty, but inside, all was shipshape. And warm. Bradshaw examined the many charts covering the walls. Old charts from Seattle's pioneering days, charts of Puget Sound, the Washington coast, Elliott Bay, and one dated 1895 indicating the depths in fathoms of the hundreds of wrecks in the Strait of Juan de Fuca. Many of the charts had little pins with colored flags marking locations.

A diving suit stood on display in the corner. It looked well used, the canvas patched, and the copper helmet had developed a dark patina. But the three glass plates gleamed. What would possess a man to put himself into such a getup and drop himself into the sea was beyond him. No treasure of the deep could be worth that.

A percolator sat bubbling atop the coal stove in the center of the room, reminding Bradshaw he'd missed his morning coffee. He moved to the stove to warm his hands, and his thoughts drifted.

The newspaper had hit his front porch this morning before he'd had breakfast, bringing news of Doyle's death and a secondhand quote from Bradshaw. The reporter had used his statement out of context in such a way as to be inflammatory and misleading, insinuating that the Edison GE bulbs were faulty. Bradshaw hadn't spoken to any reporters, but he did recognize the words to be his. He'd said them at the Bon Marché while speaking to O'Brien when only employees had been around. It was not the first time a reporter had rushed in and interviewed witnesses to a crime investigation then presented their findings inaccurately, and it wouldn't be the last. But in this particular case it was more than annoying.

Under the article had been another smaller one, given less space because it was sadly so common. A suicide by carbolic acid. The sight of it lanced him. He'd crumpled the page and tossed it into the parlor grate with a glance toward the stairs, toward his son's room. The boy knew his mother had taken her own life many years ago, but not the manner in which she'd done it.

His stomach no longer receptive to food or coffee, he'd headed out of his house, and when he opened the front door, he found standing there the same young man who had served him papers the previous day at his office. He was handed another plain manila envelope, which he accepted without argument or evasion. He'd dropped the envelope at his attorney's office on the way to the waterfront. J. D. Maddock was efficient, Bradshaw gave him that.

Now, as Bradshaw stood warming his hands at the coal stove, the smell of the coffee made him light-headed. He moved away, taking a closer look at the bulky diving dress. It was composed of two layers of thin canvas, sandwiching a layer of rubber. He was examining the way the heavy rubber collar was vulcanized to the suit when Galloway came padding in, his feet still bare.

"That was my first diving dress," Galloway said proudly, extending a strong, cold hand. They exchanged greetings then Galloway explained, "Old Gus gave me the outfit, God rest his soul, and he taught me to dive. He was tough as they come, and not afraid of anything but ghosts."

"Ghosts?"

"He saw one down below and it nearly took his life. Divers don't tend to be superstitious, mind you, not like sailors and fishermen who won't set sail if they see a cat just before boarding. When you're down deep, you can't afford to be spooked by nonsense. So when Gus said he met up with a ghost, I knew he meant it." Galloway shuddered and made a small sound in the back of his throat.

"What about you? Seen any ghosts down below?"

"No, thank goodness. But I did see one on land. Once was enough. Coffee?"

Bradshaw returned to the stove and accepted a mug gratefully. He'd never seen a ghost, and he didn't care to hear about Jake's experience, but he understood what it felt like to be haunted. They stood together drinking while outside the weather turned nasty again and sent raindrops pinging against the glass.

"Has the technology changed much since you began diving?"

"Oh, not with the suits. That old one still does the job. The compressors are better, though, so we can go deeper."

"You go down all times of year?" Bradshaw asked.

"Oh, the temperatures below aren't much better in summer, maybe mid-fifties on the hottest day of the year. Today, I think we measured forty-nine. As long as there's no danger of the hoses freezing, I work. The worst is wind. The wind makes it miserable, and dangerous."

"Are you working here? On this dock, I mean?"

"No, I was just testing out a new suit, making sure she's air-tight and well-fit before I go deeper. There's a wreck in about a hundred feet of water, went down last week with all her cargo. We'll be lightening her soon, then patching her up if she's not too bad. Hopefully get her floating again."

"That takes a large crew, doesn't it?"

"It does, more than I have. I'll be diving for the Alaska Company Wreckers. They have all the big equipment, the tugs and pontoons and pumps and sweepers."

"Do you work for other outfits often?"

"Just Alaska. I like to keep up my skills, and the pay is top dollar." He lifted his steaming mug toward the window. Lashed to the end of the dock was Galloway's salvage boat, a small steamship with the profile of a tug crossed with a trawler. It looked as strong and capable as its owner. "It's my livelihood and my home. I can't sleep on dry land anymore. If the floor isn't rocking, the room spins."

"I take it you're a bachelor."

"It suits me," he said, topping off his mug, and doing the same for Bradshaw. "I've got no patience for children, and no woman would tolerate my way of life."

"It's a young man's profession."

"That it is. You begin to lose your nerve after a certain age and so many dives, or so I'm told. But I figure I've got another decade at least before I hang up my gear, so I earn what I can. It never hurts to bring in a little extra. This is not a cheap business to run. I own my boat, and I'm equipped to take two men down at a time, do some minor repairs, retrieve cargo, that sort of thing. I employ six men full time, and others part-time who float between outfits." Galloway stretched his back and moved his shoulders as if working out kinks from muscles more developed than Henry's, and a good sight stronger than Bradshaw's.

"My men told me you're here about a treasure hunt, Professor. I specialize in those, but if it's Oscar Daulton's invention you're after, I can't help you."

"Why not?"

"I've got an exclusive contract with a client."

"And who is your client?"

Galloway's broad chest puffed a bit. "Mr. Thomas Edison of Menlo Park, New Jersey."

"I see. And when did you sign this contract?"

"Monday, with his Seattle legal representative, Mr. J. D. Maddock."

"Monday? But Mr. Maddock has been actively searching for information regarding Daulton's invention for many months, ever since Mr. Edison came to town, in fact."

"He didn't make me a high enough offer until Monday."

"You were confident he would eventually make such an offer?"

"Of course. I don't mean to boast, Professor, but I'm about the best deep diver in the Pacific Northwest. I work almost exclusively in Puget Sound, mostly right here in Elliott Bay, so I know these waters like other men know their own backyards. When Maddock first approached, I knew he needed me, but he had to try everyone else before he realized I was worth the price."

"Weren't you taking a chance?"

"What, on losing a big contract? No, it was a sure thing. I knew no one else would have any luck."

"Why were you so sure?"

"Like I said, I'm the best. They've had more than two years to find it, and they haven't."

"You've had the same two years."

Galloway shrugged, but his smile stayed as confident as ever. Bradshaw wondered if Galloway's real business, at least in regards to finding Daulton's box, was selling hope. He made money as long as treasure-seekers believed he could find it.

"Can you provide me with the names of the other divers Mr. Maddock hired?"

"I can, but you'll be wasting your money hiring them." Galloway went to a desk and his pen scratched noisily for a few minutes.

"Mr. Galloway, could you add the names of all those who hired you over the past two years to search for Daulton's invention?"

Galloway's eyes narrowed. "What do you need my client list for?"

A ship's horn sounded from a slip nearby, and seagulls cried as if in protest.

"I won't harass your clients, Mr. Galloway. Not unless one of them has committed murder."

Galloway's hand froze halfway to his coffee mug. "Is this about the electrician at the Bon?"

"Why would you think so?"

"It's front page news. The paper said you were investigating and that you blamed Edison's new holiday lights for Doyle's death. Now you're here asking about my clients, and Vernon Doyle was a client. If you're not here because of Doyle, it seems a strange coincidence."

"What was your relationship with Vernon Doyle?"

"He was a customer. He paid for a few dives. He was hoping to find the lost invention. But I don't see how the names of my other clients would help you."

"When you say he paid, do you mean he went diving?"

"No, he was afraid to dive." He said this without scorn, but Bradshaw felt an insult nonetheless. And what would Galloway make of his own terror of any sort of depth or height? Or small spaces?

"Doyle paid for me to dive and search. He believed he knew something about the invention and that he was entitled to it. Is that true?"

"I've been hearing similar reports from others. I haven't yet untangled fact from tall tales."

"Huh. Now it's your turn. What happened to Doyle that didn't get into the papers? And what has it got to do with Galloway Diving?"

"I'm afraid I can only ask questions at this stage of an investigation, not answer them. How well did you know Vernon Doyle?"

Galloway shrugged. "Had a drink with him now and again, but his wife doesn't know. She's not fond of drink."

"When did he last hire you?"

"Oh, this fall. October?"

"Can you check your log book?"

"We can find the dates on the chart."

He strode across the room, still oblivious to being barefoot. Surely the wood floor was like ice. He stood before a chart of the bay near West Seattle with the wavy lines indicating various depths. Numbered flags were pinned near the Maryland Street dock where the ferry from Seattle landed daily. Bradshaw made note of the dates and number of dives, while Galloway cocked his head and studied the map. Bradshaw could only imagine what Galloway knew of those waters and what lay deep below. There were fish of all sorts in the bay, and seals and killer whales. What else lay below? Giant octopuses, ghosts? Whatever Galloway was paid, it was not enough.

"So, what do you think? We looking in the right area?"

Bradshaw shook off the nightmare images of the deep and studied the chart. He found the Marion Street dock and followed a dotted line from it to the landing in West Seattle. "Yes, I suppose. The general vicinity."

"Passengers on board that day say there was a commotion a few minutes before docking." He looked at Bradshaw for confirmation.

Bradshaw shrugged. "I really couldn't say." He'd been pre-occupied, trying to stop a murder. He'd had no sense of the passage of time or the distance traveled across the bay. It was only an eight-minute trip from dock to dock. It was entirely possible that just a few minutes elapsed from the time Daulton threw the basket overboard until the ferry docked, but it had all passed in a blur.

Galloway said, "I read about it when it happened, like every-one else. I still don't know exactly what it is I'm supposed to be looking for other than it's in a cigar box. Some sort of electrical invention?"

"Yes. Was it you who found the basket?"

"No, a fisherman found that a day or so after it went over. Of course, it was made of wicker and floated."

"The batteries would have gone straight down. They haven't been found either."

"Batteries?"

"Three dry cell telegraph batteries, strapped together."

"That's the first I've heard of batteries, Professor."

"The reporters were fascinated with the invention inside the cigar box, not the ordinary batteries." Daulton had made his device portable with the telegraph batteries, but Bradshaw had not seen it in operation with them. "How deep is it here?" Bradshaw pointed to the flags at the outer edge of the search.

"The maximum most deep divers are willing and able to go, about a hundred and twenty feet. That takes the best gear and four men pumping air. A man can't stay down long at that depth. Ten, maybe fifteen minutes at a time. That box must be deep, and that's why the others have failed. It's why I've failed, too, I'm afraid. I've put in my time and searched everywhere accessible. But until I got the new compressors yesterday, I didn't have the air to go down any deeper. How come you've never looked for it, Professor? I've never heard of you hiring a diving outfit to search. Is it a tall tale? If the thing is worth something, why aren't you looking for it?"

"Because I don't want to find it. You've covered the area thoroughly."

"It looks like that on paper. In reality, it's dark down there, and where it's not muddy, it's rocky with crevices big enough to trap a man. In some places the bull kelp grows as thick as forests."

Bradshaw tried and failed to block the image of the massive, long, thick tendrils of seaweed wrapping themselves around a man and pulling him deep into the depths. He felt an icy fog brush against his face and feared it meant the coming of a faint. He nodded and breathed and swallowed hard and the feeling passed.

Oblivious to Bradshaw's internal battle, Galloway went on, "The thing could be two feet away, but if you don't look in the exact right spot, you won't see it."

"Yet you seem confident of finding it for Edison."

"With Edison's backing, I can afford a more thorough search, and better equipment. That new suit I was testing came compliments of the Wizard. And the new pumps. I'll be able to go deeper than anyone in the region and expand the search. As soon as I finish the job for Alaska, I'll find that cigar box for Edison, Professor. You wait and see."

"I would still like to see your client list. I will use discretion."

Galloway hesitated but at last allowed Bradshaw to copy down the complete list of his clients who'd asked to search for Daulton's lost box, going back to the spring of '01. He only recognized one name, other than Vernon Doyle. Troy Ruzauskas. The Bon Marché's window dresser.

Chapter Eight

Eager as he was to hear what the Bon's window dresser had to say about his interest in diving for Oscar Daulton's invention, Bradshaw was due up at the university to oversee the Dynamo Lab, and with term exams next week, he knew his students would be full of questions. Because of the changeable weather and myriad places to visit today, he'd left his bicycle—his preferred method of transportation—at home. He hiked up from the waterfront and caught a streetcar on the Lake Union Line at Eighth, transferring to the University Line once across the bridge.

He found the campus alive with holiday spirit, due in part to the decorating efforts of the Delta Alpha Sorority, who were still stringing garland as he climbed the steps and entered the main doors of the Administration Building.

Inside, he followed the winding concrete steps down to the basement labs, where more joviality awaited him. His students, four boisterous juniors, were entertaining an elderly white-bearded fellow with their class yell.

Rip! Rah! Roar!
Seek No More
Come Adore
Nineteen Naught Four!

The white-bearded gentleman was not Father Christmas but Grandfather Bagley, one of the State University's earliest supporters. His full name was Reverend Daniel Bagley, for besides being one of Seattle's first pioneers, he was also a Methodist minister, and his evangelical spirit included his passion for supporting institutions of higher learning. He'd been instrumental in establishing the Territorial University, which ultimately became the State University. He was beloved by the students and he visited frequently to encourage and inspire.

"Professor Bradshaw," Grandfather Bagley called out, his eyes crinkling with laughter, "It's hard to believe these young lads will one day be running our country. Have you an invention to tame them?"

"I do. When they get out of hand, I send them to the bicycle there in the corner, mounted to a dynamo. They charge batteries while riding out the nonsense."

"Excellent, Professor! I will be on my way then, and leave the rascals to you."

Grandfather Bagley's departure rang with enthusiastic holiday wishes, and then Bradshaw kindly but firmly turned his students to task, taking a small glimmer of delight from their eyes by saying, as he pointed to the diagram of an electric generator, "This will be on the exam."

Two hours later, Bradshaw grabbed a quick lunch of steaming vegetable soup and a cold roast beef sandwich at a diner near the university before heading back downtown. He met up with Detective O'Brien at the Bon, and they found a relatively quiet location on the second floor between the Ladies' Furnishings and Millinery departments.

The chatter and buzz of the hectic store was mostly below them, rising like the warm-up notes from an orchestra. Leather chairs were conveniently placed near the balcony that overlooked the main floor, with the intention, no doubt, of providing a place of rest for weary husbands, not two investigators looking into murder. But they dropped into the chairs gratefully. Bradshaw's position gave him a perfect view of the latest frilly and puffy fashions displayed on lifelike female mannequins. Toward the back, a headless female form was dressed in a simple gown of pale green. No silly frilly furbelows marred the elegant lines of the dress, and Bradshaw instantly envisioned Missouri in it. He'd never bought a woman an article of clothing before. How would he determine the correct size?

He did not ask Detective O'Brien, although, being married and the father of four girls, surely he would know.

Distracted by the gown, he missed some of what O'Brien was saying, catching only the end of his sentence, "...when I talked to the night guard, and not only did he see nothing unusual, it's my guess he saw nothing at all save the inside of his eyelids. He has two day jobs that together run from seven in the morning until ten at night, and he starts here at midnight. He confessed he can sleep standing up and even while walking. Mr. Olafson fired him about an hour ago."

"What about the store detectives?"

"Competent women, and discreet. They've dealt with a lot of theft lately—some from employees—and they know of several romantic back-room affairs, but they had nothing to pass on about Doyle that they thought would be helpful. He was honest with the timesheet and never took home anything that didn't belong to him. They did admit they haven't had any spare time to pay much attention to employees lately. With the holidays in full swing, they've had their hands full with shoplifters."

"Why is it you never hear much about theft from the Bon?"

"Because they do their best to keep it quiet. Not good for business to have customers arrested daily."

"You asked about Olafson?"

"The detectives said he was as upright and virtuous as they come."

"Did you get a chance to talk with Billy Creasle?"

"I did, and what's more, several of his fellow employees talked about him when I interviewed them about Doyle. The boy is universally perceived as a wonder, a prodigy. Great things are predicted for his future. They agreed he is the apple of Mr. Olafson's eye. Only from the shoe salesman did I get the sense that Olafson's interest was anything other than fatherly."

"Tell me about this salesman."

"Mr. Lewis Latimer, a stooped man in his fifties, worked here since the store moved to this location in '96. I get the impression he's been in sales his whole life and is competent at best. I interviewed him again, and he repeated that Olafson has an unnatural fondness for the young boys employed at the store, but when pressed, he said he'd never had occasion to observe any indecent behavior."

"Did you lead the conversation?"

"I provided the same opening to everyone. I said that I'd heard Mr. Olafson seems to be liked by the employees, especially the young ones."

"And from that Latimer supplied Olafson's unnatural fondness?"

"He did, and he repeated that he felt Olafson was particularly smitten by Billy, but no one else took the conversation there. All others gave Olafson high praise for his ability to get work and loyalty from the boys."

"And the boys themselves?"

"There are currently fifty of them between the ages of eleven and fifteen working part-time either as cash boys, runners, or errand boys. There are a few dozen up to the age of seventeen working in stockrooms or the mailroom or in delivery. There are far fewer girls, just a dozen or so who work in wrapping or as cash runners in the Ladies' Department. All I interviewed gave honest praise of Olafson. If any of them lied, they are far better at it than my girls."

"What's your hunch?"

"Where there's smoke…Of course, Mr. Latimer may well have reason to tarnish our view of Mr. Olafson, something we've yet to discover."

Bradshaw took a deep breath. The holiday cacophony took on a sinister undertone. His glance swept the women perusing the displays of finery, moved to the little cash girl dashing for the stairs to the third-floor office, then he looked over the balcony to the main floor where the salesmen and saleswomen manned their counters, and customers stood three-deep in line. A few errand boys, distinctive in their dark knee-pants suits and white aprons, dashed through the crowds.

"Shouldn't they be in school at this time of day?"

O'Brien had followed Bradshaw's gaze. "They get around that by providing a school here for the day workers. On the whole, it's not a bad job for a kid. Boys love to run."

"I didn't know you approved of child labor."

"Well, I don't want them down in coal mines, but I don't see the harm in paying them something to run around a department store a couple hours a day. Keeps them out of trouble."

"And exposes them to potential dangers."

"Life is danger, Ben. You can lock yourself up and avoid all trouble, or you can live. Boys need to learn how to deal with it."

"I don't see your daughters running around the store."

"Girls are different."

Bradshaw didn't completely disagree, and he knew the boys who worked at the Bon likely ate better and were better dressed because of it. He just hoped the lessons learned here didn't include the darker, uglier side of life. "If the shoe salesman's accusations prove valid, it could be that Vernon Doyle witnessed something between Olafson and Billy or one of the others and threatened to tell. It could be a motive for murder."

"The upshot is, even if Olafson had nothing to do with Doyle's death, I have to investigate. Convictions of indecent assault upon a child are almost impossible without third party testimony or physical proof. I won't record a word in my notebook until I have something substantial, in case it turns out to be nothing but maliciousness."

Moral depravity, perversion—those were the terms used by the press when reporting on such cases. Bradshaw knew in his soul that he wouldn't kill to protect such a secret, but he would kill anyone who ever attempted such a thing with his son. And gladly accept the sentence, if any. If ever there was justification for lethal action, surely assault of a child would be one. He took another deep breath and turned his mind back to the case.

"When you spoke to Doyle's wife, did she mention any particular friends or acquaintances?"

"No, she was fairly shaken."

"We need to find someone who knew him well. Vernon Doyle may have been places and with people his wife knew nothing about." He told O'Brien about Jake Galloway's mention of drinking with Doyle. "A man with that complexion has spent many hours with a bottle."

"Uh-oh. Mrs. Doyle is a temperance gal. Saw the sash hanging on the coat rack. Looks like we'll be adding the Tenderloin to the search. With drinking comes gambling and it could be his debts followed him to the store. I told Mrs. Doyle you might want to see her."

Bradshaw nodded. "Vernon Doyle may have been having an affair with Mrs. Adkins, a seamstress here." He told O'Brien what Billy told him.

"Now there's a motive. If she was being pressured into the affair, she might have found a way to permanently end it. I will speak to Mrs. Adkins."

"What does the chief window dresser, Mr. Troy Ruzauskas, have to say about the scorched cloth?"

"That it wasn't his fault, and neither was the last near conflagration."

"Who does he blame?"

"He doesn't, not specifically. He's angry and flummoxed by the accusations."

A bevy of women swept by, smelling of perfume from the Fragrance Department mingled with the damp wool of their outerwear, and chattering of an upcoming engagement for which they all required new gowns. Bradshaw's eye was drawn once again to the simple, elegant gown in the back of the department, and he imagined Missouri wearing it, standing in the parlor in the soft glow of the—

"It's called a chemise, Ben."

Bradshaw's glance snapped back to O'Brien.

"It's not a dress, it's an undergarment. That's why it's on a headless mannequin. You know, to make it less vulgar on public display. You give that to Missouri for Christmas, and Mrs. Prouty will clout you with her frying pan."

Bradshaw cleared his throat, and gave a final, resigned glance at the forbidden garment. "Wh—"

"It's gone on too long, Ben. You're just torturing yourself."

"This isn't—"

"I wasn't around when you went to pieces over your wife's death, but I saw the aftermath, and it wasn't pretty."

"This isn't—"

"Yes, it is. It's exactly the same because she's not right for you. She's too young, too modern, too free-thinking. The longer you drag out this purgatory, the worse hell it will be when it ends. And you'll go back to being the dour, plodding, miserable man I met a couple years ago. Yes, Missouri Fremont helped you get better, but you can't seriously think you'll ever find a way to marry her."

Bradshaw sat stunned at O'Brien's directness. "This really isn't the appropriate time to be having this discussion."

"I didn't bring it up, you did. Your mind isn't on the case, it's on that undergarment you think is a dress, it's on the conversation you haven't yet had with Father McGuinness because you know how it will end."

A sharp pain radiated along Bradshaw's jaw and down to his shoulder, and he realized that the buzz in his head was the grinding of his teeth. Not willing to face his own anger nor the truth he would see reflected, he could no longer meet O'Brien's eyes. As they sat, not speaking, not looking at each other, a saleswoman approached and asked if they needed assistance. Detective O'Brien flashed his badge, and the woman left them alone.

Bradshaw said curtly, "What did the window dresser have to say about Doyle's death?"

O'Brien paused a moment, as if weighing his options. His heavy sigh signaled a truce. He said, "Ruzauskas and Doyle conferred on the placement and timing of the holiday lights at midnight, at which time Ruzauskas went home—alone—with the intention of returning the next morning to see the lights, but he overslept and didn't awaken until his landlady pounded on the door to say he was wanted by the police."

Bradshaw said, "Billy was here that night until midnight, too. Do we have a time of death?"

"Coroner says he's near certain Doyle died between two and four. Rigor wasn't far established and the stomach contents not much digested. Doyle was seen in the men's lunch room at half past midnight, having a bite."

"Did anyone see Mr. Ruzauskas leave the store?"

"He left through the employee entrance, signed the book. So did Billy Creasle."

"Ruzauskas is a diver. Did he tell you? He hired Galloway Diving several times to take him searching for Daulton's box."

O'Brien's eyebrows flashed up. "Now that's interesting."

"I agree. There were fifty or more employees here in various capacities, mostly in stocking and shipping, the night Vernon Doyle died. I'm not ready to disregard them all, but I believe we're safe in eliminating anyone from suspicion who had no close relationship with Doyle. The location of the switch and the time at which it was thrown indicate an action of intent triggered by strong emotion, not casual irritation."

"But must it have been an intent to kill? Could it have merely been an intent to turn on the tree lights?"

"Doyle was in the process of twisting together bare wire. The lights were in his hands, not on the tree. Most people these days understand the dangers of electricity, wouldn't you say?"

O'Brien shrugged. "Many know it's dangerous, and nothing else. And everyone working in this store has become comfortable, even nonchalant, about flipping switches and pressing buzzers. Someone could have come by and…" O'Brien tilted his head, and Bradshaw could see he was trying to imagine a scenario in which some employee might stop by to say hello at two in the morning and throw the switch with no ill intent. He shook his head. "So we know it was homicide or murder."

"It's possible someone could have managed to enter the store after hours, or hidden themselves away until after closing. We may investigate those scenarios if premeditation arises as a possibility. But so far, it looks both intentional and unpremeditated. No one could have predicted Doyle would be in a vulnerable situation, and exposure to electric current isn't always fatal. The pulling of that switch was the equivalent of shoving somebody down the stairs. There's a certainty of harm but no guarantee of death."

"So who do we have then? Olafson to silence Doyle? The seamstress in a lover's spat or to end an affair? We've only got hearsay about both of those possibilities. Neither one of them were here, or so they say. You've talked to Billy, who found the body. The only other person in the store that we know might be connected to Doyle was Ruzauskas, and he left at midnight and didn't return, at least not officially, until after the body was found. He's here now, if you want to talk to him."

"I do." He got to his feet, and O'Brien followed suit.

"Do you want to look over my notes?"

"No, I trust you've told me what I need to know, Detective." Their eyes met briefly, and Bradshaw was first to look away.

"I'm sorry, Ben, but it had to be said. It's Christmas and I want to close this case. I can't do it without you."

Bradshaw couldn't think of a polite response, so he said nothing.

O'Brien said, "If our killer wasn't someone on the store's night crew, then who? The doors are locked and no one gets in at night except through the employee entrance."

"Do we know if the lockup procedure was performed in full at closing on Tuesday night?"

"According to Mr. Olafson, yes."

Bradshaw pondered a moment, thinking of locks and doors and ways they were opened.

"Do all the entry doors require a key to open them from inside the store?"

"No. Two main entrances and all the windows can be unbolted from within. Has to do with fire insurance, I believe. But they're alarmed, and the alarm switches are locked."

Bradshaw said, "The alarm switches are locked in the electrical cabinets near the doors. The same cabinets that control the show windows. And Vernon Doyle possessed a key, and he had the cabinet open all night."

This time, when their eyes met, they were thinking only of Vernon Doyle. Bradshaw said aloud what they were both thinking. "He let in his killer."

Chapter Nine

Bradshaw rapped on the partially open door of the third floor office and called, "Mr. Ruzauskas?"

"Yes, Professor Bradshaw. Please, come in."

He stepped in carefully, turning sideways to slide between easels to reach the open bit of floor space. Colorful sketches of artfully arranged window displays covered every inch of the wall, and Bradshaw allowed himself a moment of admiration.

"Did you do all these?"

"I did."

The designs set appealing scenes of hearth and home, celebrations, relaxation, and adventure, and they revealed an artistic talent as impressive as any he'd ever seen in a museum.

He turned to the window dresser, perched on a stool before an easel bearing draft paper with a scant few pencil lines. Younger than Bradshaw expected, the designer was in his mid-twenties, perhaps, and stage actor handsome, with a shock of blond hair, a clean-shaven angular face, and blue eyes filled with an open, honest expression. Yet he seemed unaware of his looks, and he'd dressed as if he'd reached for his clothes in the dark, finding them in a crumpled pile on the floor.

Bradshaw said, "I won't keep you long from your work."

"Oh, it doesn't matter. I'm not getting a thing done."

"Detective O'Brien gave me the details of your earlier interview, and I just wanted to clarify a few things."

"All right. I'd offer you a chair, but there isn't one, only my stool here."

"It's quite all right. You left the store at midnight, after discussing with Mr. Doyle the arrangement of the holiday lighting?"

"Yes, and he was alive and well when I left. And there was no cloth anywhere near the footlights in that show window. All those handkerchiefs were in the pockets of the mannequins, where they belong. I know for certain because after the last incident, which also was not my fault, I always triple check my work to be sure nothing is near the lights."

"What happened the previous time?"

"A mannequin was moved too near the front of the window and the hem of a skirt draped over a light."

"When did this happen?"

"A few weeks ago, during the Thanksgiving sales. The store was packed with customers."

"Was it determined who moved the mannequin?"

"No, but I got the blame when the dress caught fire. Thank goodness Mrs. Adkins smelled the smoke that time or I would have been given more than a warning. I've been told that my job is now in jeopardy, so if you could shed some light onto how that handkerchief was scorched, I'd be grateful."

"Mrs. Adkins? The seamstress?"

"Yes, that's her."

Was it a coincidence that the alleged mistress of Vernon Doyle was present at the time of that near conflagration? Bradshaw asked, "Do you know of anyone who would like to see you lose your position?"

"What? You think someone deliberately put that cloth near the lamp?"

"It's an option I must consider," he said vaguely. The cloth had been placed with deliberation, not carelessness, but had the intent been to harm Vernon Doyle or Troy Ruzauskas? "Is there anyone here at the store who would like your job?"

"Oh, come now, Professor. Who would risk burning down

a department store to get a job? A bit self-defeating, wouldn't you say?"

"Neither time did a full fire develop. You say Mrs. Adkins smelled smoke during that first incident?"

"That's right. She does all the adjustments to make the clothes look good on the mannequins. A customer wanted to buy a skirt from off the display. It was the only one left in the store. Mrs. Adkins was called to unstitch it."

"And she was doing so when she smelled smoke?"

"The customer smelled it, too, and goodness knows who all had been mucking about in that window. Customers have no respect for store property when they see an item they want."

"Did the smoke set off the sprinkler system?"

"No, thank goodness. Can you imagine the sodden mess? Mrs. Adkins pulled the dress away, and it burst into flames, and she screamed, and the customer screamed, or so I'm told. I wasn't there. I wasn't even at the store. Luckily, Billy heard the shouts of fire and came running with a water bucket."

"Billy Creaslc? That was a quick response."

"We're all trained in fire safety. Mrs. Adkins should have grabbed the bucket, but she panicked. The sprinkler system doesn't go into the windows, so water and sand buckets are kept nearby."

"On Wednesday night, you're sure there was no handkerchief on or near the footlights when you left at midnight?"

"No, they were where they belonged, in the pocket of the smoking jackets of the male mannequins. Maybe Mr. Doyle removed one, but I don't know why he would have, and of course he can't tell us whether he did or didn't."

"Were the window lights on when you left?"

"I left soon after Mr. Doyle shut them off from the main box. They'd been on for some time. The window was quite warm. The lights are turned on at seven in the morning. You've probably been told that. When the weather is sunny, Mr. Andrews may turn the lights off during the day for a few hours, but they are turned on again before dark and remain on until midnight. After I left, Mr. Doyle was going to wire the new Edison electric holiday lights onto a clever timing device that was supposed to cycle on and off all day. Those holiday lights were going to be attached to the tree, and they get hot. Doyle and I are very aware of the potential for fire. We always take care."

"You're an amateur diver?"

Ruzauskas blinked, looking slightly startled by the question. "Yes, how'd you know?"

"I was at Galloway Diving today and saw his client list."

"Are you a diver?" Ruzauskas' face lit with hope.

"No."

"Oh," he said with disappointment, then shrugged. "Well, I'm an amateur, but I may have to turn professional if I lose my job here. What store would hire me if they thought I was a fire starter?"

"What is your interest in diving?"

Troy's expression changed, softening, cheering. "It's exciting. You should try it. It's like traveling to another world. The creatures down below are spectacular. I've been doing some sketches and painting underwater scenes—" he got up from his stool and reached behind a pile of canvases, pulling out one from the back "—but it's hard to capture."

The canvas depicted a blue-green world of sparkling light, jagged rocks softened by plants and inhabited by creatures Bradshaw didn't know the proper names of.

Ruzauskas said, "The light is faint in Puget Sound, but the quality and texture is exquisite, especially in shallower depths. I've read about places in the world where the water is a crystal clear blue, and the fish and fauna bursting with color. I'd love to dive in such a place someday."

"Did you ever discuss diving with Mr. Doyle?"

"Quite a bit, actually. He wouldn't hear of diving himself. Said the idea of being underwater so deep frightened him. Many people feel that way, I know, at least until they try it. He did say he was interested in sunken treasure, though, and wanted to know if I'd ever seen any. I take that back, not just any treasure, one in particular. That lost invention of your student, Professor, the one they hanged for trying to kill McKinley."

Oscar Daulton had plotted to kill President McKinley, it was true, but he hadn't been successful. Another anarchist had done the deed a few months later. But Daulton had succeeded in killing three men, and it was those murders for which he had been sentenced to death.

"When was this?"

"Oh, gosh, end of summer? That's when he began talking about it."

"Did you ever search for that lost invention?"

"A few times. I got caught up in the excitement of it. Mr. Doyle said if I found it, we'd go into a partnership and get rich. He knew Oscar Daulton, you know, and he felt sure he could figure out the invention if he could get his hands on it."

"Did he say Daulton told him how the invention worked?"

"Not until recently. I remember a few times over the past year or so when he complained he wished he'd asked Daulton more questions, but I take it the boy was secretive. Then when Edison came to town, suddenly Mr. Doyle had been Daulton's best friend and confidant."

"Why do you suppose he changed his story?"

"Made him feel important. And I think he didn't like the idea of some outsider coming in and finding the treasure. Stealing it out from under our noses, was how he put it. He said they'd never find it, and so far he's been right. But then, he didn't find it either."

"Do you still dive?"

"For Daulton's invention? No, that search is in deep waters. I'm qualified to go down, but it's more expensive because it takes more men at the pump, so I only went a few times. I'm saving up to buy a house." Troy dropped his head. His hair fell over his eyes but didn't cover the smile that infused his features.

Bradshaw knew what that smile indicated. He asked, "What's her name?"

"Beatrice." He pronounced the name as if it were poetry.

"And does she have a last name?"

"Warren. Miss Beatrice Warren."

Bradshaw knew of the Warrens. They were one of Seattle's wealthiest families, with ties to shipping and the railroads. Their new home on Queen Anne Hill had been featured in a national magazine.

"Have you set a date?"

"It's not that simple. I have to prove myself worthy, able to care for her, provide a home, at least one servant. Two would be better. A cook and a maid. She says she doesn't need them, but she's never done for herself. She thinks it would be fun to live simply, but it wouldn't be fun long, and I don't want her to feel her life with me would become nothing but work and drudgery. And when our children come along, we'd need a nurse, but I don't see how I'd ever afford a nurse, not as a window dresser, and one can't depend on one's art to sell, so I wonder if I'm just fooling myself believing I can ever really support her in the way she deserves."

"Are you trying to prove this to Miss Warren or to yourself or to her father?"

"Mr. Warren has been remarkably accommodating. He's one of those wealthy chaps that doesn't believe in coddling his children, thinks giving them too much spoils them. Of course, that also means he doesn't plan to give Beatrice much of a dowry, not that I want it for me, but for her. Mrs. Warren is different. I doubt I'll ever live up to her standards, and I'm sorry, Professor, I don't know why I'm baring my soul to you. This whole thing—Mr. Doyle's death, and Mr. Olafson threatening to fire me over the scorched kerchief—it has me in a fuddle."

"I understand," Bradshaw said. He understood more than the young man knew. He understood the fear, the desperation, the feeling of unworthiness. But in his own case, the chief obstacle between him and the woman he loved was religion, not money. A difference of faith was not something one could alter with determination. Money, on the other hand, could be earned, or stolen, or extorted. If Vernon Doyle had stood in this young man's way to wealth in some manner, or if Doyle had known something that would soil his reputation in the eyes of the Warrens, he might have just confessed a motive to commit murder.

"If you think of anything that might prove helpful to the case, will you let me know?"

Ruzauskas nodded, and combed the hair out of his eyes with his fingers.

As Bradshaw passed out of the store, through the throng of holiday shoppers, the noise, the music, and the gay decorations grated against his nerves. He wanted to get away, from everyone, and if he went home, he wouldn't be in the mood to be cheerful or even kind. He also knew he didn't truly want to be completely alone with his tormenting uncertainty. So he trudged down the street to the J. M. Taylor Printing Company, where he was told the proprietor was not in, but that he could be found at the university. Bradshaw hopped a crowded streetcar.

It was a quarter past four when he arrived on campus, and dusk was about to give way to darkness. Lights glowed from many of the windows of the Science and Administration Buildings, but Bradshaw's destination lay a short walk beyond them.

The Observatory had been built with locally quarried sandstone left over from the construction of the Administration Building. It was a grand little building topped with a gleaming copper dome. Yellow light spilled from the transom above the door in welcome.

Inside, the Transit Room door was closed, as was the door to the Pier Room, so Bradshaw headed up the stairs to the dome, where meager lantern light danced. The lower portion of the building was wired for electric lighting, but not the upper Observatory.

"Professor Bradshaw! How very good to see you!" Professor Joseph Taylor's greeting was warm and effusive, like the man himself.

"Good evening, sir. I was told I could find you here."

"One of my favorite places on this great Earth. You're just in time to lend me a hand. Grab a rope."

Bradshaw did as instructed, taking hold of a rope that dangled from the base of the copper dome.

Taylor had already opened one narrow section of the roof, from the apex to the base, to the nighttime sky. Bradshaw tugged the rope and moved forward slowly, setting the copper dome turning on the bearings in the grooved track that circumnavigated the circular tower.

"Go all the way around once, if you please," said Taylor, "I just greased the balls." The dome roof rotated with a whisper-smooth, deep hum, and an occasional creak from the metal panels.

Taylor pointed, indicating where Bradshaw should slow to a stop, and then Taylor put his eye to the lens to focus the telescope. Eleven years his senior, Taylor yet reminded Bradshaw of his father. He had small, close-set eyes, crinkled at the corners from a lifetime of smiling, and a dashing mustache that curled up at the tips. An outgoing and social man, with many friends and no falseness about him, he'd assumed the role of Bradshaw's unofficial mentor. Bradshaw first met him the Fourth of July of 1894, at the cornerstone laying ceremony for the Administration Building. As the university's first mathematics professor, first Professor of Astronomy, and the first Director of the Observatory, as well as holding an esteemed position with the Freemasons, Taylor had been given the honor of laying the cornerstone. He wasn't currently teaching at the university, but he remained closely associated with the Observatory through various astronomy clubs.

Taylor had a habit of cocking his head and looking at Bradshaw with both admiration and amusement. The admiration, he knew, for Taylor had explained, was for Bradshaw's teaching style that built confidence in his students, for his several patents and practical electrical skills, and of late, his ability to solve electrical puzzles and crimes. Taylor's amusement lay in Bradshaw's dislike of social interaction. As a man who thrived on conversation, Taylor found Bradshaw's hermit tendencies befuddling.

"I haven't seen enough of you of late," said Taylor, turning away from the telescope to cock his head and give Bradshaw a grin. "Since you began your new career as Seattle's Sherlock Holmes, as a matter of fact. How are you?"

The question was not just politely asked, but honestly so.

"Confused," he said, and felt better for saying it aloud.

"Come take a look," said Taylor. "Feel your insignificance against the vastness of the heavens, and you'll gain a bit of perspective."

Bradshaw put his eye to the lens. Cracks in the storm clouds created a window into the blackness of space. Even in that small window, it seemed a thousand stars winked.

Taylor said, "I've heard it said there are more stars in the heavens than grains of sand on the Earth."

It was a staggering thought.

"Yet among them, do any contain life such as we have here on Earth?" Bradshaw asked. "Or are we alone?"

"Come now, Bradshaw! Leave it to you to find a gloomy thought while stargazing. Tell me what has you confused and let's see if a solution can be found." Taylor took a metal rod from a hook, opened a small door in the base of the telescope and began winding the weights which regulated the clockwork-style mechanism within.

Bradshaw considered speaking of Missouri, but the Catholic Church was vehemently opposed to both the Masons and the Odd Fellows, with which Taylor was also affiliated. The grounds for the church's opposition were ideological, and Bradshaw knew Taylor found them unsubstantiated and ridiculous. They'd once enjoyed a vigorous friendly debate on the subject, and while Taylor would never be disrespectful, he certainly would find it difficult to understand Bradshaw's allegiance to Catholicism if it opposed his choice of wife.

"Did you ever meet Oscar Daulton?" Bradshaw began.

"No, I never met him," Taylor said. "Does this have something to do with the search for his invention? I heard Thomas Edison paid you a visit to inquire about it."

"That's where it may have begun, with that visit. Edison has a representative here, Mr. J. D. Maddock, who is now actively looking for it." Bradshaw explained about his summons to the Bon Marché and everything he'd learned subsequently that held a possible connection between the hunt for Daulton's device and

Vernon Doyle's death. He didn't speak of Doyle's alleged affair, or the accusation against Olafson. Neither was relevant to the search for Daulton's device and could be kept private.

"Such a troubled young man," Taylor said, shaking his head. "It's a shame his genius was so warped and may have led to this. I didn't know him, Bradshaw, but I've met his type. If you can get to them young enough, you can save them. I've taught boys at nearly every age, or had them in my office as principal. When one slips out of your grasp and goes awry, it's heartbreaking. Professor Ranum knew Daulton." He spoke of the current Director of Astronomy. "He's mentioned that Daulton spent a good deal of time here, alone."

Daulton had found several places on campus where he could be alone. As Bradshaw had told Edison, he'd searched them all, including the Observatory, for anything the young man had left behind or hidden. Daulton had written extensively on other aspects of his disturbed life, but his journal contained not a hint of his inventions. He wrote of winning the war against oppression, but always stopped short of describing the weapons he planned to use, other than secrecy.

"I want to locate Daulton's box."

Taylor's eyes flashed with interest. "Now that's an about-face, and the source of your confusion, I'll wager. How can I help?"

"Galloway Diving has been searching near the ferry landing and into the bay, to a depth of about a hundred and ten feet."

"You believe they should be looking elsewhere?"

"More than two years' worth of dives and they've found nothing but the basket."

"I don't imagine something that small would be easy to find in the dark depths. Most of Elliott Bay is far beyond the reach of divers, hundreds of feet deep. Maybe a thousand, in some parts. It's only the edges that man can reach. How close to the landing were you when Daulton tossed the thing?"

"I don't know."

"Perhaps it sank below the mud."

"That's very possible. The batteries likely would have, if they hit mud rather than rock or weeds. They weighed two pounds each, and their cylindrical shape would drop more quickly and penetrate better than a flat-bottomed box."

"How much did the box weigh?"

"I never lifted it, and I can only guess as to what was inside. I believe it was heavy and would sink fairly well, but whether there was something inside providing buoyancy, I don't know. It vanished when it hit the water, and did not linger, the same as the batteries."

"Who calculated the location?"

"Jake Galloway, based on newspaper and personal accounts of the day when Daulton threw the box overboard."

"There's an art and science to finding sunken treasure. Galloway has a good reputation."

"It could be he's better with the art than the science. Would you be interested in looking at the data and making a guess?"

Taylor beamed. "I would. But surely you know the math as well as I, and I recall a certain waterfall over which you did not plummet because of your grasp of hydraulics."

"But I don't have time to research the tides and currents of Elliott Bay, nor experience with a sextant, nor do I know the captain of the *City of Seattle.*"

"Aah, you see how being active socially has its benefits? Can you provide a range of guesses as to the weight and buoyancy of Daulton's mysterious cigar box?"

"I can."

"Can we take a ferry ride and recreate the event? If I clear it with the captain?"

"I was hoping you'd ask. Do you have the time?"

"For this I do. I'll begin my research at once."

"Thank you. I have preparations to make. It might take a bit of experimentation. Shall we say near the end of next week, if the weather allows?"

"Agreed. If our findings indicate a location not yet searched, will you go for a dive, Bradshaw?"

"I'd sooner dance naked at a society ball."

"An image more gruesome than any monster of the deep. But if you have no intention of diving for it, why try to establish its location? You don't mean to give the information to Edison's man?"

"No, I don't. But I'd like the mystery solved. I'm tired of thinking about it, and if Vernon Doyle's death is related to the hunt, then the device is still killing, even from the seabed. Let's first see what our calculations tell us before I decide what to do with the information."

"Speaking of mysteries, occasionally when I'm up here in the dome alone, I hear a strange clicking sound. It's rather like static, a sharp crackling. But I can't pinpoint it. I heard it just before you arrived."

They stood quietly, listening, but heard nothing.

Bradshaw asked, "Could it be the metal of the dome expanding or contracting with the change in temperature?"

"It doesn't seem to come from above. And there's a different quality to this clicking. It's more, oh, sharp, less creaking."

"Hmm. Well, if you hear it again, count the clicks, and time the seconds between the clicks."

"Will that tell you the nature of the sounds?"

"No, but it will make the sounds less irritating if you treat them like a science experiment."

Taylor laughed. "You show potential, Bradshaw. We may yet find your funny bone. And say, I've been hearing rumors about you and Henry Pratt's niece. Could she have anything to do with your confusion and venture into wit?"

Bradshaw shrugged and held out his hand, "Sir, I thank you for your assistance and I look forward to next week."

Taylor accepted the shake and the less-than-subtle change of subject with good grace. "Take care, my friend."

On his way back downtown, Bradshaw's eye was caught by a small shop open late for the holiday season. The glowing window display was filled with colorful bars and fancy boxes of soap. If he couldn't buy that gown for Missouri, because it wasn't a gown but an undergarment, maybe he could buy her soap. When the streetcar slowed, he leapt off, and backtracked to the shop. Inside the store, his senses were bombarded with warmth and fragrances. He chose a box of lilac-scented imported soap that smelled of spring, wondering if it was too intimate a gift. It was surely more appropriate than a chemise. When she'd lived in his home, the scent of lilac often lingered in the bath and near her room. The kindly sales clerk wrapped the soap box in lavender paper, tied it with delicate gold ribbon, and topped it with a flowery golden bow.

With the box safely nestled in his coat pocket, he walked to his office, finding it dark and empty. Henry had left a note reporting he intended to spend the night asking about Vernon Doyle in the Tenderloin. For a few hours, Bradshaw worked at his desk, the fragrant gift beside him. When his eyes grew weary, he bundled up again, and took the last streetcar up to Capitol Hill.

Only the porch light glowed at his house, as he'd hoped, and yet he felt guilty for avoiding his son. Inside, he climbed the stairs, stepping over the third one that tended to creak, then looked in on Justin, who slept soundly. In his own room down the hall, he switched on the electric wall sconce, and immediately spotted the telegram on his dresser. Mrs. Prouty believed all of Missouri's correspondence contained "swooning," so she placed letters and wires from her in his room. Like so many others in his life, Mrs. Prouty was ambivalent about his relationship with Missouri.

He set down the soap, opened the wire, and felt his weariness harden into a heavy weight. She was not coming home. Not as planned. She'd written in abbreviated language to reduce the cost of the wire.

WRIGHT BROS ATTEMPT FLIGHT NC COLIN
INVITED ME OTHERS HOME DELAYED 1
WEEK LOVE MISSOURI.

Chapter Ten

Bradshaw woke Friday morning, the third day of the investigation into Doyle's death, with a growling stomach, which didn't bode well. This being a Friday during Advent, it was a day of fasting, and that meant he was restricted to one full meal at dinnertime with fish, but no meat.

He bathed and dressed, then went downstairs to the kitchen where the smell of Justin's warm oats and maple syrup enveloped him in a tortuous embrace. Bradshaw was only allowed a warm beverage this morning, and two ounces of dry toast. He usually skipped the toast but could not be so noble this morning. He ate his slice slowly, savoring the sourdough flavor, grateful for Mrs. Prouty's gift for bread-making. He sat at the kitchen table across from his son, watching him devour a great mound of syrupy oats, two thick pieces of toast slathered in butter, and a fried egg. Children were not held to the fasting rules, and for this the Jesuits were surely grateful. A room full of lads with empty stomachs would not be teachable.

"Three days," said Justin, once he'd cleaned the last drip of butter from his plate with his last bite of toast.

"Three days?"

"Until Missouri gets home."

Bradshaw's stomach clutched and his hunger fled. He'd had a whole night in which to consider the implications of Missouri Fremont traveling to North Carolina to meet up with Colin Ingersoll. "A change of plans, son. Missouri won't be home until the twenty-first or second." He told Justin about her invitation to North Carolina, forcing enthusiasm into his voice. It was a wasted effort. Justin scowled.

"She said she'd be home twelve days before Christmas."

"I know, but with each attempt, the two Wright brothers have been getting closer to success. They may achieve powered flight. This could be historic. A once-in-a-lifetime opportunity."

"So is Christmas. It only comes once a year, and this one will never come again. A boy only gets so many, Dad."

"That's true. I hadn't thought of it that way."

Justin crossed his arms and asked, "When you're married, will you make her stay home?"

Bradshaw stalled by drinking his coffee. He cleared his throat. "First of all, it's not when, but if. You know I care very much for Missouri, but we haven't yet decided to marry." He'd had to explain this several times to the boy ever since his relationship with Missouri had changed. In his son's young eyes, there was no reason for delay or any question of an outcome. Justin loved Missouri, he saw that his father did, too; therefore, they would marry. "And secondly, a man does not treat his wife like a child."

"But Roy said when his sister got married they had to say vows, and she had to say she would obey her new husband. She didn't want to say it because she's a suffragette, but they made her say it, and now she has to do whatever her husband says."

"Roy? The new boy at the end of the block? His family belongs to the Episcopal Church, I believe. The Catholic marriage ceremony doesn't include the word *obey*. Even so, in all Christian marriages, wives are to be treated kindly and with respect." Had he given his son the impression that women were servants to men? He certainly hadn't intended to teach his son anything but respect for women.

What relationships had Justin witnessed? What relationships had Bradshaw modeled? The only female Justin regularly observed Bradshaw with was Mrs. Prouty. Mrs. Prouty certainly did all the work about the house, but he paid her a good wage and rarely made demands, only requests. Which, admittedly,

Mrs. Prouty acquiesced to, sometimes willingly, other times with a grumble. Yes, she obeyed his requests as if they were demands, and he was the master of his home. Someone had to be in charge, and it was his home after all, not Mrs. Prouty's. Although, in truth, it was her home. She had no other. This had been her home for more than a decade. What must that be like? To know the home you live in is not yours, but owned by your employer, and that you live there as a condition of your employment? But Mrs. Prouty was not really an employee. She was like family. He would never think of letting her go, hiring another housekeeper. She knew that, surely.

And household dynamics, with the man in charge, was a tradition for a reason. Men typically understood the world better than women. Men were better at finances and management and leadership. And yes, Catholicism supported this. Husbands and wives filled different family needs, but they did so with respect. As his thoughts continued, he found them becoming more and more defensive. He heard Missouri's laughter, saw her rolling her eyes, heard her telling him she knew he didn't truly believe that men were naturally better managers. But he did. Didn't he? Men and women had roles in life. That was that. And to that, he distinctly heard Missouri say, as if she were standing before him, *I think he doth protest too much.* As usual, she made him question the very foundations of his beliefs, and she was twenty-five hundred miles away. What would life be like if they married? If conversations such as these were real? He could well imagine a sort of emotional vertigo taking hold, feeling dizzy all the time because he would no longer have the stability and structure of his beliefs. She would say that of course men and women were different, but those differences were not limitations. Women should be as free as men to pursue their heart's desires.

And then he imagined her smiling at him with both pity and love, stepping up to him with a challenge in her eyes and a tease on her lips …He shook his head and with a deep breath said in a tone he hoped would make his son smile, "Can you imagine Missouri promising to obey anyone?"

But it wasn't Justin who replied, it was Mrs. Prouty. "Not for a minute," she declared, then untied her apron from around her ample waist. Bradshaw glanced around, and Mrs. Prouty said, "He ran off to school a minute ago, just as the first mail arrived." She waved a sheet of paper and he caught a glimpse of Bon Marché letterhead.

"A personal invitation, Professor! It's a secret sale. I'm going downtown to catch it, and I know just what I'm getting, too. That music box I've been wanting for so long, with the carousel. It's way beyond my means, usually, but with this letter, I'm going to get it. I'll stay all day, if I have to, to be one of the chosen shoppers."

The Bon was likely trying to make up for lost sales yesterday and erase the stigma of a death in their store. It must be quite a sale to get Mrs. Prouty willing to be extravagant and out of the house before her dishes—he mentally stopped himself—*her* dishes? Was this one reason why Justin so easily accepted that women were subservient to men? Having a housekeeper around, but no mother figure to show him a relationship different from one between a man and paid help?

She hurried off to take advantage of the sale, and Bradshaw, after a glance at the sky to see that it was blustery but not pouring, pedaled his bicycle to the university to review for his freshman students the term's work on magnetism. Afterward, he climbed the stairs to his office and telephoned Henry, but the operator said there was no reply at the requested number. Henry was likely still asleep. Interviewing in the Tenderloin was hard work.

Bradshaw bundled up, hopped on his bicycle, and headed back to town, toward the Cascade neighborhood of South Lake Union. It was time for one of his least favorite parts of investigations. It was time to meet the widow.

In many areas of Seattle, keeping mud out of the house required constant vigilance, and Republican Street was no exception. Blocked from the main part of town by Denny Hill, the hill where the tunnel supporters were losing to the demolish supporters, Vernon Doyle's neighborhood was a mix of industry and homes, and the result was not harmonious for the homeowners. Noise, steam, construction, and functional but unattractive factories and businesses marred the coziness of residential lots. When the landscape architect John Olmstead had come to Seattle in the spring to advise on the development of parks, he'd opined that this part of town was best suited for industry, and Bradshaw had to agree. He would not want to live here.

Doyle's house had no front yard to speak of, just a strip of scraggly grass and dirt between the street and the road. Bradshaw propped his bicycle against a utility pole and picked his way across the muddy strip to the cement steps leading up to the door. It was a narrow house with cedar shingle siding, two stories high, if you counted the tall attic space, which, from the curtains in the window, appeared to be used as living space.

Mrs. Doyle opened the door on his first knock. Her gentle appearance surprised him since her husband had been rather rough. She was small and slender in a black mourning gown, her dark hair showed streaks of gray where she wore it swept up in the current style, but her rounded cheeks and warm brown eyes gave her a tender countenance her husband had lacked.

"Yes?" In the flatness of her voice her grief was revealed.

Bradshaw introduced himself, and she nodded in understanding, but her eyes remained kindly and somber. "The detective said you would be by sometime. Please, come in. I'm sorry things aren't more tidy."

He stepped into an immaculately clean parlor, with gleaming floors, bright wool rugs, and the welcoming warmth of a small wood-burning stove. She took his coat, hanging it from a coatrack where he spied the temperance sash O'Brien had mentioned. He left his rubber overboots by the door before taking the seat she offered him by the stove. Although there were two weeks yet until Christmas, red glass and shiny silver ornaments hung from a metal stand in the corner, and boughs of evergreen and holly berries decorated a sideboard.

"I'm very sorry about your loss, Mrs. Doyle."

"Thank you. That's kind of you." She wrung her hands, twisting the simple gold band on the ring finger of her left hand. "I hear myself saying thank you, but it's like somebody else is speaking. It's been three days since Vernon didn't come home, but I still don't quite believe it. He'll walk in the door any minute now, and I'll wake up from this dream."

He noticed she didn't say nightmare, or even describe the dream as awful. "I understand what you're feeling, Mrs. Doyle. The shock of a sudden death can be hard to accept." And was it simply the suddenness of it that made it hard for her to accept? Had he heard grief in her voice, or merely the trauma of the unexpected? Or the shock of having done something so terrible it didn't seem real?

"I haven't told the boys yet. I think about it. I sit down to write, or several times I've put on my coat to send a wire, but then it seems so wrong. Like I'm about to tell them a lie."

"You have two sons?"

"Yes." Her eyes went to a framed photograph on the wall of two boys a bit older than Justin, with mischievous smiles, so difficult to capture in children. Getting them to hold still for the length of the exposure was nearly impossible.

"That's by Edward Curtis of Curtis and Romans Photographers," she said, and there was pride in her voice. "I don't think he's there anymore, though. They say he's off photographing Indians before they're all gone. His brother takes pictures, too, but not portraits. He does buildings and streets and things." She smiled tenderly at the photograph. "My mother gave me the sitting as a gift seven years ago. They grow up so fast, and then they move away, but in your heart, they stay your little boys."

"Where did they go?"

"Junior, our eldest—his name is Vernon, like his father, but he goes by Junior—he's in the army, in Virginia. Fort Myers. They've assigned him to the Signal Corps, and he says he loves it, but I'm not—I wasn't supposed to tell his father. Vernon always wanted Junior to follow in his footsteps, but Junior didn't want to be anything like his father. It turns out, he has Vernon's cleverness with mechanical things, though, and the army saw that right away. He's working with the wireless telegraph, learning how to send and receive signals."

"That will be a good career for him. And where is his brother?"

"Charlie got the itch to see the world, and went off tramping. He's not as clever as Junior at schoolwork, but he more than makes up for it with energy and, oh, a hunger for life, you might say. But he didn't get any further than Ohio before he a met a girl." A wry smile put a touch of life in her eyes. "He's working at a lumber mill, of all places. He could have stayed right here and done that."

"But the girl wasn't here."

Mrs. Doyle's sad smile momentarily brightened. "No, she wasn't here."

"They'll want to come home for their father's funeral."

Her smiled vanished. "No, they won't." She covered her wedding ring with her other hand, and didn't meet his eye. "They didn't get along, truth be told."

"I'm sorry."

"You know how it is with boys, and Vernon could be—" She twisted her ring, and chewed her lip. "He could be difficult. They both left as soon as they finished school." Her voice had gone flat again.

He would like to comfort her, tell her that her sons would surely want to come home to see her, but he didn't know that to be the truth.

"Do you have other family in Seattle?"

"My mother passed last year. Vernon has some kin in eastern Washington, but I didn't tell them. They surely read it in the paper. They get the Seattle papers over there. I haven't heard from them, and I don't expect to. Vernon didn't get along with them, either."

"What about friends?"

She flashed him a small smile. "You are kind. I am not alone in the world, Professor, but I do thank you for your concern. I have friends who are near and dear to me, and they have been checking on me every day. They will be coming tonight with a meal and plan to sit and keep me company awhile."

"That's good."

"I've been keeping busy. Sticking to my routine. If I try to think about tomorrow—I'll have to find a job. I've never had a job. What would I do? I can't imagine. I don't know how to do anything, except work around the house. I'm too old to go into service. Aren't I?"

He opened his mouth to reply that his housekeeper was more than a decade her senior, but he realized she might not find that a comfort, and so he held his tongue.

"I've never had a maid, not even a daily. I don't know what's expected of them. I've always done without help. With the boys gone, it's much easier, and I save on the household budget. Vernon works so hard at his job, such long hours, and for very little pay. You'd think a big store like the Bon Marché could afford to pay better. The tent factory he worked for a few years back paid twice as much, but of course it burned down and Vernon had to find work where he could."

Bradshaw had seen the Bon Marché's payroll ledger, and he knew for a fact that Vernon Doyle had earned a respectable salary, indeed a wage higher than most electricians, and more than the tent factory had once paid.

"He's highly skilled," Mrs. Doyle went on, and seemed relieved to find something about him to be proud of, "but he says—he said—stores like the Bon like to give bonuses rather than a regular high wage. It helps them manage through bad times. He was always saying a big bonus was just around the corner, but it never was, and I see how busy that department store is from morning until night. I think they were taking advantage of him."

"How did he get along with everyone at the store?"

"They all admired him, Professor. You must know how it is, working with electricity. You and my husband are to be admired. Not many men are brave or intelligent enough to work with such a dangerous thing. And he's always so very careful. I don't know how this could have happened. Detective O'Brien said it might not have been an accident? Is that true? How can that be?"

"That's the question I need to ask you, Mrs. Doyle. Do you know if anyone was angry with your husband?"

She shrugged and shook her head. "Most people liked him well enough, I think."

"But he could be difficult, like he was with his sons and family?"

"Oh, no. He was different outside the home."

Bradshaw understood her meaning. Wasn't he the same? Weren't most people? With masks of social appropriateness and good manners worn in public, and true emotions, often the most hurtful, unleashed at home? Wasn't that why he'd chosen to work late last night, so that he wouldn't expose his son to his confused and angry mood?

"Mrs. Doyle, might it be possible for me to look at your husband's personal papers? His accounts?"

She twisted her ring, not looking at him. "The detective must be wrong about someone killing him. It must have been an accident. Can't you tell things like that, Professor? With electricity?"

"His death was not an accident. I examined the scene. I may find something in his personal effects that will lead me to who did this."

She put a hand to her mouth, and he could see her struggling with the decision. Finally she said, "You can look, if you really think it will help you. He kept no journal or diary that I know of, and I manage all our accounts and bills. I'm handy with numbers, and good at keeping a budget. Vernon didn't like me to admit that. I don't suppose it matters now. I don't want you to think he couldn't manage our budget."

"Of course not."

She led him upstairs to the door of the attic bedroom. "When the boys moved out, Vernon set up this room as his own so that he wouldn't disturb my sleep when he worked late shifts at the store." Her eyes lingered on the door, and she looked about to change her mind. "He won't let me go in to clean. I don't know what you'll find in there. I've been putting off—" She pressed her lips tight, and covered her face with her hands.

"Would you rather go through the room alone first?" He knew he shouldn't offer. She was giving him the opportunity to search and perhaps find a clue to Vernon's death. If left alone, she might hide or destroy something important that she believed to be useless or embarrassing. But he would want to be given that opportunity, that respect, in her circumstances.

He was relieved when she shook her head. "Would you like coffee? I'll go make coffee. She left him on his own, hurrying away to set a pot percolating. Escaping from whatever lurked in the room.

It wasn't as bad as Mrs. Doyle feared, though surely not up to her standards. The single narrow bed with a handmade quilt was made up, the wood floor and braided rug relatively clean. A secretary desk and chair, a small bookshelf, and a long wide dresser, made up the rest of the room's furnishings. A cardboard box on the floor held the remnants of an electrician's work. Lengths of wire, half-used rolls of tape, attachment plugs, fuse links. There were a few assorted tools, pliers and wire cutters, but Bradshaw doubted they represented the whole of his tool collection.

He sat in the chair without hesitation. Usually, he had to push past the feeling that he was violating the deceased's privacy, but that emotion had been tempered by anger. It was looking like Vernon Doyle had not been a decent husband or father.

The papers on the desktop were innocent enough. Portions of newspapers, advertisements from the Bon and elsewhere, crumpled and pulled from pockets. Business cards from fellow electricians, salesmen, the local hardware and electrical supply stores. He made note of them all in his pocket notebook, then piled them neatly to the side. He moved on to the over-stuffed cubbies and slots at the back of the desk. He found a letter from a cousin in Spokane dated a year ago, containing bland family news and not much warmth, and letters from organizations he belonged to, such as the Electrical Union. And he found two recent letters from J. D. Maddock, Attorney at Law.

The first letter asked for an interview concerning "a matter of mutual interest which may prove financially rewarding." The second letter, dated one week ago, referred to an in-person meeting in mid-November, and said, "I am prepared to reconsider the terms of my offer." No particulars were given. The letter had been designed to deliver little information and much temptation to motivate the recipient to return to the sender's office.

If Doyle had paid the visit to Maddock's office, the visit hadn't gone well for Maddock. He'd sought Doyle out at the Bon, and their discussion had grown so heated that Billy had scolded Doyle for his use of foul language. Bradshaw set the letters in a separate pile.

In a lower drawer, he found a file stuffed with sketches. A few were neatly drawn as if by a steady and skilled hand. More of them were rough, sloppy, ludicrous. A drunken hand, an inebriated mind. The style and letter shapes of both the neat and the rough revealed the same man had drawn both, and the external design of all of them—rectangular boxes with two projecting metal rods—told Bradshaw that Vernon Doyle very much wanted to recreate Oscar Daulton's mysterious invention. He'd done an excellent job replicating the exterior. In fact, it looked exactly as Bradshaw recalled seeing it for that brief time at the student exhibition. However, the internal designs, even those neatly drawn, didn't represent anything new or revolutionary. Nothing capable of boosting the voltage of a direct current. While Doyle's practical skills and knowledge were solid, his understanding of theoretical principles was not. It was no wonder he'd not gone into partnership with Edison's representative. Despite his boasting, he had nothing at all to sell.

Beneath the sketches winked a shiny metal lockbox. Bradshaw's pulse quickened. He placed the box on the desk, but a search of the desk and room produced no key. With only the slightest qualm, he pulled his own keys from his pocket, isolated the pick attached to the ring, and sprang the lock with a few quick twists, revealing a green passbook from Union Savings and Trust, and cash. Nearly five hundred dollars in assorted bills.

An examination of the entries in the passbook revealed he'd made regular deposits of his paychecks dating back to 1901, when he was first hired by the Bon Marché, withdrawing half of those deposits in cash. Those withdrawals likely represented the money he presented to his wife as his pay. Over the past two years, there had been many other withdrawals, both large and small, but with no notation as to what use the money had been put. The final balance recorded was a mere $8.26.

Beneath the cash lay a dirty white envelope, stained by grimy fingerprints and spilled drink. Inside Bradshaw found only a floral-scented square of card stock embossed with La France Rose Perfume, such as department stores regularly handed out. He slipped the envelope in his pocket and returned the unlocked box to the drawer.

The second lower drawer clinked when he pulled it open as whiskey bottles rocked and tipped. A slight whiff of alcohol drifted up to him. All the bottles were corked. All the bottles were empty. Except one. It was shorter than the others, and made of dark glass. Bradshaw pulled it out to see the label. "Electrozone. It will cure you of cancer, female complaints, scrofula, diphtheria, consumption, asthma, and compulsions."

He uncorked the nearly full bottle and gave it a whiff, wincing at the sharp odor of chlorine. Made through electrolysis with sea water, Electrozone was an expensive sanitizer and effective antiseptic. While the United States military trusted it to rid Havana, Cuba, of yellow fever, Bradshaw was skeptical of its ability to cure all, especially the compulsion to drink. It certainly had not helped Vernon Doyle.

The smell of coffee wafted up to him. He returned the Electrozone to the drawer and met Mrs. Doyle downstairs in the parlor, where she'd carried a tray with the coffee and an assortment of fruit cookies brought to her by friends.

She poured for him, and pressed him to eat, but she took nothing herself, sitting upright, looking everywhere but at him.

"I discovered nothing I didn't already know or suspect, Mrs. Doyle."

"Oh." She picked at her dress. "Thank you."

"There's cash in the desk. Enough that you shouldn't have to worry about finding work right away. And a savings pass book, but if the entries are correct, little money on account."

She nodded and said thank you again, but so softly the sound didn't carry.

"Did your husband have a home workshop?"

"A workshop?"

"A place he kept his tools, built things. In the basement? Or a shed?"

"Oh, no. We have no basement, and the shed has only gardening tools. There's a drawer in the kitchen where we keep a hammer and nails and a few other things."

"May I see?"

She showed him the drawer, which was similar to the one in Mrs. Prouty's kitchen, with basic household tools for hanging pictures and making simple repairs. "He kept his electrician tools at work, so that he didn't have to cart them back and forth each day."

The evidence upstairs and the lack of home tinkering space told Bradshaw that to Vernon Doyle, electricity was a job, not a passion. A job that earned him respect and a good salary, a job he boasted of, but it went no deeper. He was no inventor. His drawings represented a desire for fame and glory. Discoveries came not from a desire to impress, but from the obsession to express an idea born of inspiration. And Vernon Doyle had not been inspired.

They returned to the parlor, and for the next twenty minutes as they drank, he gently asked questions of Vernon Doyle's habits and acquaintances, but he learned only that Doyle had treated his wife like a poorly paid housekeeper. She did everything, from the yard work to bill paying, and had done so even when their children were small. She handled all the chores typically done by the man of the house, as well as her own. This information was given him without complaint, but with plenty of excuses. Vernon worked so hard, she said, or their yard was so small it was no work at all to keep it up, or she enjoyed working with numbers, and then back to Vernon being such a hard worker she didn't like for him to have to worry about the household.

She had no life outside this, as far as he could see, other than her temperance activities. And Vernon's life outside the home was a mystery to her. When Vernon had left the house, on a workday or otherwise, he'd never told her where he was going.

"And you didn't ask?"

"Oh, no. It made him feel pestered. If he was asked to work a night shift on his off day, he would tell me, or send word home. He was good about that."

"I'm sure he was." Billy claimed to have witnessed Vernon Doyle arranging for his wife to be told he would be working late on a night he'd met his mistress.

He got to his feet, encouraging her to wire her sons, and he prayed they would return home to support her even if they despised their father.

He stepped from the warm, tidy coziness of the Doyle home into the cold mess of Republican Street and reclaimed his bicycle. He'd just begun to pedal when an elderly woman in a wool coat and hat, standing on the porch of a house across the street, waved him over. He waited for several wagons to pass before pedaling over to her.

"You've been at the Doyle house?" the neighbor asked. Her face was thin and wrinkled, with a hardness that spoke of a difficult life. Her small dark eyes were sharp and clear.

"Yes, ma'am."

"Are you with the police?"

"No, but I am assisting them."

"Is it true someone killed Vernon?"

"Yes."

"Good. I never liked the man. She's better off without him." The old woman nodded her chin toward the other side of the street.

"You see what goes on in your neighborhood?"

"Am I a snoop, do you mean? Funny how the habit of keeping an eye out is disparaged until something like this happens. Then everyone's glad you were paying attention."

"Indeed, Mrs.—?"

"Carter. And you are?"

"Professor Bradshaw."

"You don't say. Well, take it from me, Professor, Mrs. Doyle has been given an early Christmas present."

"Any possibility she gave the gift to herself?"

"She hasn't the guts."

"Who do you think did it?"

"Haven't a clue. But I can tell you who liked him. No one. No one in that house anyway. There was a time," she said, "before the boys left, when Vernon Doyle took to the bottle, and they all suffered for it."

"Some men become mean with alcohol."

"Oh, it wasn't like that. Just the opposite. He was mean when sober. He was much nicer to the boys when he was in his cups. Goodness knows what that taught them. There she was, preaching about the evils of drink, and there was Vernon, singing and carrying on, slobbering on his wife like she was a dance hall girl looking for a customer."

"Are you friends with Mrs. Doyle?"

"I see what I see. The boys had him figured out. Even snuck him alcohol. It'd make things better for them for a time, but worse for her. She hated his slobbery attention. She joined the Temperance folks, tried to stand up to him."

"Tried?"

"He sobered up at home. Made it hard on the boys. Never gave it up completely, if you ask me. Just got good at fooling his wife and kept his drunkenness out of sight. Well, she knows, I'd bet the house. Only she doesn't want to admit it. She was that glad when he stopped slobbering on her."

A benefit of cycling, especially in a city built upon hills, was mental clearing through physical exertion. Far more reliable than Electrozone for the treatment of most disorders, in Bradshaw's view. Doyle's marriage might have been happier, and his desire for drink more resistible, had he pedaled more and rode the cars less.

Bradshaw arrived at home tired but refreshed, ready to analyze his notes, but the moment he arrived at his back gate, he knew something was amiss.

The gate stood open to the alley, and he knew with certainty he'd not left it that way. Mrs. Prouty was a stickler for closed gates and doors and windows, unless she was airing the house, so he entered the kitchen door prepared for some sort of emergency. He found the kitchen and dining room empty, so he went down the hall to the parlor, calling to Mrs. Prouty, his anxiety growing with each step.

He received no answer, but understood what was wrong as soon as he entered the parlor. His desk drawers were open, his calendar and papers and books scattered on the floor.

"Mrs. Prouty!" He ran upstairs, calling for her, finding all three bedrooms in disarray, Justin's the least, his own the worst. He turned on his heel and flew down to Mrs. Prouty's room, a Victorian haven of rose wallpaper off the kitchen—it was empty and untouched—and then down to the basement, where the greatest damage had been done.

His workbench had been thoroughly ransacked, tools and materials dumped from their sorting boxes. His microphones and wire recorders and various gadgets lay scattered. It was impossible to know all that was missing, but one object's absence did strike him: the cigar box filled with melted sulfur he'd experimented with two years ago when he realized Oscar Daulton might have used that element as an insulator in his invention.

The rest of the basement had suffered less damage. Mrs. Prouty's jars of this summer's fruits and vegetables had been spared and winked colorfully in the electric light. But in the corner, the storage trunks had been forced open, and their contents flung to the cement floor. They were items of little value—old clothes, rarely used odds and ends. One trunk, however, didn't belong to Bradshaw. Or rather, it did, but he didn't feel it was his possession. It was Oscar Daulton's, and its few meager possessions—Daulton's army uniform, a cheap suit, a few books of poetry—were now heaped upon the floor. It took only a moment for Bradshaw to search through the items to see that just one of Daulton's possessions was missing. His journal.

From upstairs came the sound of the kitchen door shutting, and Mrs. Prouty's sturdy steps marching inside. Bradshaw flew up the stairs to prepare her for the state of the rest of the house.

Bundled still in her dark coat and hat, she held clutched in her hand the advertisement that had sent her so eagerly from the house this morning. He could see the Bon Marché letterhead, for she waved it before his face.

"I will never shop at that department store again!" she bellowed. "I felt like a fool, standing there with my arms full, waiting for a sales woman to say to me, 'Today's your lucky day.' Do you know how many approached me to ask if they could help me while I stood there, silently pleading for them to tell me it was my lucky day?"

"Let me see it."

She unloosed her grip, and he plucked it from her.

"None. Not a one! I didn't hear them say the words to nobody. Why, I don't believe the Bon gave a thing away all the morning long! It was a ruse to get us down there. A dirty trick!"

He examined the ad with a swift glance, taking in key details. "It's a fake," he said, and her outrage was ignited anew.

Chapter Eleven

The neighbors, the few that had been home, had seen nothing. No suspect conveyances in the street or alley, no person lurking about, no one entering or leaving the Bradshaw residence. The intruder had come at a time when many were out at work, or running errands, and when neighborhood sounds raised little curiosity. No doors or windows had been forced, and it was quite likely the front door had not been locked. Daytime burglaries were almost unheard of outside of the seedier parts of the city, and like many other homes, the Bradshaws' was rarely locked except at night.

As Mrs. Prouty set about straightening the house, Bradshaw installed his burglar alarms. They were simple devices. The opening of a door or window closed a switch and sent an electric current to an alarm bell. They were essentially the same as the one first patented a half century ago by a man named Pope. Bradshaw had tinkered with improvements and various signaling methods over the years, installing them throughout the house, but he'd never left them up long because accidental triggering of the alarms put Mrs. Prouty in an unpleasant mood. But she made no protest now as he worked.

Once done, he helped Mrs. Prouty restore order. Nothing was broken. It appeared as if the intruder had not come to steal valuables. The silver hadn't been touched, although what little cash there'd been in the house had been taken. The intruder had been searching for something and found what he sought in the basement. They'd just completed putting Henry's rarely used bedroom to rights when Justin arrived home from school, bringing a blast of cold air, exuberant energy, and a ravenous hunger.

At the kitchen table, over hot cocoa and slices of Mrs. Prouty's sourdough slathered in butter, Bradshaw explained about the break-in. He'd considered not telling Justin, but decided keeping the boy safe meant he needed to be aware of potential dangers. If he could not make the world a safe place, he could at least try to give his son the skills needed to protect himself.

"He was even in my room?"

The look of apprehension on his son's face, and the way his blue eyes begged to be told otherwise, sent a protective pang through Bradshaw, but there was no way of hiding the truth. It was likely he'd not put everything back the way Justin had them, and the boy would see, and know he'd been lied to. "Yes, but the intruder was interested in finding papers of mine, not anything of yours."

"What if we'd been home?"

"The intruder knew we weren't. That's why he came when he did. Burglars want to meet you even less than you want to meet them. But what if we had been home? Or if you'd been home alone? What would you have done?"

"Hide?"

"Possibly. What else?"

"Run for the police?"

"That's what I'd do. Run to the nearest neighbor at home and have them fetch the police."

"I could run to Broadway. There's always a policeman there, and I bet I can get there in under a minute running."

"Yes, you are fast."

"Could I set a trap?"

"What sort of trap?"

"With a trip wire and rope and a bucket to fall on his head."

"Hmm, there might not be time for that. But if you can't run away, or hide, making a lot of noise might frighten him away."

"What sort of noise?"

"Scream at the top of your lungs and pound the walls with whatever's handy."

"Really? Can I practice?"

"No. You are already expert at those skills."

Permission to scream and pound the walls, if necessary, eased some of Justin's anxiety, but still he glanced up at the ceiling uncertainly.

"Come upstairs with me, and I'll show you that all is well and protected."

It was with focused determination that Bradshaw later returned to his basement workshop, found a well-thumbed issue of the *Western Electrician* and turned to a familiar article. He located a crate of odd electrical parts, a clock mainspring, and a box of his patented microphones. He chose an empty cigar box from the many he'd collected over the years for various uses, three dry-cell telegraph batteries, and a can of shiny white enamel paint.

Then he set to work.

When he had first moved into this house, it had been new, smelling of fresh wood and plaster and paint. The basement, too, had smelled new and fresh. But now, a decade later, the house was beginning to age nicely and to settle, the wood to mellow under layers of Mrs. Prouty's polish and wax, and the basement had begun to smell like a basement should, like metals and oils and rubber and a hint of mustiness that never fully developed, thanks to Mrs. Prouty's diligence.

He wanted to grow old in this house. Modest, though it was in a neighborhood that was increasingly opulent, it was his castle. His sanctuary. Perfectly sized for a small family, with a small yard and garden, within walking distance of the streetcar, Justin's school, their church. He was comfortable in it the way he was comfortable in his old clothes. It was part of him.

And it had been invaded.

The clanging of his burglar alarm sounded upstairs, was quickly silenced, and then Detective O'Brien clamored down the stairs.

"A bit like locking the barn door, Ben. You don't think the thief will return, do you?"

"You miss the purpose of the alarms entirely."

"No, I don't. Did you rig Justin's window?"

"His was the first. And the opening of his door turns on the wall lamp."

"Is this the ad?" O'Brien picked up Mrs. Prouty's false advertisement from the workbench.

Bradshaw said, "It was designed to lure Mrs. Prouty out of the house at a time when I was scheduled to be at the university and Justin was at school. It would have been easy for anyone to arrange."

"Anything missing?"

"In the rest of the house, a couple dollars in change. Down here, two cigar boxes, one filled with hardened melted sulfur. The other had a recording device I was working on. And Oscar Daulton's journal."

O'Brien whistled.

"There's nothing in it that reveals his invention, but whoever stole it wouldn't have known that."

"What did he write about?"

"Frustration with the world. Peace. Silence. Mostly anger. He copied down his favorite poems. In jail, he was obsessed with one in particular, by Emily Dickinson. He must have written it a dozen times." Bradshaw's hands stilled and his thoughts turned inward as he recited the poem:

> I took my power in my hand
> And went against the world
> 'Twas not so much as David had
> But I was twice as bold
> I aimed my pebble, but myself
> Was all the one that fell
> Was it Goliath was too large
> Or was myself too small?

"That's uncanny." O'Brien rubbed his arms. "And untrue. Three men were felled by his pebble. All of Seattle, I suppose, knows that you were the only friend Oscar Daulton had in the end, and that you inherited his possessions."

"I don't know about all of Seattle, but anyone following the newspaper stories knew it."

"Why didn't you put a lock on his things?"

"Because there was nothing worth stealing. No one was interested in him as a human being, only as an inventor and assassin."

"If Oglethorpe hadn't been such an ass—"

"He might have lived, and he might have discovered the secret of Daulton's box. But he tried to steal Daulton's invention and thereby provoked his own death, which eventually led to the damn thing landing in Elliott Bay. What's your point?"

"No point. So what's this?" O'Brien peered at the assortment of parts Bradshaw had spread before him.

"The secret of Daulton's device has done enough damage. If it's no longer a secret, maybe the madness will stop." He pointed at the article in the open journal.

"The Submarine Signal Company," read O'Brien. "And how will a fog signal help you learn the secret?" He continued to read as Bradshaw assembled. "Hydrophone? An underwater microphone?"

"A standard carbon microphone in a watertight container. My detective microphone ought to work as well or better."

"But what do you want to hear?"

"This." He indicated the cigar box and explained about the clockworks he would mount inside, powered by an eight-day mainspring. He needed something rugged, something that would work no matter what its orientation, and it had to be small enough to fit into the cigar box so that it could mimic the approximate size and shape of Daulton's invention. The clock was now resting inside the cigar box. He picked up the box and released the pin that set the gears in motion. A ticking sound immediately issued. He handed it to O'Brien, who examined it curiously.

"You're going to throw it overboard?"

"That's the plan. Professor Taylor's going with me. We'll hire one of the wrecking outfits to follow it, and they'll send down a dive crew."

"Pardon my saying so, but won't it be hard to hear the ticking underwater?"

"Set it on the workbench."

O'Brien did so, and the ticking grew louder.

"Sound carries far better through liquids and solids than air, although it does take more energy to generate a sound wave. I've placed the clock flush against the box, to maximize the resonance of the ticking, and—"

A deep gong rang from the clock in the box.

Bradshaw grinned, pleased with the volume. "It's the hour gong from a parlor clock. It's set to strike every thirty seconds. The mainspring will run a clock for eight days, and I calculated the additional bell will bring that down to six. The biggest trouble will be attempting to hear the ticking through the other noises in the sea, especially the ships."

"You know, it's sometimes quite fun being friends with an inventor. You have an ingenious solution for everything."

"I wish that were so. I haven't any solutions at all for our current case or the break-in."

"Do you think it's related to Doyle's death? Mrs. Prouty being lured away and your house searched?"

"Don't you?"

"Well, yes, but I'm not you. I go for the obvious. Isn't this too obvious for you?"

"Sometimes it is what it appears to be. Doyle was killed and my home was searched because someone is desperate to learn the secret of Oscar Daulton's invention." But even as he said it, he knew he wasn't certain. His fear had spoken, not his logic. "I don't know, Jim. It could be that they are only tangentially related. Doyle's boasting could have drawn attention, and then his death, no matter how it came about, brought me to the scene investigating and the newspapers keep spreading speculation and gossip. Someone may have thought I learned something about Daulton, taken something from the scene. I don't know. Doyle's death might be completely unrelated to Daulton. Henry is finding out what he can at the Bon, and I'll send him to the Tenderloin again tonight. And I don't believe Maddock is above burglary to get what he wants, just like he's not above using our legal system to bully for Edison. It's the sort of behavior Edison encourages. The window dresser is sweet on a girl he can't afford, and I've seen men do stupid things when they're desperate over a girl. That said, the fact remains my home was invaded and searched, and that puts my family in jeopardy, and I won't have it."

O'Brien picked up the false advertisement again. "Looks real enough. The letterhead, anyway."

"Mrs. Prouty tells me that letterhead is available free of charge in the Bon's new women's waiting room. Anyone could have helped himself to the paper. The wording mimics their ad copy, with the exception of the secret sale. A comma is missing from the third sentence. Otherwise, the spelling and grammar are correct, and the layout of the paragraphs and select use of capital letters reflects an eye for design and an understanding of the psychology of ads. The ink is faded and irregular, suggesting the ribbon in the typewriter had been well used, and the precision of the return and centering of the body of the letter tells of an expert hand at the keys. The letter arrived at my door in an envelope addressed to 'Preferred Loyal Customer,' and my house number. The postage is first class, two cents, and the postmark is this morning, the earliest post, the main post office in Seattle."

"You figured out everything but who typed it."

"I'm working on that."

O'Brien said, "The Bon's owners returned today, and I filled them in. Mrs. McDermott speaks Chinook jargon. Did you know?"

"Is that relevant in some way?"

"No, just interesting. An admirable woman with good business sense. Both she and her new husband spoke well of Mr.

Olafson. They trust him, as did the late Mr. Nordhoff. I asked in a general way if she'd ever heard anything untoward about Olafson, and she said he was highly regarded and respected. They consider themselves lucky to have him. I haven't spoken to Billy about this yet. I thought he might find it easier to confide in you."

"I'll talk to him again tomorrow."

"The Nordhoffs brought the penny to Seattle when they opened their first store."

"Pardon?"

"Before they set up shop, no one had bothered to bring enough pennies to Seattle to make it a commercially viable coin. Nordhoff brought bags of them so he could entice shoppers with penny goods, and other stores had to follow suit to compete. I remember when it happened."

"Relevant?"

"Interesting."

Chapter Twelve

Armed with a ham sandwich from home and a flask of coffee from the Cherry Street Grill on the first floor, Bradshaw entered his downtown office in the Bailey Building and found Henry asleep on the cot in the back room, wearing a stocking cap. He poured a mug of the coffee, and the aroma pried Henry's eyes open.

"Good morning," said Bradshaw. "What time did you get in?"

Henry moved his half-open eyes to the mug, hauled himself to a sitting position, then took the mug, and a drink, before saying, "About three. What time is it now?"

"Eight. Sorry. I've got a full agenda today. I'm on my way to the Bon before I head up to the university." He made room on the nightstand for the sandwich and noticed a brass object shaped like an oversized bullet.

"What's that?"

"Huh? Oh, won that last night. A genuine German torpedo siren whistle. Makes the most obnoxious high-pitched whooping sound you've ever heard."

"You're not thinking of giving it to Justin, are you?"

"Keeping it for myself. Never know when such a thing will come in handy, especially in some of the places you force me to visit." He swallowed a mouthful of coffee and sighed. "Last day?"

"No, another week before the Christmas break."

"I meant before Missouri comes home."

"Another week until then, too. She wired. Apparently, the Wright brothers in North Carolina are attempting flight again.

Colin Ingersoll has been working for them. It's my understanding he's been sworn to secrecy about what he sees, and apparently they trust him since he was allowed to invite her."

Henry scowled. "Dang nabbit, that girl. You got nothing to worry about, you know. She's stubborn and independent but honest to a fault. I tried to teach her the value of a white lie, but she just can't do it. If she'd given up on you, she'd have told you."

"She's fond of Ingersoll. If I hadn't spoken up, she'd likely have married him."

"Not yet, she wouldn't have. She's determined to become a doctor. You've got time, but not much. Talked to the padre yet? No need to answer, I can see you haven't. So, do you think they'll do it this time? Fly, I mean."

For a moment, Bradshaw's mind let go of his worries of Missouri and the case long enough to imagine the achievement. He'd seen sketches and photographs of the Wrights' earlier aircraft models, and he felt a twinge of excitement and inventor's jealousy over the vision of a craft taking flight. Such a thing had the potential to change the world.

Henry brought him back down to earth, saying, "Squirrel came up trumps yesterday as usual and sent a whole file on Mr. J. D. Maddock. It's on your desk. It's men like him that give the legal profession a bad name. Do you know how many lawsuits he's filed on Edison's behalf? A hundred and twenty-two! Do you know how many he won? None. Zero. Zilch. Know how many inventors and companies he's left bankrupt? How many patents and inventions found their way, in one way or another, to Edison's companies?"

"A hundred and twenty-two and counting?"

"Maddock's job isn't to win suits but to shut down the competition by making it too difficult for them to go on. He's good at it. And you've read about all the trouble Edison's been giving his competition with motion pictures. Ben, I don't mean to scare you, but I hope you've got your house and personal accounts separated from your patents because if his record holds, you and your boy and your housekeeper will be moving in here, and I'm not sharing my cot with Mrs. Prouty."

"He can't win."

"Haven't you been listening? He doesn't need to win, he just needs to push on until you're too broke to stand. And that suit about defamation, that one's going to be a hard go. The reporter swears you blamed the Edison outfit for Doyle's death, and he's not backing down."

Bradshaw shook his head and waved a dismissive hand.

"You know, Ben, as cynical and curmudgeonly as you are, you've got a core of innocence in you. You believe good and right will triumph over evil and greed, and that just ain't so. Maddock is on the attack and you'd better get your affairs in order and protected before it gets bloody. We've got no evidence he's ever killed before, but there's a first time for everything."

"Do we have anything yet on Maddock's activities the night Doyle died?"

"No, but I'm on it. I've found the lunch counter where he usually gets his grub, found his barber and tailor, and I've got a list of his neighbors in the office building. I thought I'd leave them to you. They're the sort that would respond better to a professor than an ex-miner. Maddock's a quiet man and not a drinker, darn his eyes. But if there's proof he went out in the night, we'll find it."

"Has he made any statement yet through his attorney?"

"Nope. Can't O'Brien get him down to headquarters for a chat?"

"Not without reasonable suspicion. He knows his rights."

"The fact he was seen arguing with the deceased that evening's not enough?"

"I'm afraid not. We've got to find more of a connection between Doyle and Maddock, and it's most likely to be found in the hunt for Daulton's box. So far, there's a connection through Galloway Diving. Both men did business with him. Can you ask around about that? Galloway said Maddock looked into the other diving outfits before upping his offer. What about Billy Creasle? Did you learn anything from your friends at the Bon?"

"The Notions girl is not only a looker, but smart, too. I may have to stock up on a few things."

"And she said that Billy—?"

"Oh, right, she thinks he spies on everyone at the store and tattles and gets people fired. Says she's got a little brother just like him. Too smart and ambitious for his own good. If he can't find any dirt, he makes his own. Last year, she's pretty sure he switched products in an order, you know, swapped a cheap pocket watch with an expensive one, to get the sales clerk fired so he could have his job. There's a hierarchy to positions and departments. He made a big leap, though, from the watch counter to assistant window dresser."

Bradshaw took his small notebook from his pocket and jotted the details of Billy's alleged shenanigans.

"Did she report this to anyone?"

"No proof. Her word against his, and most everyone at the store likes the lad, including the manager, Olafson."

"Yes, that I know. What about Mrs. Adkins, the seamstress?"

"She stayed at the Washington with Doyle. Billy wasn't lying about that. Roosevelt's room. He signed the register as Mr. and Mrs. John Smith, but the staff wasn't fooled. They knew who he was and who she is. She's stayed there before as Mrs. Smith."

"I don't suppose she was reprising her role as Mrs. Smith at the Washington on the night Doyle died? O'Brien says she claimed to be home alone all night, diligently stitching."

"Huh! The other gals say she's got an undeserved reputation for inseams and cuffs and they don't understand why customers ask for her by name, but since she gets paid the same as them per garment and she's slow and doesn't cut into their share, they tolerate her, but not warmly. I've got a sample of her handiwork." Henry handed him the sleeve of a man's white shirt, the sort with an attached cuff. He examined the stitching and found it decent, but he was no expert. He rolled up the sleeve and tucked it in his pocket.

Henry said, "Her husband works for one of the big fishing outfits. They've got no kids and she works for her pin money, spends it on fancy restaurants and such."

"Her husband doesn't dive, does he?"

"Nah, he's not really even a fisherman. He's a cook. Makes darn good money, and he must dish out good grub or he'd not last a season, they'd toss him overboard with the chum." Henry shuddered as if a wave of seasickness were washing over him. He'd once spent a season on such a boat, belatedly learning that the smell of fish in such large quantities tripped his gag reflex. "He's gone for weeks at a time, leaving her on her own." His expression changed abruptly, and his eyebrows waggled.

"I get it, Henry. Anything on Ivar Olafson?"

"Respected, tough but not unfair. He's been with the Bon almost since the beginning. Good with the cash boys and runners. He was married in the old country, but his wife died before he immigrated here ten years ago. Don't know about children. He's educated, business and music. Worked for Frederick & Nelson for a few months when he first arrived. Squirrel's looking into what he did before coming to Seattle."

"Talk to all former employees fired in the last few months, and find a few former cash runners and delivery boys who no longer work at the store."

"What am I fishing for?"

"Anyone who feels unjustly fired or as if they're hiding something, refusing to talk. Are you going out again tonight?"

"I could."

"Do. See what's the scuttlebutt on recent robberies. We got burgled yesterday."

"No!"

Bradshaw filled him in on the previous day's events and Henry punctuated the tale with colorful interjections. When Bradshaw checked his pocket watch, he saw an hour had passed since he arrived. He got to his feet and pointed at the cloth-wrapped sandwich. "Mrs. Prouty's sourdough, smoked ham, and New York cheddar."

Henry grinned. "Hook up the iron for me on your way out."

Bradshaw did as asked, screwing the plug of the electric flat-iron into the light socket near Henry's desk. The iron would be used not to press Henry's shirt but his sandwich, toasting the bread and melting the cheese.

When Bradshaw left the Bailey Building, he found the streets flooded with sunshine and shoppers. With twelve days until Christmas Eve, the stores were outdoing each other with flashy placards and displays, and men and boys wore sandwich boards, touting store sales. Musicians and singers made merry with holiday melodies, and street peddlers hawked their wares.

Was it the spirit of Christmas he felt, as he navigated the crowded sidewalk, walking in the street when necessary? Certainly this sudden spring in his step and lightness of mood he felt could not be due to his frustrating case with its lack of clues nor to the fact that he had been served with two vicious lawsuits and his home had been burglarized. No, there was something else at work here.

He'd always liked Christmas. As a child, the anticipation had been about what he might find in his stocking or under the candle-lit tree on Christmas morning. Now, as a parent, the joy was even greater, seeing Justin pad down the stairs and run into the parlor, his eyes bright with wonder at the glowing incandescent lights on the tree. Bradshaw always added a few extra strands of lights very late on Christmas Eve so that Justin's first sighting in the morning was magical. Justin boasted of their electrically lit tree to his friends and schoolmates and a showing was arranged each year after Christmas. This year, Bradshaw had thought of adding the lights Thomas Edison had given him, but after seeing other such festoons clutched in Vernon Doyle's dead hand, he changed his mind. And this year, Missouri would be spending the day. She had spent the past two Christmases with them, but this year was special. This was the first Christmas he could look at her without disguising his feelings, the first year she knew he loved her. And the first year he knew she loved him.

It wasn't rational, he knew, to feel a tingle of anticipation when their future together was so uncertain. So unlikely. But it *was* the season of miracles. When a jeweler's festive window display winked at him, diamonds set in gold bands sparkling like glittering snowflakes on red velvet, the words "special dispensation" danced in his head. He ducked into the store and knew immediately which ring would look right on Missouri's hand. A slender band, a simple setting, a precisely cut exquisite stone.

With a small plush box safe in his pocket, he strolled amongst the shoppers and hawkers and bell ringers, and allowed himself to believe. And then acting on that belief, he took a breathless detour up Profanity Hill to the county courthouse, realizing only as he gained the steps that he couldn't get a license, not without Missouri, and he was fairly certain a medical exam was now required.

He laughed at himself, at his ridiculous race up the arduous hill. He didn't know if it was the steep climb or the boldness of his act, but he found he had to sit on the steps for a few minutes to catch his breath. It was no hardship to appreciate the view of Elliott Bay and the snowcapped Olympic Mountains in the distance. The city, for all its messy construction, glittered and winked in the winter sunlight. An unfamiliar sense of joy washed over him.

He felt for all the world like Ebenezer Scrooge at the end of *A Christmas Carol*, behaving in a giddy fashion completely out of his nature. And he hadn't even been visited by any ghosts. Or perhaps it was the ghost of Vernon Doyle haunting him, repenting for the mistakes of his own miserable life, driving Bradshaw to take such bold steps.

"Well, Mr. Doyle," said Bradshaw, gaining his feet, "if it's you inspiring me, I suppose I owe you the favor of finding your killer." And with that, he headed back down the hill and hopped a northbound streetcar up Second Avenue toward the self-proclaimed Big Store, the Bon Marché.

Chapter Thirteen

Christmas took a decided turn for the retail worse when he entered the store. Saturday at the Bon Marché was a sight to behold, and one he would normally avoid. Much of the congestion could be blamed on the jolly elf himself, who was holding court in Toyland downstairs. Bradshaw climbed against the tide up the stairs, intending to ask Mr. Olafson to bring Billy Creasle to him. But on the landing, he spied Billy on the first floor below him, dressed in a fine dark suit that added perhaps six months to his young age, but no more. He held the elbow of a customer, a poor woman from the looks of her clothing. The woman was shaking her head, and another woman in a tailored suit joined them. Bradshaw understood at once what he was witnessing. Young Billy had spotted a shoplifter and summoned the store detective. A moment later, Mr. Olafson joined them. Bradshaw watched the discreet capture unfold. As oblivious shoppers went about their business, the shoplifter was guided to a corner where she pulled items from the folds of her clothing, and then the female detective walked her to the door.

A few minutes later, Bradshaw and Billy were alone in Olafson's third-floor office. Bradshaw stood near the window, watching Billy pace restlessly.

"Do you spot many shoplifters?"

"You'd be surprised, Professor. There's likely several out there at this very minute stealing something from us."

"You don't seem upset about it. You seem rather excited, in fact."

"Well, it gets your blood racing when you spot a thief. And we have to be careful not to let on to the other customers. You hold it inside, till it's all over, and then you feel a bit like a caged animal. Or like you just won a foot race."

"Why do they steal, do you suppose?"

"Lots of reasons. The woman we just caught was hungry and she's got six or seven kids to feed. We've caught her before. She only takes food. Since we moved the Grocery Department upstairs, it's harder for her to sneak out. But we get rich people stealing, too."

"Why do the rich steal?"

"Because they can. Because they don't care. They don't steal the same way the poor steal. Not usually. They do things like complain they were sent the wrong tablecloth, even though it's the exact one they chose, and then they say it ruined their party. The store refunds their money but doesn't make them return the tablecloth. That's stealing in my book. Or they simply walk out of the store with some item, and the store does nothing about it."

"Why wouldn't the store stop a rich thief?"

"Because you can't very well chase down some rich woman and accuse her of stealing, can you? We've got one customer who is a genuine kleptomaniac. That's somebody who can't resist stealing. I can't tell you her name, but you'd be shocked if I did. Her husband has a big reputation in this city."

"Why does that matter?"

"They're some of our best customers, and so are their friends. She rarely takes anything of much value, and we can easily make up for any losses."

"Does she know you're aware of her theft?"

"Goodness, no. That would take the fun out of it for her. She steals because she's bored and it gives her a thrill. That's what the kleptomaniacs need, to feel that thrill. She doesn't need any of the things she takes."

"You allow her to steal because she doesn't need to steal?"

"Yes."

"What about the poor woman? Was she allowed to keep any of the food she stole?"

"And give her the impression she can come back for more? Tell her friends they'll leave with a tin even if they get caught? It's not as backward as it sounds. One woman brings the store a profit, the other costs us. It's as simple as that. The Bon Marché caters to shoppers of all sorts. We've got penny tin horns for the children of the poor and ten-dollar dolls for the rich. A man can get a decent suit for less than five dollars or pay fifty dollars, or more, for quality. When you have a spread of clientele like that, you can't treat them all the same, because they're not. You must understand business, Professor. We don't help ourselves or the poor by letting them steal from us."

"It all sounds like a complicated game."

"I suppose it is, Professor. You've got to keep your eye on the profits when running a department store. It's a people game, and it's all about making impressions."

"It sounds as if the lines between right and wrong become blurred."

Billy shrugged and sat down, looking as if the excitement was draining from him.

"Is it the same for employees? Do some get away with breaking the rules while others don't?"

Billy shrugged again.

"Are there ways of getting ahead that fit the blurry description?"

Billy looked away.

Bradshaw pulled his small notepad from his pocket and flipped through the pages. "You started as a cash boy six years ago, at the age of twelve, and since then you have worked in nearly every department, from delivery to your current notable position of assistant window dresser."

"That's right. It's important for a store manager to know every job there is in a department store, and I mean really know it, not just from the job description, but know what it's like to do it, the ups and downs, the troubles and such."

"My sources tell me there were some lucky coincidences in your promotion history. For instance, a man named Saunders was fired when it was found he'd sold an expensive pocket watch at the price of a much cheaper one to a friend. He denied he'd done it."

"That happens."

"You were given Saunders' position."

"That's right."

"Earlier this year, a woman with fifteen years' experience in department stores was hired as assistant window dresser. She was let go after it became public knowledge that she'd had a child out of wedlock."

"So?"

"Are those examples of blurred lines?"

"I don't know what you mean."

"Then I'll ask you directly. Did you set up Saunders so that you could have his job? Was it you who made your predecessor's history public?"

"Saunders was an incompetent clerk, and Miss Tyler had no vision."

"Is that your justification for getting them fired? You didn't believe they deserved their jobs?"

"If they hadn't done something wrong, they wouldn't have been let go."

"Billy, the more honest you are with me, the easier it will be for you. I'm not concerned with past indiscretions, I'm merely trying to establish if you've developed a habit of hastening people out of jobs you want for yourself."

"What has any of this got to do with Vernon Doyle's death?"

"That's what I'm trying to figure out. Right now, I can think of two reasons you'd want to kill Mr. Doyle."

"Me!" Billy jumped to his feet. "Me? You think I killed him? I did not. I did not! He was dead when I got to the window. I swear it. Give me a Bible, I'll swear on it. He was dead when I got there."

"Either Mr. Doyle witnessed you doing something to sabotage Troy Ruzauskas' position or he learned something that caused you great personal distress and you wanted him silenced. Which was it?"

"Neither, Professor! I had nothing against Mr. Doyle and anyone who says otherwise is a liar. His death has nothing to do with me!"

"I know this is difficult for you."

"Difficult? It's stupid!" Billy paced, throwing his hands up. "I've got to get back to my windows. It's the busiest time of year. Mr. Olafson won't like it if I get behind."

"Mr. Olafson knows this is more important than window displays. And he's not the sort of man to punish you for speaking to me. Is he?" He watched Billy closely.

Billy sat again, seeming suddenly weary. "No, he's all right."

"Are you sure? Some of the boys have complained about him. The runners and cash boys have made accusations. They feel—uncomfortable—around him."

Billy didn't flinch or blush or cringe. He scoffed. Looking Bradshaw directly in the eye, he said, "Professor, where are you getting your information? Mr. Olafson is great with the cash boys and runners, and he's been like a father to me ever since I started here, giving me advice, and giving me a chance on positions others said I was too young for. I think someone's giving you the runaround and trying to pin the blame on me. I've never said a word against Mr. Olafson."

"Mr. Olafson asks for nothing in return for his generosity?"

Billy pulled another face that, to Bradshaw's grateful mind, was completely void of any embarrassment. "What do I have to give?" he asked innocently. "Can't a fella be decent without there being some sort of motive? Never heard of Santa Claus?"

Bradshaw allowed a small smile. "What about Santa?"

"He's good and generous and kind, but he expects you to be the same. That's Mr. Olafson. He's like Santa without the red suit, all year long. You don't get promotions you don't deserve, and he expects you to work hard at your job, but you get jolly fair treatment and genuine thanks for it."

Bradshaw believed him. Billy was hiding something, but it wasn't anything sordid about Mr. Olafson.

"Billy, someone deliberately placed a handkerchief on the floor lamp in that window so that it would catch fire when Mr. Andrews turned the lights on at seven."

Billy looked down at his hands. His knees began to bounce restlessly.

"It was removed before it caught fire. Did you place and remove the handkerchief?"

"It wasn't my fault. You said yourself that Mr. Doyle was dead long before I found him. You said so. I couldn't have saved him even if I'd found him earlier, when I'd arrived at the store."

"You saw him lying there when you placed the handkerchief over the lamp?"

"I didn't have anything to do with his death. Can I go now?"

"Did you have anything to do with the handkerchief?"

"No."

"Please look at me and answer once again."

Billy's brown eyes met Bradshaw's, unblinking, hard, and guarded. "No," he said, and he stormed out the door.

Bradshaw stood pondering. Billy's alibi, that he was home asleep the night Doyle died, could not be confirmed or denied. His mother and sisters insisted he'd been in all night, but the boy had a window in his room and could easily have slipped in and out without notice, hurried down the hill to the Bon, tapped on the window to get Doyle to open the door to him. But it wasn't plausible that this act was premeditated. Billy couldn't have known Doyle would be in a vulnerable position holding that wire. Had he gone to speak to him about something? Something that had him so worried he'd get out of bed at two in the morning, just two hours after climbing in, on a stormy winter night, to confront Doyle? And then, when the conversation didn't go his way, thrown the switch at an opportune moment? But what about the handkerchief? Would Billy have attempted to stage a fire if he'd killed Doyle? If Billy had not placed it there so that he could play the hero as he'd done the previous month, and cast blame on Troy, thus easing his way into the chief window dresser's job, then who did place the handkerchief? And who removed it without reporting the body?

Billy was hiding something, Bradshaw still felt it, but he didn't believe it was murder. He left Olafson's office and made a tour of the store, from the third floor offices and daylight Grocery Department down to Delivery in the basement. He counted typewriting machines as he went, and kept his mind open to details. While in Toyville, he bought Justin drawing paper and a box of the new art crayons by Crayola. He found a model automobile kit with working doors and trunk and a small electric motor that turned the rubber wheels. At three dollars, it was expensive for a toy, but he knew the boy would get many hours of enjoyment from it, even after the assembly was complete. And what better investment for his patent royalties than a gift that brought joy and education to his son?

His final purchase was in the Music Department.

"Such a lovely choice, sir!" said the female clerk. "This carousel music box has been very popular. Would you like it wrapped in Christmas paper?"

"That's not necessary. I purchased several items in the Toy Department less than ten minutes ago. Can you have this delivered with them? To Mrs. Prouty at my home."

"Yes, sir, we have your address on file. On Capitol Hill? I'll let them know to deliver them all together. They'll arrive before school dismissal time, so there will be no surprises ruined."

"Could I attach a message to the music box?"

"Of course."

The clerk handed him a small white note card and he wrote simply. "Today's your lucky day."

The clerk politely inserted the card into an envelope without reading it, and his payment was handed to a young runner who raced off upstairs to fetch Bradshaw's receipt. His purchase was placed in a metal basket and whisked away for wrapping and delivery.

The Bon certainly provided excellent customer service, yet, as always on an investigation, he was beginning to learn far more than he wanted to know. No longer would a trip to the Bon Marché be a pleasant journey through aisles of brand-new products and being helped by smiling, courteous faces. He'd now know the inner workings, the resentment behind the smile, the jealousy between clerks, the sordid details of their lives.

He found Mr. Olafson in the Music Department playing a rousing rendition of "Up on the Housetop" with children and mothers gathered around, and a boy of perhaps nine beside him on the bench. Bradshaw tried to observe objectively, and while he witnessed nothing at all untoward, and he believed Billy had not been assaulted by the man, he knew his perspective was tainted by the shoe salesman's accusation. The seed of suspicion had been planted.

Mr. Olafson ended the song with a dramatic tumble from the bench, bouncing up like a jack-in-the-box and bringing a round of applause from his audience. He spied Bradshaw, and after handing out candy canes to the children, he extricated himself from the crowd, and they found a relatively quiet corner in which to talk.

Mr. Olafson had been told of the incident with Mrs. Prouty and he said with a shrug and a soulful expression that conveyed his sympathy for Bradshaw, "It's not the first time someone has tried to fool us with a homemade advertisement, but this one looked better than most, and we did run a similar letter ad this summer. Being under your employ, we felt it best not to ban her from the store in future. I trust it will not happen again."

"My housekeeper did not make the ad. It arrived in the mail."

"Oh? Professor, my apologies. I didn't mean to accuse—I, well, so it was a prank then? That does explain the other one. Gracious, I hope there aren't more."

"What other one?"

"Last evening before closing, another woman had one just like it. I thought it was the same one because it was all crumpled, liked she'd pulled it from the trash. She put up a fuss when we told her it wasn't a legitimate ad."

"May I see the Women's Waiting Room?"

Olafson looked confused, but acquiesced, escorting Bradshaw to the second floor. A long narrow space overlooking the atrium had been outfitted with a row of writing desks and potted palms. Every desk was in use, and the chairs along the walls filled with chatting women.

"This area has proved highly popular since we opened this month," boasted Olafson. "We had our saleswomen write the advertising, and I must say they know their customers." He pointed to the sign at the entrance:

> *Welcome to the Women's Waiting Room—just the cutest place imaginable for a meeting place for women. Here are combined many features of convenience for women who feel the fatigue of shopping. Do not fail to visit this pretty waiting and retiring room, and ask your friends to meet you here.*

Bradshaw didn't know about attracting women, but it certainly would repel men. He pointed to the letterhead on the nearest writing table. "Do many take this paper away with them?"

"Every day. The ladies can post their letters here, of course, but some prefer to write at home, and some simply want the paper." Olafson shrugged. "We like to think of it as inexpensive advertising."

Bradshaw asked, "Is there paper available for your gentlemen shoppers?"

"There are writing materials available at the counter in the Men's Department, but we don't provide a room such as this. Men don't write for the same reasons as women. And they don't like to gather to gossip, unless it's over beverages, of course. They sometimes want to dash off a note to a colleague, but rarely do they write expansively."

"Do you sell typewriting machines?"

"Certainly."

Among displays of paper, pens, staplers, and other office supplies was a shelf containing the latest models of typing machines. Little signs forbade touching the keys without permission, but one model sat at a table with a chair. A little boy sat pecking at the keys. Olafson shooed him away, softening the lad's disappointment with a candy cane.

"All day long, the machine is played with. Tap-tap-tap! It is good for sales to let customers try it out, but the children think it's a toy. Some of them are good little typewriters. It's the tool of their generation, I suppose, but what is to become of their handwriting if they are all using machines?"

The wastebasket beside the machine was full of crumpled sheets. Olafson tsk-tsked, but Bradshaw was pleased. He sat in the chair and began to methodically uncrumple and read the contents of the basket, but he found nothing similar to Mrs. Prouty's false advertisement. "Do you ever supply store letterhead here?"

"Oh, no, just the inexpensive plain. As you see, it all ends up in the waste basket."

"Could you remove the ribbon for me, please?"

Olafson fetched the harried clerk who efficiently replaced the ribbon, winding the old one onto a spool with the use of a lead pencil and depositing the spool onto a clean sheet of blank paper in Bradshaw's hand.

"I only attempted to change a ribbon once," Bradshaw said, "and was rewarded with black fingers."

The clerk smiled. "Try it a few times a week, you'll get better." He hurried off to waiting customers.

Bradshaw sat, setting aside the old ribbon. He fed a clean sheet of blank paper into the machine, pulled Mrs. Prouty's ad from his inner breast pocket, and began to slowly copy it.

He was not a trained typist, but he'd had enough experience with machines at the university that he knew how to operate one and could find the necessary keys. His slowness, however, seemed to annoy Mr. Olafson.

"I have much experience on the machine," Olafson said tactfully in his Swedish-laced diction. "I could type that for you."

"I would appreciate it," Bradshaw said, relinquishing the chair.

Olafson flexed his fingers, hovered the tips over the keys, gave Mrs. Prouty's ad a fixed stare, then began to type. The keys were soon clicking with a smooth rapidity. With as much skill as he played the piano, Olafson operated the typing machine, swiping the carriage return with a graceful swoop. In just a few seconds, he pulled the paper free and handed it to Bradshaw with a slight bow.

Bradshaw thanked him, then held the page next to Mrs. Prouty's. While the ink of the newly typed letter was dark and crisp in comparison to the other, there were distinguishing commonalities. Most noticeably, in both letters, the uppercase *B* and the lower case *e* were missing portions, and an inspection of the keys revealed lint adhered to their striking surfaces.

"Whoever typed this," Olafson said, nodding at Mrs. Prouty's ad, "used a heavy hand. You can see the dents in the paper, compared to mine, with its lighter touch. Of course, with that old ribbon, the typist might have thought force was required to get ink onto the page, so it might not be a clue as to the identity of the typist. I will instruct my clerks to change the ribbon more frequently, despite the cost and inconvenience. We cannot sell typewriters that require such vigorous pounding!" He waved a clerk over and gave the command immediately, and Bradshaw asked the clerk if he'd been working the previous morning, or the evening before that.

"I was here yesterday morning."

"Was the waste basket empty when you arrived?"

Olafson said, "Be truthful! It is important the Professor learns the truth. No one will be reprimanded for neglecting to empty the basket. This time."

"But it was empty, I'm sure of it. I checked it myself, and the supply of paper, and the ribbon looked as if it could last another day."

Olafson said, "But not this morning?"

"No, sir. When I arrived, I found a special order waiting, and I thought it best to fill it right away before seeing to my daily cleaning duties."

Olafson nodded firmly, agreeing, yet not fully pleased. "It should have been emptied last night."

"When were the keys last cleaned?"

"Three days ago. With the brush that comes with the machine."

Bradshaw asked, "Did you notice anyone sitting here using the machine for any length of time? Or anyone who brought paper with them? In particular, store letterhead?

The clerk said, "At this time of year? As soon as those doors open, we're overrun. I can't even hear the keys being tapped most of the day at this time of year, let alone see who's sitting at the machine."

"Thank you. If something or someone does occur to you, will you let me know?" He gave the clerk his card then turned to Olafson.

"I have two favors to ask. I'll need an empty ribbon spool and use of your office again."

"Certainly, come."

Olafson took an empty ribbon spool from the shelf behind the counter, then led Bradshaw upstairs to his own office desk near a large window.

"I have also the incandescent lamp. Please, sit. Use this." He tore off his blemished blotter to reveal a fresh page, then left Bradshaw to his inspection of the old ribbon.

Using one lead pencil to unspool and a second to re-spool, he deciphered the letters pressed into the ribbon. It had been reused several times, so there were double and triple strikes in places, and the words of several typists blended. But he was able to read enough to find the section of ribbon where twice Mrs. Prouty's letter had been typed.

He inspected the ribbon sections immediately before and after the typing of the letters, finding "A quick brown fox jumps over the lazy dog" and several "dear santa please." Names were typed, some of them in full, but only one in full near the section of ribbon under inspection. This fellow had taken the chair just after the false ad typist and had pecked out "dear santa I am arnold ryker I am 11 year old I want a." No more could be deciphered through the double and triple strikings.

Bradshaw found "Ryker" in the Polk Directory and from the address made a guess as to young Arnold's school. The boy was summoned to the principal's office. Small for his age and possessed of a sharp, rather suspicious eye, Arnold remembered the man at the typewriter because he typed so fast. He wore a dark winter coat and hat, and he was shorter sitting than Arnold was standing beside him, even with the hat, which was a crusher. His hair might have been dark, the boy didn't recall, the man's hands were his focus, not what they looked like but what they were doing, moving on the keys, and the boy wanted to learn. Bradshaw held up his hands, which were pale, long-fingered, beside the principal's hands, which were darker, broader, meatier. The boy said he thought Bradshaw's were closer in appearance to the man's at the typewriter.

"Only he had freckles," said Arnold. "Lots of them. And I'd never seen freckles on a hand before."

Bradshaw thanked the lad and gave him the miniature toy mechanical dog he'd purchased at the Bon for fifty cents. The boy's face lit up. "Gee, Mister. Thanks!"

He had another in his pocket for Justin, but that one would be slipped into a stocking hung by the chimney with care on Christmas Eve.

He returned to his office in the Bailey. Henry was out, and the office cold. He turned up the steam, set the electric kettle to boiling for his Postum, and sat at his desk to go through Squirrel's file on Maddock. As Henry had said, Squirrel had come up trumps, with newspaper clippings, personal notices, and a list of official records that spelled out the man's life.

Born in Akron, Ohio, Maddock attended the usual series of schools, and he apprenticed at a law office while studying patent law and engineering. He established his own law practice, working solo, married in the First Baptist Church, and the following year welcomed the first of eight children. In 1898, he became one of Edison's many legal representatives, and in August of this year, just prior to Edison's visit, he relocated to Seattle, established the office at the Globe Building, which was also his personal residence. He had a home under construction on Queen Anne Hill, so it was presumed he would be moving his family out as soon as construction was complete.

Oh, joy, thought Bradshaw. John Davenport Maddock intended to stay permanently in Seattle, poking his legal stick at everything electrical. Bradshaw closed the file and sat for a moment, trying to focus his thoughts on the case, but they kept drifting to the personal task he'd not yet faced. He pulled the ring box out of his pocket and set it on the desk before him. He opened the lid and the diamond winked in the incandescent light.

A few minutes later, having come to no conclusions or resolutions, he snapped the box shut and shoved it deep within his coat pocket. He locked the Maddock file in the wall safe then headed for the Globe building. It was a fruitless journey. Maddock's neighbors had neither seen nor heard anything that cast the least suspicion on him. He was a model tenant. He'd given them all boxes of Edison's holiday lighting outfits. In their eyes, he could do no wrong.

Chapter Fourteen

It was time.

With every case, there came a time when enough information had been unearthed that Bradshaw felt ready to begin compiling a list of suspects, their possible motives, means, and opportunities. On Monday morning, Bradshaw knew it was time, but he wasn't feeling positive about the outcome. Still, he spread a large clean sheet of paper on his office desk, and began to lay out a graph. He used to do this at home in the parlor at his rolltop desk, but now that he and Henry had an office, he preferred to compile and store the list here, in the wall safe. Not only did this prevent his young son from seeing notes of violence, it kept private the very personal and often sordid information he uncovered that ultimately had nothing to do with the solving of the crime.

At the top of the paper, he wrote, The Case at the Bon Marché, then filled in his list of suspects and their motives. When complete, he sat back examining them.

Billy Creasle. Motive: silence Doyle. If Doyle had discovered that Billy had forced fellow employees out of positions he wanted, or if Doyle had learned of something between Billy and Olafson, then Billy would feel threatened with exposure. After his last interview with Billy, Bradshaw no longer believed the shoe salesman's insinuations, but he did believe Billy had criminally hastened his rise through the company. And the scorched handkerchief? Had that been Billy?

Ivar Olafson. Motive: silence Doyle. But if there was nothing to the shoe salesman's accusations, then Olafson had no motive, at least none that had come to light.

Maggie Adkins. Motive: lovers' quarrel. A crime of passion. That certainly fit the conditions of the fateful night. Had she gone to him that evening for a secret assignation? To break off the affair?

Troy Ruzauskas. Motive: nothing evident. Troy wanted money to impress the mother of the girl he loved, and also to support her in the manner she was accustomed. He'd been diving for Daulton's box and discussed the treasure with Doyle. Had they gone into some sort of secret partnership? Had Doyle made boastful promises he couldn't keep and angered Troy?

J. D. Maddock. Motive: greed. Doyle wouldn't play Maddock's game, likely because he didn't have the knowledge he boasted of. Maddock, not knowing this, could have become increasingly frustrated and marched down to the Bon in the middle of the night to confront the electrician once again and lost his temper when he failed to get what he wanted. This seemed reasonable. Maddock could have returned to the Bon and typed the letter to Mrs. Prouty. Only, Maddock didn't have freckled hands. Bradshaw clearly recalled that the attorney's hands were pale and thin. He could have hired the freckle-handed man to type the ad so that he, or the hired man, could break into Bradshaw's house. Yes, Maddock had motive to both kill Doyle in a moment of anger and to steal from Bradshaw's house anything related to Oscar Daulton.

Usually at this stage, his mind swam with possibilities and his gut pointed him in the direction of the guilty party, no matter how unlikely. None of the suspects' whereabouts had yet been confirmed for the time of Doyle's death. They all claimed to be at home, sleeping.

Maddock seemed the most likely suspect, but Bradshaw felt nothing. He had details and facts all lined up with logical conclusions, but his gut was not involved at all. The thoughts held nothing visceral.

He stared at his list unmoved, at least unmoved in regards to Vernon Doyle's death. He felt pangs of fatherly anxiety for Billy who was far too eager to get ahead, and those thoughts led to a cold dread about the accusations made about Ivar Olafson, who, even if he was innocent of the accusations, might find his life ruined by them nevertheless. He felt a commiserating heartache for Troy Ruzauskas, who loved a girl he might not win. And he felt a loathing for J. D. Maddock. He wanted Maddock to be guilty and he was by far the prime suspect. But Bradshaw didn't feel it.

He didn't feel it.

At the end of the list he wrote: Other Bon Marché employees: 400 plus. General population of Seattle: 100,000.

Maybe O'Brien was right. Maybe he was too distracted about Missouri to focus. He put his hand in his coat pocket and felt the velvety soft box. Where was the giddy joy he'd felt just the day before yesterday that had sent him into the jewelry store and racing foolishly up to the courthouse? He was as low today as he'd been high then. A special dispensation? Why not believe in elves and Santa Claus? He got up, opened the wall safe, and locked the ring box inside.

He dropped into his chair with a sigh. His emotions were consumed and so apparently was his intuition. Or maybe it had been a mistake to open an office. Maybe he should have stayed with electrical forensics and left the rest, the finding of the criminal, to the police and other investigators. Why hadn't it occurred to him that his intuition might fail him? The responsibility of an investigation wasn't something he could abandon simply because he didn't feel it.

He thought maybe he needed something stronger than Postum to awaken his brain and was considering going out for coffee when footsteps thundered down the hall and the door burst open, bringing a gust of damp sooty air. There were times when Bradshaw wished Henry Pratt would practice restraint. It was like partnering with a rambunctious child. But it wasn't Henry bursting in. It was Detective O'Brien.

Without preamble, O'Brien said, "Mrs. Doyle is in the hospital. She's asking to see you. We've got to hurry, she might not make it."

Bradshaw jumped up and grabbed his coat and hat, following O'Brien into the hall. "Wait," he said. He turned the key in the office door and set the dead bolt. Then he ran with O'Brien down to the street, leaping onto the Second Avenue car just as it was pulling away. O'Brien rode the street and cable cars of the city with daring recklessness, trusting his years of experience to keep him from being crushed or shocked or trampled as he leaped and dashed. He never sat, but always stood holding a strap, prepared to jump. He and Bradshaw held straps now, watching for their corner.

"What happened?"

"She was attacked. Someone broke in."

"Broad daylight again? Did she get an advertisement?"

"No, but she did get something from the Bon. A letter from the payroll department saying she was to come down straight away to sort out money owed to her husband."

"Was it legitimate?"

"We don't know yet. She had the letter in her pocket. Looks like she was on her way to the Bon then returned to the house, as if she forgot something. The patrolman posted in the neighborhood saw her leave, and he stationed himself closer to the house. He saw no one enter. About ten minutes later, he saw her hurrying home again. He stopped her because she looked agitated, and she told him she'd forgotten her coin purse for the streetcar. He circled the block again, and when after a quarter hour she didn't come back out of the house, he knocked on the door. He got no response, so he went in and he found her on the floor in a pool of blood."

"Did she say what happened? Who attacked her?"

"She's barely spoken other than to say your name."

At Madison, they switched lines, narrowly evading a full lumber wagon as they ran into the middle of the street to reach it. They rode silently up to Fifth Avenue to Seattle General

Hospital, where two nurses uniformed in striped gowns and white aprons and caps greeted them at the door to Mrs. Doyle's hospital room, warning them in hushed tones that the patient was very weak and should be kept as quiet as possible.

Bradshaw approached the iron bed slowly. Mrs. Doyle lay still, her head wrapped in a white bandage, one arm in a sling across her chest. Her gentle face was furrowed as if with pain, and her skin was white, chalky, bloodless. He was afraid he was too late, but when he said her name softly, her eyelids slowly raised.

Her lips moved slightly, and he bent low to hear her.

In a voice below even that of whisper, she breathed, "My photo."

"The photograph of your sons has been stolen?"

Her eyes told him yes.

"I'll find it," he promised, because he could see she needed to believe he would. It was his fault. His distraction had landed her here. "Can you tell me anything about who was in your home? Who attacked you?"

She winced trying to shake her head. She gasped, "Behind."

"He came up behind you? You didn't see him."

Again her eyes said yes, and she seemed relieved he understood. She closed her eyes with a small exhalation.

The nurses rushed over and felt her pulse, then told Bradshaw and O'Brien they would have to leave. The next twenty-four hours were crucial with such head injuries.

As they moved somberly down the hall toward the main hospital entrance, a chill shot through Bradshaw. He said, "It's got to stop."

"The insanity over Daulton's invention? I agree. This must be connected to Doyle's boasting. Someone needs to find that cigar box, and it had better be you. The photograph Mrs. Doyle wants, is it the one that was on her mantle, the Edward Curtis of her boys when they were little?"

"It's her most prized possession."

"Why would the thief want it? The photographer has some fame, but a personal portrait wouldn't hold much value to someone not of the family. A few other things were taken, we think, but not sure what. Valuables like silver weren't taken, but desk drawers were ransacked and papers may be missing."

"Our thief was looking for information, not valuables to sell. The same as at my house. He might have believed something was hidden behind the photograph. If that's the case, then the photo and frame will eventually be discarded. Let's see what the Bon Marché has to say about the letter from payroll. Do you have it on you?"

They stepped back into the lobby of the hospital to get out of the weather while Bradshaw examined the letter. It had been typed with an old ribbon, the ink was faded, and the capital *B* and small *e* were flawed in the way Mrs. Prouty's letter had been. Bradshaw's stomach twisted.

A half hour later, the Bon's senior accountant said neither he nor any of his staff had ever seen the letter before and weren't responsible for it, although it was genuine Bon Marché letterhead. It was what Bradshaw expected, but he needed to ask anyway. He must be thorough from this moment on.

Downstairs, the harried department clerk, because of the previous inquiry, had been paying a bit more attention to the typewriting display. As O'Brien went through the wastebasket, Bradshaw, with growing anxiety, and a sense of futility, began to examine the ribbon, which the clerk then extracted for him.

It took just a few minutes. "It's not on here," Bradshaw said. He put a hand to his mouth and closed his eyes, staving off a fit of self-loathing. He'd missed it. Two days ago, he'd surely held a warning in the palm of his hand and he'd missed it.

And O'Brien realized it, too, although he kindly withheld accusation from his tone when he asked, "Where is it?"

"My office safe."

Bradshaw felt a firm hand on his shoulder. "Don't blame yourself. You couldn't have known."

But he should have. He should have examined the entire ribbon with more care. If one false and luring letter had been typed, why not more? He shouldn't have assumed.

He cleared his throat. "There are too many possibilities in this case, Jim. There are hundreds of employees, thousands of customers. And it's possible that there are no witnesses and no incriminating clues to uncover. These letters and burglaries may be connected to Doyle only by the publicity surrounding his death and the attention Daulton's box has been getting."

"If we have two cases, we'll solve them both."

But Bradshaw couldn't let go of the look in Mrs. Doyle's eyes.

"I have a bit of good news. We can take the window dresser off our list of suspects. I spoke to his landlady. She said he came in dripping wet all over her floors just after midnight on the night Doyle died. His coat and shoes were soaked through, and he left them to dry by the kitchen stove as he always does, according to her. In the morning, when the police came to question Troy, the landlady fetched his coat and hat and they were bone dry. All her tenants keep their coats and shoes in a wardrobe off the kitchen, unless they're wet, then they are hung near the stove to dry. She said she would have noticed a wet coat in the wardrobe or his room, when she went upstairs to clean, so we know he didn't go back out into the night."

"He never had a clear motive anyway."

"True, but it's nice to confirm his alibi nonetheless. Cheer up, Ben. If J. D. Maddock turns out to be our villain, those lawsuits against you will go away."

"Will they? If they were legally filed, his arrest won't stop them. Edison will simply hire another attorney."

Henry was at the office when Bradshaw arrived in a black mood, grunted hello, and retrieved the typewriter ribbon from the wall safe. He sat at his desk and began to examine it.

"I might have a lead on your burglar, Ben."

Bradshaw looked up, frowning but interested. Henry grinned. "There's talk in the Tender about a new second-story man newly arrived from Chicago. He's known for day jobs, and for advance work. His favorite trick is to send wires or letters to his marks to get them out of the house. The second-story tag got put on him because he's been known to enter through top-floor windows or attics, but he's just as likely to stroll through a front door."

"You don't say." Bradshaw stared at the ribbon, not seeing it, pondering Henry's news. "How new is he?"

"Hard to say, but it sounds as if he arrived about the same time as our good attorney, Mr. J. D. Maddock."

"I don't like coincidences. What does he usually steal?"

"That I didn't learn."

"Tell O'Brien. Mrs. Doyle's been attacked. By a burglar. Does this second-story man have a moniker?"

"They've dubbed him Tycoon Tommy because he talks more like a rich businessman than a thief, but no one knows what he was called in Chicago."

"What does he look like?"

"Average height, wiry, brown or red hair, there wasn't a consensus."

Redheads often had freckles. "Anything else?"

"What, no 'atta boy'?"

"Atta boy, what else did you learn last night?"

"Don't take it out on me, Ben. Just tell me what's got you so mad. Is Mrs. Doyle seriously hurt?"

"Yes. And I should have known it was coming."

"How the hell could you have known?"

Bradshaw held up the ribbon.

"Oh. She got a letter, too?"

His answer was to continue his examination of the ribbon.

Henry pulled up a chair. "Well, I learned old Vernon Doyle was one mighty fine drinker. His favorite haunt was the Considine on Washington, and three times a week, the days depending on his work schedule, he could be found having a jolly good time. I wish more drunks were like him, happy in their cups instead of mean son of a—well, you know. Everyone was his friend when he was drinking, but he didn't gamble or slip into a box with a gal. He had what you might call superstitions. He thought a man only had so much luck assigned him in life and he feared wasting it on cards, plus his brother died of a particularly gruesome strain of something a man dreads, so he shied away from communal women for the most part. It's said he did occasionally visit the Folly. They've got a doc on staff and the girls are guaranteed safe or your money back."

Bradshaw grunted.

Henry said, "Two bucks don't buy a cure. Anyway, it's generally believed that Doyle's claim to knowing Oscar Daulton's secret is a crock, but I say generally because a few men weren't so sure. Doyle had hired Jake Galloway to dive, and Jake doesn't come cheap. Some say that if Doyle was spending a lot of money, there had to be something behind it because he didn't believe in wasting luck gambling. With Doyle dead, a conspiracy theory is growing and Doyle's electrical genius is growing by the minute."

"Doyle knew nothing. He boasted to get attention, it was his way. And he likely didn't consider money spent on dives to be wasted. Daulton's invention is down there somewhere, it's a fact. Somebody will eventually find it, and he wanted to be that someone. His desire for Daulton's box, and his search for it, in no way indicate he had the knowledge of how it worked."

"Well, he was taking a gamble for a man who didn't like such things."

"Luck's influence can be greatly reduced through science and method."

Science and method were exactly what Bradshaw intended to use to find Daulton's box. He was nearly done assembling his locating system, and when he tossed it from the ferry in the reenactment, he hoped it didn't mark a spot too deep for divers to search.

A pattern of letters on the ribbon grabbed his full attention. D-o-y. He peered closely, trying to decode the layered letters that followed. He soon knew he was looking at the ribbon that had been used to type the luring letter to Mrs. Doyle. He leaned his elbow on his desk and dropped his face in his hand. He should have seen it.

Mrs. Prouty and Justin were in the kitchen when he arrived home, having a bedtime snack. Justin didn't look up from his gingerbread. Bradshaw reached into his jacket pocket and found the mechanical dog he'd intended for a stocking gift and placed it before Justin with the key. The boy's face didn't light up as he'd hoped, but he did pick up the key and give the mechanics of the toy a winding. The internal spring and gears whined and hummed and sent the dog walking stiff-legged.

Mrs. Prouty said, "I didn't hear a thank-you to your father, young man."

In a small polite voice, Justin said, "Thank you." He got up and fetched the dog from the other end of the table and gave it another wind.

"It seems the spirit of Christmas has visited you, Professor," Mrs. Prouty said with an uncharacteristic blush. He feared for a moment she'd learned about his venture into the jewelry store and sprint up the hill, possessed by the spirit of Vernon Doyle, but then he recalled the music box. She patted his hand, and said quietly, "You shouldn't have. But thank you."

Justin didn't question their exchange, and Bradshaw found that disturbing. The boy was perpetually curious. He simply picked up the little dog, its legs still moving with a whir of gears, and said, "'Night."

Bradshaw watched him go, heard his feet pad softly up the stairs and his bedroom door click closed. He feared his son's sadness was due to missing Missouri. His devotion to Missouri was not purely that of a child for a mother figure. He also loved her with the innocent crush of a boy for a girl. And because she was not always there, he never took her for granted, and he never resisted her guidance, or became angry when she told him to complete a chore. That would change if they married. Or would it? When a boy got the mother of his dreams at the age of ten and a half, did he appreciate her more than a child who had always had a loving mother? Bradshaw had never gazed with rapt adoration at his own mother, he knew. He'd loved her, he loved her still, with the inner certainty of a child, so secure in his parents' love he was able to move to the other side of the country, leaving them behind. He thought of Justin doing the same to him some day, and he wondered at the pang of betrayal he felt. If his parents felt that way, they'd not let on. They'd sent him and their grandson off with best wishes and a few batted-away tears.

Mrs. Prouty said, "I hope he's not coming down with something."

But Bradshaw did. He knew it was a selfish and horrible thought for a father to have, but he'd prefer that Justin's behavior implied an oncoming cold rather than misery over Missouri's delayed homecoming. What if Missouri never came home, not in the way Justin wanted? Not in the way they both wanted? How would either of them recover from that?

"I brought the nativity scene down from attic, Professor. It's in the parlor."

He nodded and got to his feet. He found the parlor warmed by a small fire in the hearth and the mantle prepared for the scene with a simple runner of burlap. From the storage box he first removed the wooden stable he'd made himself at the age of twelve from scraps of lumber and twigs. His parents had sent him the stable and a new set of ceramic statues as a gift the first year he and Justin moved to Seattle. They were identical to the ones he'd grown up with. Next he unwrapped the ox, the lamb, and the donkey. He placed them inside the stable, nestled near the walls. Next came Joseph with his staff, then the baby Jesus in his manger, positioned in the center. But where was Mary? He dug carefully through the box, finding the sack of decorative straw, and the angel, which he hung from the peak of the stable. He looked at the little scene, so incomplete without Mary. Without the mother. Just the father and child. A lump rose in his throat. He dug again into the box, gently exploring the packing, and near the bottom he felt her. He unwrapped the little statue of the kneeling figure dressed in blue and white, her hands crossed over her heart, and he set her where she belonged.

Chapter Fifteen

A chorus of young voices rose from the schoolroom below, filling the chapel with angelic hymns. The scent of incense lingered from Early Mass. Bradshaw sat in the front pew, breathing in the comforting scent. The sense of calm he always felt when alone in a church was there, surrounding him, but it did not fully release the tightness gripping his heart.

Reverend Father McGuinness, garbed in his simple Jesuit black robe, appeared from the sacristy, and Bradshaw rose, following him out a side door to a neat little office, the white plaster walls bare of all but a crucifix. He was invited to sit. He sat.

"If you didn't come to me soon, I was going to summon you," said Father. "I've heard of your changed relationship with your friend Henry's niece. Miss Missouri Fremont? I trust that is what you have come to see me about this morning?" His voice was gentle but stern. A tone Bradshaw had often taken with Justin.

"There has been nothing improper, Father."

"Hasn't there? Impropriety has many forms. One need not perform an act, one need only cast a look that holds a promise you cannot deliver."

Bradshaw dropped his eyes to his hands. He hadn't expected such a fast reprimand.

"Have I ever seen Miss Fremont in church?"

"She's not in Seattle at present. She's attending the Homeopathic Medical College in Pennsylvania." It was a stall, of course, and not really addressing Father McGuinness' comment. It also seemed a lie to leave out the fact that at this moment she wasn't in Pennsylvania but on her way to North Carolina to join a young man who was in all likelihood in love with her.

Father McGuinness cocked his head patiently, his fingers steepled.

Bradshaw said, "Miss Fremont is not a member of our church, or any church."

"Is she an atheist? A freethinker?"

"With her, it's more a matter of vocabulary." A rose by any other name, he thought.

"What does that mean, Professor? Is she a heretic, denying one or more Catholic doctrines? Or a full apostasy from the faith? Is she a believer in Christianity or has she abandoned it completely?"

"I don't really know. She has a unique way of seeing things."

"Things? You mean God? Religion?"

"Everything. She sees connections between—everything." He remembered her kneeling in his flowerbeds when she first arrived in Seattle, lovingly turning over the soil and nurturing the lily-of-the-valley. It was then she first mentioned the cycle of life, the importance of understanding the cycle in connection with all living things, and it had been the first time he'd applied the scientific principle of the conservation of energy to the human soul. His mind had awakened, as had his fear that perhaps his vision of the world was obscured by self-imposed blinders.

"If she has not embraced a respected form of Christianity there is no use in discussing this further, Professor." Though the words were spoken gently, they were final, fatal.

Bradshaw hastily said, "She was baptized a Catholic." But he knew he sounded childish and defensive.

Father McGuinness sat silently, waiting. Bradshaw had nothing more to offer.

"Does she intend to return to the Catholic faith?"

"I—no."

"She is not a young woman of our faith, practicing any Christian faith, and yet you are courting her?"

"We've discussed the possibility of a future together. We understand our differences might be insurmountable, but we—I could no longer deny my feelings for her."

"And what are those feelings?"

He opened his mouth to speak, but found his voice choked. He felt his face tremble, and he pressed his mouth tight. He cleared his throat and tried again. "I love her." His words emerged hoarsely, and his eyes stung with tears that he blinked away. He looked everywhere but at the priest as he composed himself.

"My son, what are you hoping to hear from me?"

A miracle, Bradshaw thought. But after clearing his throat again, he said, "That there is some way we can marry."

"Of course there's a way. You can have a civil wedding, you can find a minister of some other religion to join you. I can't stop you from marrying. What you are truly asking is how you can marry without committing a grievous sin and without risking excommunication."

"Yes."

"If you believed I had a solution, you would have come to me months ago, Professor. You know the answer as well as I."

"I thought there might be some exception. A special dispensation. Mixed marriages are sometimes allowed."

"If she were of another Christian faith, and if she were to agree to raise any children in the Catholic faith, then a dispensation might be possible. Marriage to a heretic, Professor Bradshaw, is impossible."

"My son loves her, too."

"More's the pity, Professor. And I must say I'm disappointed in you. It's one thing to allow your affections to be inappropriately diverted, but to place your son in such a position is cruel."

"I didn't, not intentionally. He's been fond of her from the first moment he met her." As had he. They'd both been entranced the moment he opened the door to her. "She's been wonderful for him. He trusts her. He confides in her. Besides Mrs. Prouty, she's the closest thing to a mother he's ever known."

"Children are loving and trusting by nature, but it's your job as a parent to protect him from things he can't yet understand. A close relationship with a pagan cannot be healthy for a boy who has only recently entered the age of reason."

"I grant you her beliefs don't have the structure of a religion, Father, but she's not a pagan. And her influence on my son is only to the good. She teaches him about respect for nature, and about generosity, and kindness."

"Which makes it all the more difficult for the boy to understand that in turning away from God she is choosing to live a sinful life. Miss Fremont should be removed from the boy's life as gently, and quickly, as possible."

A tightness gripped Bradshaw's throat and chest. He tilted his head back, his eyes on the ceiling. He swallowed and tried to breathe. When he lowered his chin, he found the priest still watching him with pitying eyes, his fingers steepled.

Bradshaw said firmly, "I cannot remove Miss Fremont from my son's life. To do so would break his heart."

"Hearts are mortal, Professor. Souls are eternal and far more fragile."

Bradshaw got to his feet and marched to the window, clenching his fists.

"Does she cause you to doubt your faith?"

"Not my faith. But I admit I question some rules of the Church."

"Our rules were not chosen at random, Professor. They were given, or inspired, by a higher power, to help us stay true to our faith. We fast on Fridays not on a whim but because our natures tend toward greed and we require the regular habit of self-discipline. It is not sinful to eat meat on Fridays, it is sinful to show blatant disrespect to the Church. The rules established by the Church over the past nineteen hundred years provide the structure man needs to stay faithful and pure of heart. Our regimented ways, if you will, are not in themselves right or wrong, but they help us choose right from wrong. You are a father. I know you understand what I'm saying."

"I have always found comfort in the structure and traditions of the Church. But Miss Fremont doesn't require it. She trusts an inner guidance. I trust her inner guidance. We both understand this difference between us, and if her approach to her spiritual life doesn't alter mine, then what is the harm?"

"The differences between your approaches, as you call it, already have you doubting and attempting to defy Church law, Professor. And there are other differences between you, are there not? She is younger, of course, but I don't hold that as necessarily a barrier toward marital harmony. But is she conservative like you? A woman of routine? A woman who will find contentment in the home, nurturing her family? She is off studying homeopathy you say, and that she intends to have a career. Where does that leave you? What of future children? Is there anything you have in common, Professor?"

"Besides our love for my son? No. We have little in common." Yet as he said it, he didn't wholly believe it. On the surface it was true, but there lurked the possibility that deep down they agreed on many things. Only—only he feared letting go of what he believed of the world to discover for sure. And she knew that. When he looked into her eyes, he felt understood. Not judged or pitied, but understood. She'd given him time. Two entire years before her patience with him wore thin. Her ultimatum at the ocean this summer had made him face at last not just the truth of his feelings for her but his feelings toward many things. Even his coming here now and speaking to Father McGuinness had as much to do about his coming to terms with himself than an attempt to find a way to marry Missouri. She was the excuse, but this self-evaluation was a long time coming. He didn't know if such an admission would hurt or help his position with the priest, so he remained silent. But he loathed being silent. He'd been clinging to silence, to exclusion, to reticence as a form of protection for over a decade, and he was choking on it. Yet to open up now, completely, could eradicate any chance he had of convincing the priest to condone his marrying Missouri. And he wasn't ready to abandon the Church.

Father asked, "What is that common expression? Opposites attract? Do you believe that?"

"Only when it comes to magnetism."

"Indeed! I recall that demonstration you gave, Professor, at the university. But when it comes to people, truly opposing beliefs cannot sustain a lasting relationship. Differences must be of the complementary sort, not the conflicting. If one of you is thrifty and the other a spendthrift, together you might find balance."

And if one of us clings to routine and tradition because it feels safe, yet is pulled by the free spirit of the other, wondering if maybe there were an entirely different way to see the world?

"The opposing beliefs between you and Miss Fremont, I fear, will not lead to harmony but to you renouncing your faith and losing your way. You have your son to consider, Professor. He is downstairs now being educated, learning about mathematics and grammar and God. You've done well by him so far, giving him the guidance and structure all children need. In a few years, he will need such guidance all the more as he grows and begins to make decisions on his own, and to ask questions of the world. His mother abandoned him. I know you will never do so."

Of course he never would abandon Justin. Routine and tradition had been his salvation these past ten years, and it had provided Justin a secure home. And while he'd delayed this conversation about marriage with Father McGuinness, he had come to him upon his return from the ocean, where Justin had inadvertently learned about his mother's suicide. Not the manner of her death, but the fact that she had caused it. Bradshaw had been concerned Justin would dwell on the thought. Father had offered to speak to Justin, to explain the sin of suicide, but Bradshaw had said no. He didn't want the topic brought up; he simply wanted his teachers aware. He couldn't stomach the idea of Justin being told his mother had committed a mortal sin and was now in Hell. He didn't believe that himself, not anymore. At the ocean, he'd come to terms with what his wife had done, and he'd forgiven her.

He sensed Father McGuinness was studying him.

"If I'm not mistaken," Father said, "you've lost weight."

"My appetite has been sporadic."

"A war wages within you, Professor, and you know it is not a battle I can determine for you. I would like to say 'Go in peace,' but it is more suiting that I say 'Go toward peace.' Find a place of solitude, be still within yourself, and pray. When you cease fighting and accept the right path, your appetite will return."

Chapter Sixteen

He walked. His intention had been to find a quiet spot to do as the priest ordained, but once moving, he felt compelled onward. He paid little attention to where he was, following sidewalks and roads and paths around the city, up and down hills, skirting construction and ditches whenever he came upon them. He allowed himself just two thoughts, two scenarios, and he alternated between them, paying attention to his physical reaction.

The first scenario, life without the Church, enveloped him with a feeling of disorientation akin to his intermittent vertigo. This knotted his gut, tightened his chest, and made him feel as if the road were a tightrope.

The second scenario, life without Missouri, enveloped him in melancholy. His energy vanished, panic vanished, all feeling vanished. His steps turned plodding, and he knew with certainty he became the definition of dour.

One reaction was not sustainable, the other he had lived for a decade. It was familiar. Hated, but familiar. He looked up and around, and saw that he was on Broadway. His legs were taking him home. He arrived at 1204 Gallagher with aching feet and a decision. It was a relief to know what he was going to do. It was like coming home again, to himself, after a terrible bout of insanity. And perhaps that's what it had been.

He'd been insane to think he could traipse through life in blissful uncertainty. For him, uncertainty meant panic. He was a man who required structure to his day, to his thoughts, and to his beliefs. It was enough for him that he set a portion of his mind, the scientific portion, free to explore possibilities, disregarding presumptions, assumptions, and established facts, in order to delve into the future of invention and into his investigations. But to have his entire life be in such a state? No. Impossible. Not just for him, but for his son. Children needed guidance and structure, as the priest said. Someday, Justin might question certain aspects of life, perhaps even his religion, but he would do so from a position of stability. One step at a time. Not hurled off a cliff into an abyss.

He had no appetite, but maybe the priest had forgotten to tell him he would experience a period of mourning upon his decision. He thought of the diamond ring locked away in his wall safe at the office. It would have to stay there for now as a reminder of his moment of giddy madness. The ghost of Vernon Doyle had much to answer for, but all of Seattle would not be seeing Bradshaw dancing down Broadway come Christmas morning.

He opened his gate and marched up to his porch, determined to put his mind fully on his case. He would not crawl in a hole or go back to bed. He retrieved the sample of Mrs. Adkins' sewing and brought it to the kitchen to show Mrs. Prouty. She was in the beginning stages of her holiday preparations. From now until Epiphany, when she wasn't cleaning or decorating, she would be cooking and baking as if their household consisted of an army and their visitors far greater in number. He was always grateful that her skills with foods that were sweet or spiced were far better than her recipes for fresh vegetables, which she tended to boil to death. Anything that required delicacy lost tenderness and texture to her heavy touch, but Bradshaw never had the heart to complain. Today it was to be candy—butterscotch, molasses, and peanut, from the looks of the tins and jars on the table. She loved the season, frequently sang carols as she worked, and glowed as she presented her concoctions. She was now at the sink, washing up the large bowls she used for mixing while humming "I Saw Three Ships."

When Bradshaw asked for her opinion on Mrs. Adkins' handiwork, she wiped her hands, put on her reading spectacles, and held the cuff in the light of the window.

"Pshaw," she said.

"Not good?"

"Well, not very good. Not bad enough for most men to notice, but it's nothing to go boasting about."

"She has a reputation for inseams and cuffs, I'm told. Customers ask for her."

Mrs. Prouty lowered her spectacles to the tip of her nose and looked over them at him. "Male customers?"

"Primarily, yes."

"Well, there you are."

"Where am I?"

"She's offering more than stitching."

"I thought that may be the case, but not in the usual way."

"If there's a new way, I don't care to hear about it."

"I mean, I believe money may not be the medium of exchange. She is known to enjoy going out to restaurants and theaters and the like."

"Where is Mr. Adkins?"

"Often out on a fishing vessel. She has no children."

"Henry will likely get the sordid details. What has this to do with your case? Did she kill the electrician?" She handed him back the cuff, pocketed her spectacles, and returned to her washing.

"She was seen with him at a hotel. She's a suspect, but she claimed she was home alone the night Doyle died."

"You don't sound too keen on her being your killer."

"I'm not keen on anybody. That's the problem."

He sat at the table, staring at the patterns in the oak, unable to summon the energy to move. The sounds of Mrs. Prouty's washing blended with the ticking of the wall clock and the soft simmering of the kettle on the stove.

A steaming mug of Postum appeared before him, and Mrs. Prouty laid a firm hand on his shoulder. "You saw your priest this morning," she said.

He didn't deny it.

"And you didn't get the news you'd hoped for. I'm sorry, Professor, but—"

He silenced her with a look. He did not want to hear her say it was for the best, that it was not meant to be. He was not a proponent of difficulties being blessings in disguise or pain being part of some divine master plan or test of faith. And no, he'd not developed this attitude because of Missouri and her freethinking ways but from his own bitter experience with life. If it differed from the Catholic Church, so be it. Father McGuinness could not blame all of Bradshaw's heretical ideas on Missouri Fremont.

The telephone rang, and he got determinedly to his feet and marched down the hall.

"Professor Bradshaw speaking."

"It's O'Brien. Henry is here at the station. We have a lead on Tycoon Tommy, the second-story man. Meet us at Maddock's office. We're on our way."

He arrived at the Globe Building in time to see a pair of uniformed patrolmen emerge with a handcuffed auburn-haired man in a fine tailored suit. The patrolmen greeted him, and he asked if he might see the back of their prisoner's hands. The cuffs were none too gently gripped, and a pair of freckled hands presented.

Bradshaw lifted his gaze to the prisoner's green eyes, which gleamed with amusement. He thought of Mrs. Doyle lying in Seattle General, fighting for her life. He thought of the look of fear on his son's face when he realized a burglar had been in his room. He was not a proponent of police violence, but he did hope the cuffs hurt.

"Thank you," he said to the patrolmen, and they tugged on the cuffs, moving their prisoner down the street. The police possessed but one patrol wagon, and transporting a mobile prisoner was not a priority for its use. He would be walked the six blocks to the station.

Detective O'Brien and Henry emerged with J. D. Maddock, who was not in cuffs, but was looking distinctly annoyed.

"We're heading down to headquarters for a chat," O'Brien said lightly, but the look he gave Bradshaw told him events had not unfolded as he had hoped.

Maddock didn't argue. He held his mouth tight, practicing his Fifth Amendment right. His drooping eye looked to be plotting another lawsuit.

O'Brien said, "Sorry you missed the excitement, Ben. Henry will give you the scoop." He turned to Maddock and grinned. "Let's catch this car." He sprinted into the road to hop aboard the Madison cable car, forcing Maddock to scramble after him. O'Brien would likely be even more daring than usual as he hopped the cars, weaving them to Third and Yesler, in hopes of arriving at the police station with Maddock's reserve sufficiently rattled.

Bradshaw looked at Henry. "Well?"

"I'll tell you as we walk. You need to go to the Bon." They turned north, eschewing the cars in order to talk more freely. "O'Brien wants you to nail down that shoe salesman. Neither of us can find a thing to back up his claim. We think he's got something against Olafson. He could be bitter against getting passed over for promotion, but if he doesn't recant or continues with the gossip, he'll ruin Olafson and young Billy, too. If O'Brien challenges him, he says it's got to go in his notebook and I take it that means it becomes official police business. Do you want me with you? Help put the scare in him?"

"No. I've got it." He needed no help today finding sufficient anger. "Tell me about what just happened. Did Maddock hire Tycoon Tommy?"

"Hard to tell. I told O'Brien about Tommy and he knew right away who he was, but hadn't known about his habit of writing luring letters so hadn't connected him to the burglary at your house and the Doyle place. I'd no sooner got to the station, when the patrolman on duty near the Considine made his regular report from the call box on Yesler and said he'd just spotted Tommy, dressed dapper as usual, whistling a tune and carrying a package, so O'Brien told the patrolman to follow him, and he did, to Maddock's. That's when O'Brien called you and we set out. I've got one of your microphones on me." Henry patted his coat. "We were gonna try to listen in, but it was all over by the time we got there, Tommy was coming out and he still had the package."

"What was in it?"

They found themselves unable to move, heading upstream against a tide of women intent on shopping, burdened with straggling young children, or baby buggies, or packages too precious to have delivered home. They stepped into the street, preferring to dodge horse droppings and freight wagons.

Henry said, "Daulton's journal was in that package, one of your cigar boxes with melted sulfur, and two lousy sketches that looked like a drunk did 'em. Figure those were Doyle's."

"That's all?"

"What's missing?"

"One more cigar box and several of Doyle's better drawings."

"Maddock let O'Brien search his office, and the patrolman said Tommy and Maddock never left it. It doesn't look like a deal was made. Tommy claims he found the stuff in an alley behind the Considine, and being a businessman who keeps up with the news, he suspected the items might be of some value to Edison's representative."

"And Maddock?"

"He said he smelled a rat and refused to deal with him, declared that's all he had to say, then called his lawyer. The secretary with the sourpuss and tight bun said Tommy refused to let Maddock examine anything without up-front payment, and Maddock refused to buy a pig in a poke."

"What do you think?"

"I don't know. Miss Sourpuss didn't strike me as being the protect-the-boss type. If that's how it went down, then maybe Tommy was acting on his own and it backfired. O'Brien will get that kid who saw Mrs. Prouty's letter being typed to look at Tommy's hands. Not that it'll prove anything in court, but he's all the eyewitness we've got. Tommy was found with stolen property, so O'Brien can charge and hold him. He's at least off the streets until we get this case sorted out."

If they ever got it sorted out. Everything about this case was connected but only tangentially, indirectly, obscurely. Was it that obscurity that kept his instincts from kicking in? They'd unearthed deceit and theft and sordid behavior, but all their efforts had brought them no closer to naming a killer. These thoughts spun depressingly in his mind until Henry grabbed his arm and held fast. Bradshaw pulled himself from his thoughts and realized they'd arrived. They were across the street from the Bon. The windows glowed and twinkled with lights and merchandise, and the constant flow of customers kept the doorman busy.

"Henry, while I do this, find out who Mrs. Adkins has been seeing lately when her husband's out of town. Mrs. Prouty said her stitching didn't justify her reputation. She may be using her job here to meet men who will take her out on the town."

Henry put his nose in the air and said haughtily, "I did not know Mrs. Prouty's good clean mind could harbor such thoughts. I shall start with Mr. Smith, with whom Mrs. Adkins recently shared a room at the Washington."

"Maybe the hotel staff will know his real name. They knew Doyle's."

Henry shrugged and resumed his usual manner. "Maybe it's really Smith this time."

"For your sake, I hope not, there are eleven pages of them in the city directory."

◇◇◇

Mr. Olafson kindly offered his office for Bradshaw's interview of Lewis Latimer, the shoe salesman, but Bradshaw declined.

"He may be more cooperative if I take him outside."

Olafson's eyes grew wide.

"He won't be harmed, but I'm glad to know I look capable of it."

◇◇◇

Lewis Latimer was a mouse of a man. Normally, Bradshaw didn't hold a man's size against him, but in his current mood, and given the insinuations Latimer had been making, he wasn't feeling affable. Latimer was small, beady-eyed, and his greasy black hair produced a powdering of white flakes on the collar of his dark coat.

"This is the busiest season of the year," Latimer complained as he stepped out into the alley where Bradshaw stood waiting. "And it's cold out here. Why can't you say what you have to say inside?"

"Because the nature of our conversation is not suitable for indoors and I didn't want Mr. Olafson to hear."

Latimer scowled and looked away.

"A matter came to light during our recent investigation into Vernon Doyle's death, and it's now time to move forward with prosecution. I'll need names and dates and all the sordid details."

"I don't know what you're talking about, Professor. And what's this got to do with you? Weren't you here just to see about the electricity?"

"You confided in Detective O'Brien that you know Ivar Olafson to be a man of unnatural perversions."

"I did no such thing!"

"Come now, he can't hear us. That's why we're out here. I must warn you that you will be called to testify. It is obviously your moral obligation to protect the children employed by the Bon Marché."

"Now hold on there, I never said I was willing to testify."

"I'm afraid you must. You can't make an accusation like that and not follow through. How can that protect the boys?"

"I didn't make an accusation, I just said Olafson had a fondness for boys. He likes them. He's good to them. He's kind to them. Like Santa Claus."

Bradshaw narrowed his gaze. Billy Creasle had also compared Ivar Olafson to Santa Claus.

"You told Detective O'Brien that Mr. Olafson is smitten with Billy and that he has an unnatural fondness for the boys employed here."

"He mistook me! He's a good man, is Mr. Olafson."

"He did not mistake you. He interviewed you twice, and the second time you were more insistent. You can't retract your remarks now, it's too late. You surely understand the police must act."

"But it's not true! I swear it. It's not true."

"Then why did you say it?"

"The detective mistook me!"

"Let's not go backwards in this conversation, Mr. Latimer. You made the remarks with intent. Are you now telling me you were lying?"

"I didn't want to do it! It was Billy. The window boy. Billy Creasle. No-good little sneak!"

"Did he threaten you?"

"The boy has a bad habit of following people. He knows their private business."

Bradshaw paced, rubbing his jaw, pretending to weigh his options. He stopped before the shoe salesman and leaned down so he could look straight into his beady eyes. "Tell me what Billy asked you to do and why or, so help me, I will make sure what you said about Olafson is said about you and you can bet in this town I'll be believed. I've had a very bad day, and I'm not feeling charitable, so you'd better make it good."

The little man looked horrified. "He didn't tell me why, he didn't even tell me how! He just said I was to try and make the police not trust Olafson. He knows I don't like the man. Passed me over for promotion twice this year alone. Billy said if I did it he'd see I got moved to Men's Wear. I hate shoes. Hated shoes for years."

"You attempted to ruin a man's reputation for a position in Men's Wear?"

"It was that or get fired."

"Fired for what?"

"Benefits! Helped myself to benefits. I took stuff. There, are you happy? I took merchandise without paying. Took these very shoes! And Billy knew it. But they owe me. Passing me up for promotion time and again. Leaving me in Shoes. I hate shoes. I hate feet! They owe me."

"They owe you nothing. You may go now, Mr. Latimer."

The little man ducked his head and reached for the door.

"No. You are going home. You no longer work for the Bon Marché. You will not be getting a final paycheck."

"You've got no right!"

"Leave the shoes."

"What?"

"Leave them."

"What am I supposed to wear home?"

A few minutes later, Bradshaw was alone with Olafson in his office, and he revealed the details of Lewis Latimer's accusation and confession.

"Oh, dear!" was all Olafson could manage to say before dropping into his chair. He shook his head in disbelief that such a thing could be said of him. His eyes welled with tears. "To think!" It took him a moment to compose himself. "My beloved Ingmar and I so wanted children, but we were never blessed with them. And then she passed away. She was the love of my life. When I started over here in America, I had no idea how much happiness I would find with my small charges at the store. They have such hard lives, most of them. Otherwise, why else would they be working? But they are so full of joy and optimism. And potential! I try to give them discipline and kindness and show them that they can be successful in life. Billy. Billy is my favorite, I do admit it. I am fond of him, as if he were my own. I can't believe he would do this to me."

"If it's any comfort, he didn't select the manner in which Latimer was to discredit you."

"No, no. Thank heavens for that. Latimer! I should have fired him years ago. But I pitied the little man."

"He doesn't deserve your pity. I fired him, by the way. I know I didn't have the right, but I sent him home and told him he'd receive no final pay. You have the right to prosecute him for theft." He'd given Latimer's shoes to a hobo in the alley, who'd thanked him with a toothless grin.

"Oh, no. Let him be gone and the matter over. Professor, thank you for handling this situation the way you have. And Detective O'Brien. I simply can't imagine what I would have done if the detective had believed Mr. Latimer."

"You can best thank us by revealing what you know about Billy Creasle that has him so frightened he would want you discredited?"

"I promised him I wouldn't tell."

"You can't help him by protecting him."

"I've tried to guide him. He hasn't a father, you know. And he's very clever. Too ambitious, it's true, and I've struggled to get him to learn to temper his ambition. He can be ruthless. But I don't think he's bad. He works too hard to emulate some of our most successful capitalists. He's trying to grow up too fast."

"What does he not want us to know?"

"He must not have trusted me to remain quiet. I encouraged him to go to the police. Those scoundrels must have broken several laws in their treatment of him. He's just a boy. He wouldn't go, and then poor Mr. Doyle was killed, and he must have feared I would speak. He must have thought to protect himself by discrediting me. You see, he wasn't at home that night as he claimed."

"What scoundrels? Where was he?"

"I have given him a stern lecture already …."

"Where was he?"

"Billy was in a brothel on the night Vernon Doyle died. I was awoken at three in the morning by an unsavory fellow who said I was to come with him or the lad would be a floater. I had to ask what that term meant, and I must tell you, I was appalled. Billy had gotten himself into a very bad pickle and it cost me ten dollars to extricate him. That's more than the boy earns in a week, and he will be paying me back. Please do not ask me to provide the details."

"Do you know how long he'd been in his predicament?"

"I'm not sure. For the better part of an hour, anyway. He went first to another establishment that apparently serves alcohol to boys of just eighteen, to bolster his nerve, he said."

"What time was it when you freed him?"

"By the time I got the mess sorted out, it was nearly five by my timepiece, and it keeps good time. I saw Billy as far as Pike Street, and he said he would go straight home. I don't know if he did. He was upset. The brothel he'd visited, well he said that Vernon Doyle had told him about it. Apparently, Mr. Doyle told Billy the women at this establishment were clean, whatever that is supposed to mean. And the boy was angry at Doyle for what happened to him. There. I've said it. You know his secret, and I pray the boy did not seek out Mr. Doyle after I left him. I went home myself, had breakfast and coffee, then headed to work. I next saw Billy at the store when he shouted for help. He swore to me he went home after I left him and that he had nothing to do with Doyle's death. I believed him. I chose to believe him, and so I said nothing to you or the police."

"You can put your mind to rest on one account, Mr. Olafson. Billy did not kill Vernon Doyle. The coroner is certain Doyle was killed no earlier than two and no later than four."

Olafson slapped a hand to his heart and collapsed in tears of relief. Bradshaw fetched him a glass of water, and when he'd recovered, told him that it was very likely that Billy had nearly started the two show window fires, and that the boy may have used deceptive means to hasten his advancement in the store.

"Oh dear, oh dear, oh dear," was Mr. Olafson's response.

"Is Billy here now?"

"Yes, he's here. Shall I get him?"

"No. Some of his activities have been criminal, some border on criminal, and he needs to be made aware of this. A verbal reprimand is not likely to alter his course."

"You mean to have him arrested?"

"The police will spare him and the store the embarrassment of handcuffs, but I think it best that Detective O'Brien take him down to the station for a formal interview."

Olafson took a ragged breath. "Yes, yes. You're right, of course. Will you tell Billy that I kept my word? That I said nothing until now? I want him to trust me."

"I will tell him."

◇◇◇

Bradshaw was allowed to be present during the interview which took place in one of the city jail cells, a dank, dark space beneath the police station, in the basement of City Hall. The cell smelled sharply of unwashed prisoners and the foulest of bodily emissions. A single bare incandescent bulb cast a harsh light on the filth. A pile of grimy wool blankets sat in one corner. A stack of chamber pots in another. There'd been talk for years of the need for a new jail, and while everyone agreed, no one wanted to pay for it.

O'Brien believed that the boy needed a good fright to set him on the straight and narrow path. Billy was not officially under arrest. He was being held temporarily under suspicion of criminal activity, but he didn't know it, nor had he been told that the police knew he had not killed Vernon Doyle.

The boy stood trembling, unable to pace in the foul space as he was wont to do because O'Brien had forbidden him. He made do by stamping his feet in place and clenching his fists across his chest.

"I didn't kill Mr. Doyle!"

O'Brien asked gruffly, "Then who did?"

"I don't know! I'd tell you if I did, but I don't."

"Where were you that night? Don't bother concocting a lie, we have witnesses."

"Can't trust anybody. Mr. Olafson promised—"

Bradshaw cut him off. "Mr. Olafson only spoke when we demanded it from him. He kept your secret far longer than he should have."

Billy took a deep breath, which was a mistake. He coughed and sputtered. "Don't you ever clean this place?"

"Oh, it's pleasant right now, compared to how it will be later. This is the chain gang's cell. In a few hours, you'll be sharing this charming room with twenty mates who've been working like dogs all day."

The silence was filled with coughs and guttural murmurings from the other cells, horses neighing from somewhere above, and the din of traffic filtering in from the narrow barred window near the ceiling.

"You promise not to tell my mother?"

O'Brien said, "You're in no position to bargain, young man. Care to spend a week here?"

"I was at the Folly. Do you know where that is?"

"Yes, I'm familiar with the establishment and what goes on there. Did you go straight from the store to the Folly?"

"No. I went first to a club." He lifted his chin defiantly. "I had some whiskey. Can't say I liked it."

The whole story emerged, matching closely with what Olafson had told them. Billy admitted to slipping the handkerchief on the floor lamp before he left the Bon just after midnight. Yes, he said, he wanted to get Troy fired so he could have his job, because he thought he'd be better at it.

"Troy's an artist, not a salesman," Billy said, a bit of cockiness creeping into his tone. "He doesn't understand what designs catch the public's eye and make people buy. You've seen my spinning display, Professor. That's the sort of thing that will make a store a success."

O'Brien said, "You sound like all the other criminals we have locked up down here, Billy. They've all got an excuse for breaking the law."

"What law did I break?"

"Attempted arson?"

"I wasn't going to let it get to a full fire."

"It's still arson. And there's theft—"

"I never stole a thing!"

"On at least one occasion, you swapped one item for another in a customer order to get a clerk fired. That's criminal, Billy. Let's get back to the night Doyle died. You placed the handkerchief over the lamp then left the store. What next?"

"Next, I about got killed. Mr. Doyle had told me that at eighteen I should be doing what men do, if you know what I mean, and he told me the Folly was a safe place to go."

"There are no safe places, Billy."

"How was I to know? I went, only they said I cheated them, that I paid with counterfeit money. I swear I didn't, I paid with real cash dollars, I know I did, but a couple thugs came into the room before we, before I, well before, and they tied me up and said they'd find a way for me to earn what I owed. That's when I got really scared and told them to get Mr. Olafson."

Later, after Olafson came to his rescue, Billy didn't go straight home as promised but returned to the Bon and rapped on the window intending to give Mr. Doyle a piece of his mind.

"When Mr. Doyle didn't appear, I put my face to the window to see if he was still there. The window was dark, but I saw him lying on the floor behind the tree. I couldn't see him very well, but he just didn't look right. I was afraid, I mean, he was so still. I thought maybe he'd been drinking, but he never drank on the job. I didn't know what to do, so I went home."

He'd not slept. He took a hot bath and got dressed and went back to the Bon, entering through the employee entrance. He'd hoped to find all was well, but when he checked the window, Doyle was still lying there. He went about his work in other parts of the store, hoping someone would find Doyle, but at seven when nobody had, and the window lights came on, he hurried into the display to remove the handkerchief before it caught fire. It was scorched and he figured he might as well leave it to serve its original purpose, so he dropped it by the light. For the next half hour he fretted, and waited, but nobody ventured near enough the window to spot Doyle. He finally had to shout for help himself.

"Was he still alive when I saw him at five? Could I have saved him then if I'd told someone? Or when I first got to work?"

O'Brien looked at Bradshaw and nodded his head at the door. Together, they left the cell, and O'Brien slammed shut the iron door, leaving Billy standing alone inside, his questions unanswered.

Upstairs in the fresher air of the detective's room, O'Brien said, "I'll leave him in there a night or two."

Bradshaw shuddered. He'd spent the night once in that very cell. Alone. If the experience of being in the foul place locked up with twenty hardened men didn't turn the boy away from a life of deception and immorality, nothing would.

"Jim, he won't be hurt, will he?"

"Nah, I'll have Jailor Corbett keep an eye on him. I want to scare him, not kill him, and not scar him for life."

"What's happening with Maddock and Tycoon Tommy?"

"They're both sticking to their stories. The Ryker boy identified Tommy's hands as being the typist's, but it's not solid evidence. Maddock is looking mighty smug and might be telling the truth."

"If Tommy acted on his own, who did he try to sell the rest of Doyle's drawings to? And the other cigar box he stole from me?"

"He says he found only what he was carrying when we arrested him."

"Have you heard from the hospital?"

"The sisters are hopeful. Mrs. Doyle sat up today, and even ate."

O'Brien was hailed by the desk clerk, and Bradshaw left the station. He stood on the blustery corner, busy with traffic, wondering which direction to turn. He finally chose northwest and the Bailey Building.

In the hall outside his office, he found Henry in an agitated state, pacing, scratching his jaw. From the other side of the closed door came the shrill sound of women's voices raised in argument.

"You don't want to go in there," said Henry. "Not without protection. You got a stick or a club on you?"

The voices swelled, there was a shriek, and something thunked against the door.

"Explanation?"

"Well, the good news is Mrs. Adkins is in the clear, complements of Mrs. Smith, who tracked her husband to the Adkins' apartment building on the night of Vernon Doyle's death, and she can testify the two of them were there all night long."

"That's rather convenient."

"Sometimes, Ben, life throws us a bone. She's got no reason to lie, and there's plenty who will back her up. She hasn't stopped talking about it since it happened. She didn't know which apartment he'd gone into, so she stayed in the lobby until he came down in the morning, at half past six, at which time she commenced to bash him with her umbrella."

"Huh. So there really is a Mr. Smith."

"A battered and bruised Smith now living in a cheap room and begging his wife's forgiveness. Guess what his first name is."

"Not John."

"He thought it was a good trick, signing John Smith in the hotel register."

"Not good enough. So what has all this to do with what's happening in our office?"

The voices had lowered to a menacing hum.

"Well, her husband wasn't the only man besides Doyle who's spent the night at the Washington with Mrs. Adkins and signed his name as John Smith. The hotel staff knew the real names of the other men. All five of them."

"Are you telling me there are six women in there, all of whom have just learned their husbands have cheated on them?"

"Seven. Mrs. Adkins is in there, too."

"Henry!"

"Now, don't blame me. I sent them messages, saying to come see us at their earliest convenience. How was I to know they'd all show up at once?"

The voices exploded into shouts again, and a crash preceded the shattering of glass.

Bradshaw pushed Henry aside and opened the door, ducking as a black-leather heeled shoe came flying toward his head.

"Ouch!" said Henry.

"Enough!" Bellowed Bradshaw, using his most intimidating professorial voice. Seven sets of eyes glared at him from beneath furbelowed hats quivering with fury. One of the women stood upon his desk, her back to the window, another shoe poised and ready to throw. She was a petite woman with an ample figure and elaborately coiffed brown hair under a particularly ugly black hat. She was rather an attractive woman, with rounded cheeks and arched eyebrows. A flush of anger enhanced her beauty. A fact he felt sure added to the fury of the other women in the room. This was Mrs. Adkins, he presumed. He crossed the room, putting himself between Mrs. Adkins and the six angry women.

"Henry, please escort these women downstairs to the Cherry Street Grill, ask for a private room. Ladies, Mr. Pratt will see that you are served your choice of food and drink in exchange for your cooperation. I assure you, any information you relate not pertinent to our case will be kept in the strictest confidence."

"What about her?" shouted one of the women, and a chorus of support rang out.

"Mrs. Adkins will remain here to be questioned by me."

Complaints and vicious names aimed at Mrs. Adkins rose and swelled around him, drowning out his calls for calm, ceasing only when a high-pitched, oscillating whistle had them all clapping their hands over their ears.

Henry grinned, holding up the torpedo siren whistle. "Told you I'd find a use for it. Come on gals, lunch is on the Professor." He tossed Bradshaw the leather shoe that had struck him in the chest.

When they'd gone, Bradshaw gave Mrs. Adkins her shoe then offered a hand to help her down. She sat in his chair and slipped her slender stockinged feet into her shoes like a stage actress knowing she was being watched.

Bradshaw looked about and discovered the broken glass he'd heard belonged to the frame of his private investigator's license, now on the floor, downed by his bronze inkstand which luckily had contained a near-empty bottle of ink. Henry could deal with the mess when he returned. He pulled up a chair and sat before Mrs. Adkins.

"I am aware of your stay at the Washington Hotel with Mr. Vernon Doyle."

"So you know. And your partner knows I was not anywhere near Vernon the night he died, I was with Mr. Smith. If you don't believe me, you can ask his wife." She had a husky yet feminine voice, and he could see she likely had no trouble finding companionship when her husband was out to sea.

"I believe you. I know you did not kill Vernon Doyle, but I need to know everything about his personal life in order to thoroughly investigate his death."

"Why bother? Have you spoken to a single person who's upset he's gone? Not even his wife is distraught, is she? Dowdy little thing. Mrs. Dowdy Doyle, I call her. Not to her face, of course, I might be an immoral woman, but I'm not cruel. As for Vernon Doyle, he was a pig. A slobbering, swaggering pig."

"Then why were you having an affair with him?"

"I wasn't. It was blackmail. He found out I sometimes go out on the town with the men I meet at work, and he said he'd tell Mr. Olafson and get me fired if I didn't go out with him. I went just once and decided I'd rather be fired than do it again."

"He didn't follow through? You still have your job."

"I turned the tables on him. Told him I'd tell his wife what we did. Oh, he kept pestering me, but he didn't dare risk me telling Mrs. Dowdy."

"Do you have any other admirers at the Bon Marché?"

She shrugged and tossed him a small smile that he was sure she had mastered before a mirror. "I have admirers everywhere, Professor. But unlike most women, I don't flirt unless I mean it."

He kept his features impassive. Was she flirting now?

"Are any of your admirers as persistent as Mr. Doyle? Or possessive?"

"You mean did any of my admirers kill Vernon to protect me from him?"

"Or to keep you for himself?"

"I'm afraid I don't stir that sort of passion in men. I'm a plaything, not worth killing for."

"You never know how a man will react when his heart is captured."

She lifted her lovely arched brows and gave him a knowing smile. "Not you, Professor, surely. A buttoned up man like you? Has a woman ever driven you to mad impulses?"

He knew he flushed. He felt the heat rise up his neck as he recalled stepping into that jewelry store and purchasing the glittering gem now locked in his safe, then dashing up to the courthouse on a mission he couldn't fulfill.

"Well, well," she said with a laugh. "I'm glad for you, Professor. Life's awfully short, and I don't think we're meant to live like dullards."

He cleared his throat and tried to settle his flushed face into a dignified countenance. "We're talking about murder, Mrs. Adkins, not some flight of fancy. When a man's life is taken from him, even a man no one appears to miss, society suffers until the killer is brought to justice."

"Oh, pooh. Sometimes a man's death is a blessing. Mrs. Dowdy would agree with me. But you can rest assured none of my admirers did Vernon in. Besides, I never went out with any men employed at the Bon, other than Vernon. You'll have to find another reason why somebody killed him."

"Can you think of any reason someone would kill Mr. Doyle?"

"I make a point of never dwelling on anything ugly, upsetting, or dull. Other than lifting a glass of wine to celebrate his demise, I've not given Vernon Doyle another thought. Now, if we're through here, I'm late for an appointment." She rose with coquettish grace, and licked her lips. "I can see you aren't a man who believes in a casual dalliance, but keep me in mind if whoever put the color in your handsome cheeks doesn't make you happy. I've got medicine for a broken heart."

She left, but a hint of her rose scent remained. He thought of the perfume card he'd found in Doyle's home desk. A man doesn't keep such reminders of a woman he's only casually involved with. The affair might have been brief and unwanted for Mrs. Adkins, but Vernon Doyle wanted more. Had that desire led to his demise? Should he and Henry track down every man in Mrs. Adkins' life? The idea didn't inspire or appeal. Passion could kill, it was true, but removing all the men from Mrs. Adkins' life would necessitate a string of murders, not just one.

With a sigh, Bradshaw got to his feet and crossed to the wall safe. He spun the combination, opened the door, and stared at the small velvet box inside. Why, he wondered, did life have to be so complicated? Here he was, battered by restrictions about love and marriage, and there was Mrs. Adkins, called the foulest of names because she chose to ignore all the rules.

Had Henry been in the safe recently and seen the ring? He'd not mentioned it. Should he lock it elsewhere? He considered doing so but knew it was no good keeping anything from Henry. Not just because Henry was clever, but because Bradshaw would eventually tell him about the ring and his subsequent conversation with Father McGuinness.

He closed the safe and spun the dial, then retrieved his graph of The Case of the Bon Marché from the file cabinet, spreading it upon his desk. With a bold lead pencil, he made a check mark beside Billy Creasle, then Mrs. Adkins.

So there it was. If he didn't consider Mrs. Adkins' many admirers, or any of the other hundred thousand Seattle residents Doyle may have encountered, then only J. D. Maddock remained a suspect. But even if Tycoon Tommy pinned his thievery on Maddock, for Doyle's death there wasn't a shred of evidence against him.

Chapter Seventeen

"The Wright Brothers did it," Bradshaw told Professor Taylor. "I had a wire this morning from Miss Fremont."

"No! They flew? Powered flight, not just gliding?"

They were weaving their way around traffic, through a corridor of grocery and freight wagons on Marion Street, just above Railroad Avenue, heading for the West Seattle ferry. Bradshaw carried a wicker picnic basket. It held not food but his locating device and telegraph batteries.

"At half past ten, eastern time," Bradshaw said. "They got off the ground successfully three more times, then crashed and had to quit. Hold on a minute." He'd spied crates of Justin's favorite winter treat, Japanese oranges, and he crossed to see the name on the grocer's wagon: Louch, Augustine. "Is he on First?"

Taylor agreed. "In the eight hundred block."

The same grocer was also loading a barrel of Italian chestnuts and crates of bananas from New Orleans, which had arrived by way of San Francisco on the Sunset Route.

They continued on, and Taylor said, "They really did it? Controlled flight, steering and landing? Not just a dramatic hurl into the air and a lucky slow plummet to the ground?"

"Real, controlled, powered flight."

Taylor grinned, and so did Bradshaw.

"I'm getting hungry," said Taylor. "All this food, and nothing to eat!" They were surrounded by wagons and hand trucks loaded with onions, garlic, potatoes, cabbage, and squash. Butter, eggs, honey, figs, cranberries. Fresh, iced smelt, flounder, sole, cod, crab, clams, oysters, and Alaskan halibut. Taylor said the abundance was torture, but Bradshaw had no appetite.

At Railroad Avenue, they were stopped by empty, unmoving rail cars.

"There," said Taylor, pointing to a stream of pedestrians disappearing between the cars. They followed, making their way through a narrow gap and across a half dozen tracks, and finally to the terminal of the West Seattle ferry. Bradshaw bought the tickets and they stood on the dock to wait. Out in the bay, the *City of Seattle* ferry trailed a plume of black smoke. Near the wharf, a tug outfitted with cranes and pumps idled. Bradshaw lifted a hand and waved, and a figure aboard waved back. The tug, called the *Beverlee B*, belonged to the Seattle Salvage Company and was positioned to follow the ferry at a safe distance.

Taylor shook his head. "Flight! I can't hardly believe it! Why isn't there a special edition out? Where are the bold headlines?"

"The test wasn't open to the public. Miss Fremont's wire gave few details. I'm sure the news will eventually emerge. They'll want to officially establish their success." As thrilling as the idea of powered flight was, Bradshaw had been more concerned with the rest of Missouri's news. She was now on her way home. His stomach tightened.

"So how goes your case, Bradshaw?" Taylor asked, pulling Bradshaw's thoughts to the elimination of all suspects save Maddock, on whom they had no evidence. He thought of Mrs. Adkins and the six angry wives, and he thought of Billy Creasle, in jail after two nights. O'Brien said the boy was still belligerent.

Bradshaw said, "You said to me the other day that troubled young men could be turned around if caught early enough."

Taylor cocked his head. "I did."

"Is eighteen too old? There's a young man with the ability to go far, but his moral compass is off. Would you consider counseling him?"

"Tell me about him."

"His name is Billy, and he works at the Bon Marché." As the ferry neared, Bradshaw told Taylor all he knew. "I don't know if his father passed away, or abandoned his family, but Mr. Olafson tells me Billy has no father. Olafson has filled that role for the boy to some extent, but he was unaware of Billy's devious behavior until now."

"We do often turn a blind eye to those we care about. Mr. Olafson likely didn't want to see it. The boy's heroes are the giants of industry, I suppose? Rockefeller, Astor, Hill?"

"Indeed. His list also includes giants of department stores. Wanamaker, Macy, and Marshall Field. I don't know their personal histories or how their stores came to be so successful, but I have no doubt Billy Creasle does. He worships success. He has fully embraced the doctrine of the survival of the fittest, and feels no compunction at hastening the process along."

"There are aspects of that doctrine I find downright immoral when applied to mankind."

"Capitalism and morality are often at odds. Oscar Daulton wrote of it in his journal, and it was one of the few things about which I agreed with him."

"Anarchy was certainly not the answer."

"No. But in a country that equates democracy with capitalism, he felt he could never win through the democratic process."

"What did winning mean to him?"

"I don't think he truly knew what he wanted to achieve. He was miserable, he wanted justice, he wanted respect. Oddly enough, I think he wanted kindness."

"Noble goals sought through heinous means. Well, we can't let this young Billy abandon the path of goodness without a fight. With you and me and this Mr. Olafson rallying around him, maybe we can realign his compass. And here is our ride." The ferry had arrived with a blast of her whistle and a whoosh of white foam.

Passengers disembarked, then came a wagon, a hansom carriage, and a farmer leading a cow by a rope.

"I'll act as a buffer," said Taylor, "and keep curious passengers out of your way. While I take measurements, you retrace your steps and recall the conversation that took place. What was the weather like that day?"

"Clear, mild, gusty. The water was mildly choppy. Much like today only much warmer."

"Good. The timing of the tides and currents were different in the spring of '01, but my calculations show this time of day most closely matches them."

Taylor had spoken to the ferry captain by telephone the previous night and asked permission to conduct an experiment by throwing the basket overboard, emphasizing they would not need the boat to slow or stop.

They boarded and positioned themselves at the back deck. Bradshaw opened the picnic basket and removed the cigar box. He inserted a key to set the internal clockworks ticking, then firmly pressed a rubber stopper into the hole, plugging it so that seawater couldn't enter.

Then he mentally transported himself to that May day and his emotional state. He'd woken that day knowing, yet not yet able to prove, that Oscar Daulton had killed three men. He'd gone up to the university and found the proof he needed. When he then went in search of Daulton, he learned that he'd left his dorm room with a picnic basket and was heading to West Seattle with a friend, Artimus Lowe. Bradshaw had instantly understood the terrible danger of that basket. Lowe had been considered a suspect by the police, and if he were to die, if it were to appear he took his own life by leaping off the ferry, then his guilt would be presumed and the murder cases closed. And Daulton would remain free.

There had been no time to waste, nor time to wait for street-cars or hacks. Bradshaw had grabbed his bicycle and made the arduous four-mile ride, over bridges, up lung-bursting hills, and down neck-breaking streets to the waterfront, where he'd abandoned his bicycle to the tangle of traffic and raced on foot to the Marion Street dock and this very ferry, leaping aboard as the boat had pulled away from the dock.

And now, more than two years later, the ferry was pulling away again. Bradshaw recalled the pain in his lungs, the numbness of his limbs as he'd struggled to move along the deck. He retraced his labored steps and Taylor moved with him, his stopwatch ticking, his sextant at the ready in his other hand. If passengers eyed them curiously, Bradshaw didn't notice. He kept his focus inward on his memories.

He sprinted forward, as he had done then, when forcing his strained muscles to move, through the dim interior, and out into the sunshine of the forward deck, then he slumped against the bulkhead. In his mind's eye he saw them, Oscar Daulton and Artimus Lowe, sitting on the ledge of the bulwark, the picnic basket between them. He hadn't had the strength to move or speak. For how long? It had seemed an eternity, but as he panted and his head spun, Artimus Lowe had begun to speak. Yes, it had been very soon after Bradshaw propped himself here that Artimus spoke.

He'd said, "To what do we owe the pleasure of your company, Professor?" And then, "We'll give you a moment to compose yourself. No fun getting old." He'd then launched into a diatribe about Bradshaw's abandoning him in jail, saying that Daulton was a good friend and had saved him from despair.

Lowe had been a law student, long-winded, eloquent, barbed, and clueless to the fact that he was sitting beside a murderer. By the time he was done, Bradshaw had been able to begin to question Daulton. "Tell me about the Philippines," he'd begun. Understanding had flashed in Daulton's eyes. Bradshaw could see the young man knew he was caught, but he still defended himself, talking of the horrors of war and the hypocrisy of a nation that boasted of freedom and equality.

"How did you learn about anarchy?" Bradshaw had asked.

"You say it like it's something bad, Professor. They've got you fooled, too."

"Who has me fooled?"

"The people with power. The newspapers, the people with money, the military, the government. That's how they keep control. They get everyone believing what they're doing is right or noble, for the greater good. Manifest Destiny. A load of lies, Professor." Daulton's words came back clearly now, and Bradshaw listened to them, feeling anguish as he had then for this brilliant young man who truly believed his murderous actions would ultimately bring world peace.

Finally, Bradshaw had asked, "Can I have the basket, Oscar?"

Oscar shook his head and curled his fingers around the basket handle, saying, "You taught me about resistance, Professor. You taught me that unimpeded current has no limits. But resistance draws heat and light. Resistance draws attention. It eventually destroys the circuit path and the current ceases to flow. My fellow anarchists are foolish and vain to boast of their accomplishments. They leave their symbols blatantly as a signature of their work, but bragging only draws resistance. Feeds resistance. Silence is an anarchist's friend." Daulton's eyes had glazed as his vision turned more deeply inward. He'd said reverently, "Silence is his unending line of power." He'd closed his eyes, and thrown himself backwards.

Bradshaw sprang forward, both in memory and now in reality, reaching out to grab hold of Daulton. And then he became Daulton, spinning on his heel and hurling the heavy picnic basket overboard, high into the air. The lid flapped open, dropping the contents—several shiny white-lacquered objects—into the sea. He leaned over the rail and saw they were approaching the landing, a couple hundred yards from shore.

"Could be anywhere from eighty to maybe a hundred sixty feet here," said Taylor. "According to the charts I studied."

Bradshaw looked toward the *Beverlee B*, which had followed the ferry at a safe distance. The captain stepped from the wheelhouse trailing a wire attached to the headphones he wore, and he lifted his hand high in the air, giving Bradshaw a wave. The ship had been outfitted with two of Bradshaw's waterproofed microphones wired to a telephone receiver. The captain's signal meant they were picking up the ticking.

Bradshaw returned the wave then sat heavily on the bulwark as Taylor held up his sextant to take measurements, jovially telling astonished onlookers that they were merely performing a scientific experiment.

"Take this down, Bradshaw," said Taylor, and Bradshaw pulled his notebook from his pocket and recorded Taylor's findings. Once completed, Taylor sat beside him.

"So what was Daulton's plan that day?"

"He was going to shock Lowe with his device, then tip him overboard."

"Why did he throw the basket?"

"Because he knew he was caught and he didn't want the world, his enemies, to get hold of his invention. He tried to go over, too, but I stopped him."

Bradshaw imagined the contents of the picnic basket sinking. Three batteries and the cigar box, the contents encased in molten sulfur, as he believed Daulton's invention to be. He'd painted them all with a heavy coating of shiny white lacquer to make them more visible in the dark depths.

Taylor asked, "Seattle Salvage will keep track of the ticking to see if the currents or tide move them?"

"Yes, and if there is no movement, and it's not down too deep, the divers will go down on Monday." Troy Ruzauskas was scheduled for a test dive with the company on Sunday. Bradshaw had offered him a handsome wage to take part in the search. "Will you join us for the day?"

"I wouldn't miss it. You realize we've had witnesses to our odd little experiment. Someone else might beat us to it."

"I know." He wasn't sure he cared, as long as it was found, and the violence ended.

Chapter Eighteen

At ten and three-quarters, Justin Bradshaw was old enough to know that the white-bearded man in the red suit on whose lap he now sat was employed by the Leader Bargain Store, but he'd insisted on visiting him. Bradshaw had chosen Leader's rather than the Bon Marché because he hadn't wanted to enter the big store today. He was taking the entire day off from work.

"And what is it you want for Christmas? A fine red wagon? A shiny new bicycle? Or are you a musical lad? A piano or violin to make merry?"

A piano? thought Bradshaw. Did this Santa work on commission?

"No, I don't want anything from the store." Justin put a hand to his mouth and whispered. Santa's eyes opened wide and he looked at Bradshaw questioningly. "Well now, I will see what can be done. How about I have the elves make you something special, a model train set, just in case, eh?"

"No, thank you. That's all I want." He stood up and relinquished the jolly man's knee to the next child, a girl of about four, with a massive pink ribbon on top of her head, who didn't seem sure she wanted to sit there.

Bradshaw asked Justin, "What next? The lunch counter?"

"Really? But it's Advent."

"That's true, I hadn't forgotten." While Catholic children didn't fast during the season, they were expected to perform works of penance, just as they did at Lent. The penance usually included giving up some favored treat, such as candy, and the practice made Christmas morning all the sweeter. "You'll have to abstain from soda, but a modest meal at your favorite lunch counter is within the spirit of the season. It's part of the preparation for celebration. As long as we don't overindulge, we get to do anything we want today."

"Anything?"

"Anything that won't put us on Santa's naughty list. Or Mrs. Prouty's."

Bradshaw did his best to make it a jolly day. It was a distinct effort to set aside his worries, but the happiness on his son's face made it worthwhile. He had no appetite and was grateful that Justin didn't seem to notice. As he'd explained to Justin, in keeping with Advent their day was one of preparing for the holiday to come. They purchased a few gifts at the stores to supplement the most treasured gifts they would exchange, those that were homemade. They each dropped a coin in the Salvation Army kettle, and Justin chose the toys, which they purchased and delivered to the Women's Society, which was collecting them for the city's poor children. They strolled through McCarthy's, Spelger & Hurlbut, and every other store but the Bon. They marveled at all the decorations, stopped to listen to music played by musicians on street corners and inside the stores, and they examined all the latest novelties. At Bartell Drugs, Justin became serious and asked his father to wait outside for him, and he emerged with a small brown-paper bundle, which Bradshaw knew not to ask about. Their final purchases were from a farmer off his wagon. They selected a wreath for the front door that Justin would decorate, boughs of greenery, a canvas sack of prickly holly, and a Christmas tree—a Douglas fir—which, they were promised, was freshly cut that very morning. All to be delivered before the end of the day.

By early evening, the tree stood on the back porch in a bucket of water where it would remain until Christmas Eve, being subjected to Mrs. Prouty's vigorous shakings to rid it of spiders. The decorations waited in a box in the corner. Delicate glass

ornaments in a variety of shapes and colors. Handmade ornaments of paper and ribbon that Justin had made, more delicate
ornaments of silk and glass made by Mrs. Prouty and Missouri,
and a few small wooden birds and angels, carved by Henry.

Bradshaw was pleasantly exhausted. A day with a child, no
matter how enjoyable, taxed a man's physical and emotional
energy. After a meal of leftover beef stew, Justin gazed through
his stereoscope at his collection of slides of Christmas scenes
from around the world before settling on the rug before the
hearth to string a popcorn garland for the tree. Bradshaw now
sat gratefully with the evening paper, skimming the articles,
wondering when the Wright brothers' success would be brought
to light. Wondering where Missouri was at this very moment.
Imagining her in a dim compartment in a speeding train. Wishing his thoughts had not gone there. He turned his mind away
and found himself lost in the case of Doyle's death, and there
his thoughts churned dismally for a good long while. It might
be the first case he never solved.

When he became aware of his surroundings again, the fire
had dwindled to embers, and Justin was no longer sprawled on
the floor before it, although the bowl of popcorn and string were
still there. The house was too quiet. It was Mrs. Prouty's night
off, and as usual she was out with her cousin, who was also in
domestic service.

"Justin?" He called, but there was no answer. The boy had
been very quiet the past hour or so. Had they overdone today?
Was he coming down with a cold after all? Bradshaw climbed the
stairs and found Justin's bedroom door ajar, the room alight. He
tapped lightly with his knuckle, then called out again. When no
answer came, he pressed open the door and looked in. Justin's bed
was neatly made, the dark blue spread flat against the mattress,
the pillow fluffed and propped against the wooden headboard.
A glance around revealed an unusually tidy room, the dresser
drawers all closed with nothing protruding, the books on the
shelf neatly arranged, toys stowed in the closed toy box. This
state of order was a holiday gift, the result of a boy skeptical

of the naughty and nice list, yet taking no chances. The closet door stood ajar.

"Justin?"

There was no answer, but Bradshaw felt the boy's presence. He opened the closet fully to find the clothes pressed aside on the wooden rod, revealing the back wall and the little door that accessed a cubby space. This door was also ajar, spilling a meager light.

"Justin?"

There was a short pause before he heard, "Yeah?"

"Can I come in?"

"You won't fit."

Bradshaw got down on his knees and pulled open the door. Justin was inside, seated on pillows, a battery-powered lantern beside him. Bradshaw had squeezed in a few times before, but the boy was right. He had modified the space since Bradshaw last visited and a small shelf with books and gadgets prevented him from doing so now. He could only kneel in the closet looking in. Justin was hiding something, but the look of apprehension on his face didn't indicate it was a gift.

"Best show me and get it over with," he said gently.

"Promise not to get mad?"

"Yes, but I won't promise not to lecture if appropriate."

Justin reached behind his back and pulled out a small dark glass bottle. He sat very still, holding the bottle on his lap. When he looked up, his eyes were filled with anguish.

Bradshaw didn't need to see the label to know what it was. Carbolic acid.

His heart stopped. The closet floor tilted beneath him. He felt as if an ice cold washcloth was draped over his face. He knew he needed to be strong, and wise, but first he knew he needed to breathe. Second, he needed not to vomit.

He managed both, and he heard himself say in a surreally calm voice, "Can you come out so we can talk?"

Justin shook his head. Bradshaw didn't push. This was his son's place of safety, a concept he understood all too well. He moved to a seated position before the door, marginally more comfortable and stable.

Justin's young innocent face was awash with confusion.

"I just wanted to know," he said, "what it was like. It smells sweet."

"Yes, it does. It's rather deceptive, though, because it doesn't taste or feel sweet."

"My mother swallowed it."

Bradshaw felt numb. He'd dreaded this moment for a decade. He'd prayed it would never happen, or if it did, that it would be when Justin was much older, much stronger. He was a boy. A boy shouldn't know such things.

"Yes. I'm very sorry. How did you learn?"

"It wasn't hard to figure out. You always hide the paper on days when there's articles about someone drinking it."

If it were possible for him to feel any worse, he would, but he could spiral no lower.

Justin asked, "Did she think it would cure her?"

"Not cure her, no. But I think she believed it would end her pain. She had the sort of illness, an illness of the mind, that doctors don't yet know how to cure."

"You mean she hoped she would die."

"I'm not sure. She wanted her life to be different. She found the pain unbearable." It had not been a physical pain, but a mental one. She'd been unbalanced, with a desperate and sick need for attention masked by her loveliness and acting ability. Her parents had known and not told him. He'd not understood until too late, until the wedding vows had been said. And then she'd revealed her true self. It had come as a shock to him. He'd courted a charming, lovely girl, but married a monster. Each day, she had grown steadily worse, demanding, threatening, until she discovered she was with child. And then she'd been furious. He'd spent the duration of her pregnancy doing her bidding to keep the child safe, and after the boy was born, and she rejected him, refusing even to hold him, Bradshaw became both mother and father. But these were truths Justin need never know. They weren't publicly known, they were his secrets, shared with only two people in the world, Henry, and Missouri. And they would all take the secrets to their graves.

Justin stared at the bottle, his pale slender hands wrapped around it.

"Is that what you bought at the drug store?"

The boy nodded.

He'd forbidden Mrs. Prouty ever to bring it into the house. It had never occurred to him that Justin would bring it home himself.

"It cost two bits. They'll sell it to anybody." He said the last as if surprised by the fact. "Even me."

"Because it's a household cleaner. It's made from coal tar. It has antiseptic properties. Many people use it diluted for cleaning when there's sickness in the house. Doctors use it in their offices. In very small doses it can even be used in medicine, but too much is very dangerous."

"But it's a poison."

"It can be, yes. There are many things like that. When used one way they are dangerous, used another they are helpful. Most everything can be used to cause harm, that doesn't make everything inherently bad."

"Do you think—I mean, it's one of the Ten Commandments, isn't it? That you're not supposed to do? You're not supposed to kill anyone, not even yourself."

"That's true."

"People who break a commandment, it's not like fibbing or something. If you break one of the commandments, you don't go to heaven. Do you?" His innocent and distraught blue eyes begged for comfort.

"For a very long time, I believed that. I was angry at your mother for leaving us. I didn't understand her illness, and I couldn't forgive her. But over time, I came to realize that life isn't always clearly divided into right and wrong. We are none of us born with perfect minds or bodies and we are often faced with very complicated choices. Your mother was faced with something beyond her ability to control, and she made a mistake. Her death still makes me sad, but I've forgiven her."

"So you think she's in heaven?"

"I do. A life is judged by more than one act. And she did give the world something very special."

Justin gave a half smile. "Me?"

"There is a theory about the conservation of energy. Very simply, energy is never lost. It simply transforms from one state to another. People are a form of energy, and your mother passed on some wonderful energy I see in you. You're musical like her, and artistic. I'm sure she's very proud of you, and she wants you to be happy and live a full life. And do your homework."

Justin rolled his eyes. But his smile grew.

"Can I have the bottle, son?"

Justin handed it over. Bradshaw dug into his pocket and found a quarter. "Now you can buy me a present."

"I already made you something."

"You did? Well, you keep the money then. How about we go downstairs? You can finish stringing popcorn, and I'll read us a story."

"'A Christmas Carol'?"

"Exactly what I was thinking."

With a copy of Scrooge's tale in hand, they headed downstairs to the parlor, and it occurred to Bradshaw he'd spoken the truth of his beliefs to his son, and they echoed not the Catholic Church, but Missouri Fremont.

When Mrs. Prouty arrived home at ten, Bradshaw was dressed to go out.

"Don't wait up," he said, wrapping a woolen scarf around his neck and pressing his hat low. The night was cold and clear and tinged with frost. He walked briskly, hands deep in his pockets. The streetcars were still running, and restaurants and places of entertainment open. He made his way down to the corner of Second and Pike and stood across the street from the Bon Marché, which was still busy with customers taking advantage of the extended hours. The Men's Wear window display was lit up, with the mannequins depicting a jovial holiday morning, but there was no tree in the scene, nor any of Edison's holiday lights. He stood for a quarter hour, willing inspiration to come, imagining someone tapping on the window to be let inside.

Who had it been?

What did he not yet know?

He tried to keep his thoughts focused on the case, but they kept returning home, to Justin's cubby in the closet, and the sight of the carbolic acid in his hands. What if he'd taken a few minutes longer to go in search of his son? What if Justin had decided to taste it?

The thought sent a panic through him, his every nerve screaming, and his brain spiraling. He couldn't stand still, so he began walking again, and then he ran for a few blocks, heedless of looks from others on the street, until a stitch in his side forced him to slow. When a streetcar passed, he hopped aboard and was soon headed north. He stood near the door, clinging to the strap until the end of the line, then walked again, his frenzied stride leading him toward the university. He avoided the lamps that lit the walks, staying in the shadows until he reached the Observatory. When he reached for the handle, he begged to find it unlocked, and nearly whimpered when it swung open for him. He lit the lantern kept near the door and carried it up into the dome. When he had the narrow section of roof open, he collapsed against the wall, head tilted back, praying to the stars in the heavens to instill in him a sense of perspective. There were more stars in the universe than grains of sand on Earth, Taylor had said. But Earth held just one small boy named Justin Bradshaw who was all the world to him.

If only he had someone to talk to. Someone who understood not just his fears for his son, but everything. O'Brien, Henry, Mrs. Prouty, Professor Taylor—he knew they understood him to a point—only Missouri understood him completely. If she were here, she'd word her advice poetically. Something about roses and cycles and how men complicate things that are simple and try to simplify things that are complicated. She would tell him to stop trying to be perfect, stop trying to control everything. To simply be. Relax and be. And listen. In that regard, she would agree with the priest. He should stop struggling to make sense of it all because the noise in his brain was keeping out answers.

And so he sat. He breathed. The stars winked. He shivered and dug his hands deeper into his pockets. Daulton had spent time here, just like this. Alone. So utterly alone, without the support of family nor any close friends, not trusting his teachers or government. Not trusting anyone.

Bradshaw's thoughts and breathing quieted. He allowed the silence to fill him.

And that's when he heard it. The clicking Taylor had mentioned. Not the creaking of the metal dome, but a snapping sound, like static electricity. He focused on the sound as it came and went, tilting his head to try to determine where it was coming from. It was quite near. On hands and knees he slowly crawled toward it until his head hit the base of the telescope.

The sound came from within. He stood to open the door in the pedestal that allowed access to the weights. The snapping sound grew louder, then silenced. All was still within, the chain and weights unmoving. The pedestal was hollow below the level of the weights, but it was too dark to see anything. He lifted the lantern, but the light didn't penetrate far enough. He set the lantern down, knelt beside the opening, and reached inside. His fingertips met the cool base, slightly gritty and dusty. The base was L-shaped. He moved his hand into the lower part of the L, a space a little more than an inch in height. His fingertips met something within that felt hard, smooth, like glass. He was able to move his fingers around the object and carefully pulled out a glass cylinder. When he held it to the lantern light he could see hundreds of thin discs of metal, stacked together.

A closer inspection in better lighting was needed to draw a definite conclusion, but if he wasn't mistaken, what he held was a miniature version of a battery known as a Zamboni pile. He'd built many of them over the years with his students, but never one this small. In Oxford, England, a pair of Zamboni piles had been set up to ring a bell. The movement was small, the clapper making little sound as it was pushed and pulled by the electrostatic force, but it had been moving continuously since it was assembled in 1840, sixty-three years ago. This Zamboni pile, if indeed that's what it was, looked as if tiny holes had been punctured in the thin metal-coated discs. For what purpose? And is that what had produced the irregular static tick? Did the holes trigger some sort of intermittent electric discharge? And what on earth was it doing here, hidden away in the base of the telescope?

He carefully set the battery aside and reached again into the small recess. His fingers met something else, something thinner and made of paper. He pulled the object out to find it was a handmade journal designed to fit the space. He sat propped against the telescope, heart beating rapidly as he opened the journal and immediately recognized Oscar Daulton's writing. It was more hurried than usual, more frantic, as if he were greatly agitated or elated at the time of the writing.

> *They will regret laughing, they will regret ignoring the warnings, as if I didn't matter, as if none of us mattered. How easy it will be to take control and give power to those who deserve it, to each one of us so that we will never be used or abused again. Is this what Man felt when he invented the wheel? Did it make him laugh at how simple it turned out to be? Did it make him swell with pride that he could see what others could not? It is here, I see it in my mind as clearly as if I hold it in my hands, and its power is beyond imagination. Weapons will have no strength to defend against it. It is the ultimate weapon of peace.*

Page after page the writing continued, veiled and threatening. Rantings against the evils of politics and the freedom of anarchy. And the revolution of a weapon. *His weapon*. Daulton gave no specifics as to design, not even to say if the miniature dry pile battery stored with the journal was part of the weapon he wrote of. But one sentence sent a chill through Bradshaw that shook him to his core:

> *At the exhibition, they will get a glimpse of what it can do, but they will never guess the true, magnificent, destructive power of my design. And it's simple. So simple. Like the wheel. Why is everyone else so blind?*

There was no question as to what exhibition Daulton referred. He had participated in just one, the student exhibition in May of 1901. It was there he'd demonstrated his mysterious cigar-box invention that was now on the bottom of Elliott Bay.

The writing was too vague to be theory, too far-fetched, radical, and unproven to hold truth. And yet. Hadn't others had such visions? Didn't Nikola Tesla see his inventions in a flash? Fully formed in his brain down to the last detail before he ever began to sketch them out?

Bradshaw thought of his own deductions as to what was in that cigar box. He'd not experimented with his ideas, true, other than to melt sulfur, but he had thought he was likely correct in deducing the main components. But an ultimate weapon? His speculation had never gone there.

It wasn't possible. Nothing in so small a space as that cigar box could contain anything as powerful as what Daulton intimated. And yet at the exhibition, Bradshaw had seen the silent flame emitted by the device. A flame that should not have been there. What else could the components of that cigar box do that was yet inexplicable? It had been used to kill three individuals in three different circumstances that Daulton had never explained. Could it also be harnessed to kill many? To be a weapon capable of defeating armies?

Crazy. Impossible. And yet, if true, if Daulton's terrible genius had seen what others could not yet attempt to grasp, and he had conceived of an ultimate weapon, and if that was the device he'd displayed at the exhibition and later tossed overboard into Elliott Bay, then, dear God.

Bradshaw had wanted perspective, and he'd found it. All else in his life receded as one fact took precedence. Oscar Daulton's mysterious box lost in Elliott Bay potentially held the secret to a terrible weapon of unthinkable power. And Bradshaw had thrown a ticking locator into the bay, in full view of a ferry full of witnesses.

Chapter Nineteen

Sometime after midnight, clouds had moved in, insulating the city. By the time Bradshaw walked Justin home from Early Mass, delivering him to Mrs. Prouty's care, the frost had melted entirely. He didn't linger, not even for coffee. He hugged his son more fiercely than usual, then headed downtown. A cool wind gusted in from the bay and up the hill, sweeping away smoke from chimneys and buffeting his clothes, reminding him of time spent at the ocean this past summer, of how he'd hunkered against the wind to keep it from his ears, and how Missouri had tossed her arms open wide to embrace it.

More proof of the disparity of their natures he did not need. Yet a part of him had wanted to embrace the wind, to pull off his shoes and splash barefoot in the sandy surf. There was a time in his younger days, before his disastrous marriage, when he'd been far bolder, when a tingle of fear only enhanced the excitement of an adventure. Never foolhardy, he nonetheless had taken calculated risks and enjoyed life. He'd rediscovered some of that thrill through his investigations, but that boldness had yet to enter his personal life. Would it ever?

Out of habit, he joined a small group of pedestrians crossing Second Avenue—there was safety in numbers when traffic was thick, but today being Sunday, it was light—he wondered if the boldness had even abandoned his investigations. Where was the excitement? The drive to find a solution to the case? Last night he'd learned news that terrified him, and this morning?

This morning he was locking away the source of his fear and when done, he wished only to go home and go back to bed. Fear of Daulton's invention falling into the wrong hands, and the idea of Mrs. Prouty fussing over him like he was a sick child, prevented him from doing so.

He'd examined the small glass cylinder he'd found in the telescope base and discovered his initial deduction to be correct. It was a miniature Zamboni pile. Inside he'd found thin paper discs with a zinc coating on one side and manganese peroxide on the other. Typical and ordinary. The perforations in the discs baffled him, and he'd not heard it emit any static sounds. He had no idea if the battery was related in some way to Daulton's ramblings about a weapon or the cigar box out in the bay. But why else hide it away with his secret journal? Surely it had meant something of vital importance to Daulton. But what?

It was a question Bradshaw could not now answer. Nor could he take the time to ponder. Before settling on his wall safe as the temporary repository of last night's finds, he'd been tempted to destroy them. Only a profound abhorrence to the destruction of knowledge prevented him. What if someday the knowledge could be used for good rather than evil? Or if Daulton's vague ramblings held the key to stopping an even greater evil? He didn't want the responsibility of monitoring the world for such a need, but for now, having it all locked away gave him a small measure of—if not peace—then time. Or it would, once he found that wretched box lurking in Elliott Bay.

With Daulton's journal and the miniature dry pile battery safely locked in his safe, Bradshaw continued down to the waterfront where the streets were planked rather than paved because beneath them was not solid ground but a network of pillars and piers and scaffolding, swept twice daily by the tides, and always in need of repair. Railroad Avenue was to him an engineering marvel. One hundred and fifty feet wide and several miles long, the avenue was in reality a timber trestle that supported the weight of a dozen train tracks and their massive burdens, along with horses and freight wagons and constant traffic.

It was just one example of the tenacity, the audacity, of the sort of men who changed the future. Such men could see possibilities where others saw only muck. Everywhere Bradshaw looked in Seattle, he could find examples of such confidence and success. Tides and hills did not defeat such men. And such men did not allow life's cruel events to cower them or cripple them with fears. No. They faced life bravely and made things happen. How did one become such a man? How did one stand in the face of opposition and adversity and find joy in the challenge?

What had O'Brien said? That he didn't want to see Bradshaw become a dour plodding old fool again? Well, neither did he. This roller coaster ride of fears had to end. It was no way to live.

He marched on, his back erect, his jaw set. He counted no fewer than seven languages as he made his way along Railroad Avenue, and identified the flags of six countries flying from masts at the wharves. The counting, he knew even as he did it, was a diversion from an idea. A bold, ridiculous, lunatic idea, that nevertheless took hold of him and would not be silenced.

When he reached the office of the Seattle Salvage Company, his stomach was in knots.

"Your ticking device has not moved," said Captain Donovan, a tall sandy-haired fellow with touches of white at the temples. Donovan owned the company, captained the tug, the *Beverlee B*, and was his company's master diver, although he rarely went down himself anymore. A bout of pneumonia the previous year had left him with scars that impaired his breathing. His office was no shanty like Galloway's, but a modern space in a modern brick building on the avenue, across from the modern, new five-hundred-foot wharf extending out into the harbor. The floors did not shine, as polished flooring wasn't practical to such a business, but they were clean, the plaster walls white, the charts and nautical items well displayed.

"We set a buoy nearby but couldn't mark the exact spot since it's too near the traffic lane. One of my men scooted out there this morning in the launch and listened with one of your portable microphones. Still ticking and gonging like clockwork." He chuckled at his pun. "I'd say it's sitting about sixty feet down."

"Sixty? That shallow?"

"It doesn't seem so shallow when you're down below with sixty feet of water above your head. But yes, sixty is easier on a man than a hundred, and we did expect your ticker to be in much deeper water. Boulder reefs run into the bay in that area. Looks like your ticker box landed on one. It doesn't appear it was carried far by underwater currents or the tide before it settled, so let's hope it's pointing the way to Daulton's box. Your man Ruzauskas is here. He just checked out with our gear. He'd make a fine professional, if he decides to change careers."

"How many men are you able to send down at a time?"

"We've got pumps for four, but not the manpower currently. One of our divers is out sick, and we loaned another to Tacoma Wrecking, so we've got just Charlie and your man for this dive. We agreed on two originally, but I can try to find a third diver. A good man will add another ten dollars a day to your cost."

"I'd like to talk to Troy before I answer that. He's on the dock?"

The captain led him across the train tracks to where the *Beverlee B* and her diving scow were berthed. Troy was there, still in a diving suit but with the helmet and weight belt removed. His youthful face was flushed with the exhilaration of his dive.

Bradshaw looked at Troy and heard himself ask, "How would you feel about me going down with you?"

Troy's eyes opened wide with surprise, and a grin gave away his pleasure. "You? But Professor, you said—"

"And it's still true. I'm terrified. I'm afraid of heights and depths and tight places. I'm light-headed at the thought of it, but I have one thing in my favor, and that's dedication. To your safety and to our mission. I want to find Daulton's box, now more than ever. If after attempting this, I find I can't do it after all, or if I feel I will not be safe for you, I won't go through with it."

"All right. I know you can do it."

The young man was a hopeless optimist. Bradshaw turned to the captain. "What do you say? Can you teach me what I need to know by tomorrow?"

"We can try," said the captain, rubbing a doubtful jaw. "But at the end of the day, it's my call."

"Fair enough. Is sixty feet manageable for a beginner?"

"It is for some beginners. It's a game of nerves, Professor. It's not a matter of you being physically capable, but mentally able. I've never known a man with such fears as yours who's been able to do it. Sometimes men don't even know they have such fears until they put on the gear."

"At least I know what I'm about to be hit with."

"It will kill you or cure you, Professor Bradshaw. One or the other. I've got a list of instructions and safety rules to go over with you, but there's no sense in spending the time if the suit proves too much for you."

"Then get me into it before I change my mind."

The captain called over the crewmen whose job it was to dress and tend to the divers, as well as maintain equipment and serve as deckhands. Six young men of slight build and with dark hair and dark eyes, lined up for orders. Captain Donovan spoke to them in a language that sounded similar to French with hints of Spanish. As he spoke, the men nodded and shot Bradshaw a few curious glances before hurrying off to carry out their orders.

"Portuguese?" Bradshaw asked.

"Yes. The best crew I've ever had. All cousins. I've assigned Berto to you. He's the most experienced and will look after you like you're his firstborn. He speaks fluent English."

From aboard the *Beverlee B*, three of the crew had fetched a crate with a dolly and wheeled it down the dock to Bradshaw. Inside was a diving outfit, all two hundred pounds of it, neatly patched, cleaned, and stored. The pieces were respectfully removed and arranged on deck in the order in which they were to be donned. The care and soberness with which the very unpacking was done sent a high-pitched ringing in Bradshaw's ears from the clenching of his jaw. This was serious business.

One of the crewmen approached him, gave a respectful nod of greeting, and said, "Strip down to trousers and shirtsleeves, Professor."

"Are you Berto?"

"Yes, sir. I am Berto."

"A pleasure to make your acquaintance. Did the captain tell you about my fear of doing this?"

Berto's face grew somber. "Berto will take the utmost care, Professor. Berto will let no harm come to you."

"Thank you, Berto."

And so the bold, the ridiculous, the lunatic idea was put into play. As he removed coat, jacket, tie, and shoes, they were taken from him by the efficient Berto and passed to his cousins.

"Wet your hands up to the wrist, Professor," said Berto, as one of brothers placed a bucket of sudsy water beside him. Bradshaw removed his cuffs and pulled up his sleeves, then dunked his hands into the warm, soapy water.

"Now rub," said Berto, demonstrating. Bradshaw rubbed, getting his hands slick.

Two of the brothers then held the canvas suit for him to step into, and he did so, steadying himself with his forearms on their backs as they eased the suit up around his legs and up over his torso. He was directed to press his hands through the tight wrist holes, and he was glad for the slippery soap lubricating his skin. The suit was soon encasing his chest, the heavy collar on his shoulders and up to his chin. He felt as if his head was poking up through the top of a mason jar. He swallowed hard and breathed through his nose.

Berto asked, "All right, Professor?"

He nodded, not trusting his voice. The air hose and the thick rope of lifeline were unreeled and attached to the suit.

"It's time to sit."

He was directed to a large upturned crate where he sat down. Brass straps, held down by wing nuts, clamped the heavy rubber collar to the breastplate, forming a gasket that would, he was assured, seal out the chill waters of the sound. Lead-soled shoes with brass toes were set with a thud before him, and he slid his encased feet into them. He couldn't easily bend to see, and so he only felt them being secured about his ankles and calves with leather straps.

"Professor," said Captain Donovan. "We usually add the weight belt and helmet just before we move you to the ladder. That way you don't have to bear their weight for so long before going down. But I don't think you're ready for water yet. What say we simply get you into the full costume and let you get the feel of it?"

Bradshaw wondered if the captain could hear the pounding of his heart over the constant din of the waterfront. He could hardly hear anything else. Just the pounding in his ears. He said abruptly, for he was short of breath, "Yes. Good."

They told him to stand, and he was aware of the exchange of looks between the men as they lifted the wide belt with its burden of lead bars and wrapped it around his waist. Attached to the belt were straps, and these were pulled up, crossed in front and back, over the breastplate and over his shoulders. A final belt secured him as if he wore a jockstrap, and indeed, that's what the captain called it.

"The straps keep the weight belt, your diving dress, and your helmet in place once the air begins to pump. You don't want your suit rising up or your helmet trying to lift off your head."

"No, I don't," said Bradshaw. "I don't want that." Nor did he want to see the image now struggling in his imagination. Buckled in securely, the full eighty pounds pulled his shoulders toward his toes. He gladly sat down again when instructed.

"Breathe, Professor. Draw the air through your nose and down to your belly. It's only on land you'll feel the weight. Down below, when we're pumping your suit and helmet full of air, you'll float like a rubber ducky."

Bradshaw tried to chuckle, but it came out as a grunt. He did as instructed, breathing in as deeply as he could.

"The weights are your friends underwater. So don't worry about how they feel now. Got it? The weights help you go down, and they keep you vertical and safe."

He nodded again.

They gave him a minute of breathing freedom before lifting the copper helmet with its three round, glass goggle-eyes, which the men called "lights." In his world, in his mind, "lights" were entirely different things. Lights were bright, glowing things you did not submerge in water. When the captain and his men said "lights," Bradshaw thought "window." The front window had a removable glass plate and it was off now as the helmet was hefted above his head and slowly lowered onto the copper collar, pressing him down further. Immediately, the sounds of the waterfront were stifled, his own breathing accentuated in the enclosed space. His air access was restricted to the small round window. A surge of panic assailed him.

He gasped, "Nah!" or something to that effect, and immediately the helmet was lifted off of him. Nothing was said as he breathed, and licked his lips, and told himself his fear was only in his mind, irrational, controllable.

He nodded, and the helmet was hefted above him again. It came down and he felt the weight on his collarbone as he stared out the small opening, like a drowning man, sucking air from a straw. He forced himself to count to ten, but when he felt them begin to bolt the helmet on, he barked, "Off!" The helmet came off again.

After the third failed attempt, the captain said, "There's no shame in what you're feeling. It's unnatural to strap yourself inside a suit such as this and drop yourself into the sea."

"You're not helping," Bradshaw growled.

The captain laughed. "You want to keep trying?"

"Slowly."

"It's your dime. Ready?"

"Yes, but don't bolt it yet."

"You just tell us when."

This time, when the helmet went on, he bore it for an entire minute. His face grew clammy, his chest tightened, but he endured it. He took a break with the helmet off, and the captain had the weight belt removed, saying it wasn't necessary to have it on while he adjusted to wearing the helmet.

An hour later, he could wear the helmet for minutes at a time with it bolted tightly in place. But only with the little window before him open. As soon as the signal was given to one of the cousins to begin pumping air, and Captain Donovan held the round plate to the opening so that he could twist it tight, Bradshaw felt himself being locked inside, buried alive. Pure terror filled him, and his reflexes slapped the captain's hand away. Several attempts to seal the window sent Bradshaw backwards in progress, and he begged them to take the helmet off.

"You've given it a good effort, Professor. Let me see if I can find another diver for you. That way you'll have three down searching."

Hands on his knees, Bradshaw said nothing, too consumed with breathing and calming himself to even feel the shame of his defeat.

"Captain," said Troy, still clad in diving dress. "Let me talk to him for a minute, huh?"

"All right." He nodded to the crewmen. "Let's get some lunch and let the professor gather his thoughts. Berto? Could you stay with them? I'll bring something back for you."

"Yes, I shall be pleased to stay."

When they'd gone, Berto positioned himself patiently by the air compressor on the scow, and Troy quietly sat beside Bradshaw. Not rushing him. The whistle of an outbound train sounded long and piercing, like a cry from Bradshaw's own soul.

"Professor, why all of a sudden do you feel the need to do this?"

"It's rather complicated."

"It's more than just finding that cigar box, isn't it?"

"Yes, it's more than that."

"Is it about a girl?"

"Yes and no."

"You're trying to prove something to her."

Bradshaw turned to look at Troy, at his innocent young face, at the sympathy, the empathy, in his eyes. He was a young man who'd seen a few of life's hardships but nothing yet so terrible that he'd become bitter or resigned. Or riddled with fears. Bradshaw had, without revealing its potential dangers, explained to him the importance of finding Daulton's box. He'd understood, accepting payment for his diving services, willing to forego any chance at fortune should Bradshaw decide to do nothing with it. To this young man who felt he must financially succeed in order to win the girl he loved, his understanding revealed an unselfish heart.

Bradshaw said honestly, "I need to do this for myself."

Troy nodded solemnly. "If you can do this, overcome your fears and do this, then you can do anything?"

"That's about it."

"Then you'll do it. I'll help you do it. I don't care if we're here until midnight, we'll get you fully into that suit and into the water."

"Whatever I offered you to dive for me, consider it doubled."

"I'll take it. I wouldn't, as a rule, because I don't like to take advantage, but you know I've got my own girl trouble and every dollar helps. Now, how about we sit here and I put the helmet on you, not bolted, and we simply practice opening and closing the face piece?"

By the time the captain and his crew returned from lunch, Bradshaw could tolerate having the face piece closed for several seconds at a time, even with the helmet securely bolted. It was a horrible sensation, to be locked inside the helmet, unable to touch his face, or scratch an itch. It made him feel as if he were choking. The worst of it was being trapped. He could not remove the helmet by himself. He was trapped inside, at the mercy of others, with Berto pumping air to him. But Troy sat patiently, very near, looking at him through the glass, saying encouraging things, and unscrewing the little window at the first sign of Bradshaw's panic.

On his return, Captain Donovan witnessed a demonstration of Bradshaw's progress and said, "Well done, Professor. Take a break, we've brought you two sustenance."

Bradshaw couldn't eat, but he did gratefully drink the water provided while Troy ate, and they sat quietly, watching Captain Donovan and crew go about their work, preparing for tomorrow's dive. The tight bands around Bradshaw's wrists, meant to keep water out and air in, had begun to hurt, but there was nothing he could do about it except shake his hands to keep the blood flowing.

After a quarter hour, the captain called out, "Berto, let's pump some air to the Professor while he learns the signals."

The weight belt was once more strapped securely to Bradshaw, and Berto and one of his cousins boarded the diving scow. Berto stood ready, holding both the air hose and lifeline, while the cousin manned the pump, ready to turn the iron wheel that would supply the air. The captain hunkered down before Bradshaw to peer inside the open window. "Professor, Troy will close this light, and you signal to him if you want it reopened, right? Just breathe normally. There's a valve on the side of the helmet that lets the used air out. When you're down below, that used air will leave as bubbles. If you feel like you're getting too much air, give one tug on the hose. If you need more air, give two tugs. Got it? We're going to practice signaling for awhile, OK?"

"One for less, two for more."

"Those will be the same signals you give below. The helmet can hold about eight gallons of air. About five minutes' worth. Maybe more. The suit holds reserve air, too. As you've noticed, five minutes can be quite a long time. Enough for a man to get himself back to the surface if he's not too deep."

"Is sixty feet too deep?" He glanced up at the city's skyline. Several nearby buildings stood five and six stories tall. About as far up as the divers were going down tomorrow.

"Five minutes of air will get you back to the surface from sixty feet."

"Am I not supposed to come up slowly from depth? I've read about the change in pressure causing problems, pain and sickness." He'd seen the dive charts. At sixty feet he'd be subjected to more than forty pounds per square inch of pressure. Nearly three times more pressure than what one experienced on the surface. With only the air pressure pumped into the helmet to protect him from the crushing force. There were times when scientific knowledge was not his friend.

"We call that the bends, Professor, and yes, coming up more slowly is the usual way to avoid them. But if the air in your helmet stops flowing, that is a bigger problem. If you can stay calm and take the full five minutes to return to the surface, you'll arrive with less pain."

The air began to flow once more into Bradshaw's helmet, and Troy screwed on the faceplate, locking him inside. The cool air smelled of rubber and the sea and all the mingled scents of the waterfront. Troy sat before him, diligently watching him through the glass plate.

How could he tell what was too little air? Or too much? The air flowed down his neck and into the rubber-lined suit, plumping him slightly. He tugged the air hose twice, both to practice signaling to Berto and to see what more air felt like. He soon felt the air pressure increase, a subtle but distinct sensation in his skull and ears, and his suit grew fatter. He tugged the hose once, and the pressure eased.

"OK?" asked Troy, his voice muted by the helmet and air.

Bradshaw nodded.

The rest of the afternoon continued in the same fashion, with Bradshaw spending increasingly longer intervals sealed inside the suit breathing pumped air between lectures from the captain, Berto, Troy, and the diver Charlie. A seasoned veteran, Charlie was built much like Henry, and of similar temperament. He'd only come by to pick up his pay but he stayed to participate in Bradshaw's introduction to the science and practical knowledge of deep-sea diving.

As Bradshaw practiced the tugging signals for both the air hose and the lifeline, which was a rope with a diameter of a nickel that was securely attached by means of an eyelet on the breastplate, he sensed he'd become a project to the Seattle Salvage Company. A goal to accomplish. A prize to be won. He was encouraged in both English and Portuguese, and Berto never once lost patience with him as he practiced the signals. He knew by heart that three slow tugs on the lifeline meant they were to pull him up.

At half past two, the captain announced it was time to get wet. The announcement sent a flash of cold dread through Bradshaw, but Berto looked through the open window of the helmet and said, "Berto is here, Berto will send you air, Berto will pull you up. Then we celebrate."

And Troy's face appeared beside Berto's. "I'll go down first and be waiting for you at the foot of the ladder. I won't leave you alone for a second, OK?"

He watched as Troy's weight belt and helmet were attached, his hoses checked, his faceplate screwed tight. Alfonso, who had been assigned as Troy's tender, signaled a cousin, who was already turning the wheel of a pump, and Troy disappeared down the ladder into the cold water.

And then it was Bradshaw's turn. He clomped to the ladder with his leaden feet, the air hose and lifeline trailing behind him. The captain screwed on the faceplate, locking Bradshaw inside the helmet. Then Bradshaw turned around to descend facing the dock. A few steps down, he stopped, gripping tightly to the rails.

The captain stared soberly through the small window and said with a raised voice to be heard through the helmet, "It will get very loud as soon as your helmet goes under. That's normal. The weight belt will pull you down. That's good. When you get to the foot of the ladder, let go. Berto will slowly lower you down. It's about thirty-five feet to the bottom."

"Thirty-five feet?" He hadn't thought it would be so deep. But of course it made sense. These piers were designed for large ships.

"The tide is coming in. The depth, including the ladder, is now about forty feet. When you get down a few feet, you need to pop your ears. The pressure begins to build quickly. At thirty feet, your ears will get mighty painful if you haven't managed to relieve them. If they pop that deep, it's a terrible loud crack. But don't worry. It's normal. As you descend, yawn and swallow to relieve them and you'll be fine. Troy is down there waiting for you. Are you ready?"

"No."

"In diving, Professor, we take men at their word. Are you ready?"

"Yes."

"Breathe normally. That's the secret to diving. Relax and breathe. I'll give you a rap on the head when it's time to go down."

Bradshaw stared out the little window at the ladder rung, felt hands check his air hose and the lifeline, and then before he was ready, he felt and heard a single hard rap on his helmet.

He didn't give himself time to think. He began slowly chanting. Breathe. Breathe. Breathe. He moved his trembling weighted foot down another rung, and he felt the water rise to his knees. Then another to his thighs, and the air flowed into his helmet and down into his suit, puffing him out. He stepped down again, clumsy both from the weight and his trembling. He stepped down again, breathing, chanting, and the water rose up to his neck, then up to the windows of his helmet, and then with the bravest step of his life, he was under.

A roaring filled his ears, and as he breathed out, musical bubbling joined the roar. He had a flash of memory of another time in which he'd heard such sounds, when he'd been underwater, fighting for his life. He'd been without diving gear, wearing a wool suit purchased at the Bon Marché, in fact, tumbling in churning water. That had been Oscar Daulton's fault, too.

He stayed in place, gripping the ladder, trembling head to toe, until he had his thoughts back under control and could focus again. There was sufficient light to see. He was only a foot under the surface. A tug on the lifeline from Berto asked him if he were OK. He loosened the grip of one hand, groped for the lifeline, tugged his reply, then continued down.

Then his foot groped for the next rung only to learn it was not there. He was out of rungs. It was time to let go.

With a whispered, "Hail Mary," he let go.

The weight belt and lead boots pulled him down slowly and softly, and he felt the gentle, guided resistance of the lifeline, which told him Berto was controlling his descent. The noise distracted him. The roaring quality changed as he felt the pressure in his ears build. He worked his jaw and swallowed hard, trying to relieve the pressure, and just when he thought it might become painful, he heard a crack, just as the captain predicted, and his hearing cleared. Before he could blink, he touched bottom and found himself staring out his little window at Troy's little window. Bubbles flowed up from their helmets.

Troy waved, and Bradshaw waved.

He could hardly believe it. He'd done it. He was down below the surface, breathing, anxious and excited, trembling with nerves, but not panicking. The air kept coming, and he kept breathing. He felt buoyant, literally and figuratively.

Troy tugged on his own lifeline, signaling for tools to be lowered, and Bradshaw tilted back his helmeted head as best he could to gaze up through the greenish water to the light above. Down came two long prods on a rope. They each untied one, and as they planned, Bradshaw followed Troy for a stroll. Walking proved to be easy, a bouncing, almost weightless sensation. As the captain had said, the lead weights were as nothing now. Indeed, he did sense that without them, he would bob to the surface like a cork.

The underwater world was rather murky, a grayish green, and visibility perhaps ten feet. He'd been told this would be the case diving off the dock as the water was churned by traffic and polluted by all manner of effluent best not contemplated, and he didn't. He concentrated on moving carefully, on staying upright, and on breathing, never taking his eyes from Troy who led him on a tour. There wasn't much to see. This portion of the waterfront had been rebuilt just last year, so the timbers were still new and bolstered by twenty to thirty feet of broken concrete, rocks, and sand. He saw not a fish or crab or even seaweed. But he was underwater, beneath Elliott Bay, a place he never believed he would ever willingly be. And he found it, as his students would say, keen. It would be inaccurate to say he felt no apprehension, or that he gave no thought to the gravity of his location and dependence on Berto and his cousins up above who faithfully pumped air to him, but the absence of panic was in itself a triumph.

They stayed down for twenty minutes, practicing with the prods to poke through the mud and gravel. Since neither Daulton's box nor his batteries had been found, it was likely they'd sunk beneath the mud, or slipped between rocks. An experienced diver could feel the difference between a rock and some other material, say a plank of wood, but Bradshaw knew he'd be digging up a lot of rocks.

Troy led Bradshaw back to the ladder and together they sent up the prods. Then Bradshaw signaled with three slow tugs. The air pressure increased, puffing his suit, making him more buoyant, and the thick rope of his lifeline tightened slightly around him as Berto began to reel him in. He felt himself moving easily, slowly, upward. He reached for the ladder, and as soon as he put a foot on the rung and took over the ascent, the full burden of the lead weight resisted him. It was by far the most arduous climb he'd ever made up those few rungs, even with the lifeline pulling firmly, and he was glad of the hands that hauled him up the final steps onto the dock. The helmet and weight belt were quickly removed from him. By the time they had the lead shoes off him, Troy was up, too, and suddenly the serious crew broke out in smiles. Words of congratulations echoed. Troy and Charlie and the crewmen beamed at him, and the captain extended his hand. It felt hot in Bradshaw's ice cold one.

"Be here tomorrow at ten," said the captain. "And you can go down and find your ticker."

"Thank you," said Bradshaw, and the look in the captain's eye told him the depth of those words were understood.

"As much as you likely are in need of stiff drink now, Professor, I must warn you off. A hearty meal and a good night's sleep are best the night before a dive."

The hearty meal he would be denied, it being Friday and a day of abstinence. But when he arrived home, he ate every morsel of fish and vegetables allowed him. To Mrs. Prouty's prying questions about his exhaustion and the red rings about his wrists, he said that he'd been doing water experiments all day. He spent an hour with his son in the parlor before a warm fire, playing a game of chess, which the boy won, and at seven o'clock, announced he was turning in for the night.

"Before me?" asked Justin.

"Before you."

He hauled himself upstairs, wondering who might have witnessed him learning to dive today, and if anyone had made the connection between his diving and the wicker basket he'd tossed from the ferry into the bay. He thought of the ticking cigar box and batteries, reflecting light from their white enamel paint. Two things eased his concern: Tomorrow he and the crew of the *Beverlee B* would stake their claim at the dive site indicated by his ticking locator, and the *Beverlee B* was the only ship equipped with listening devices to hear the ticking.

He managed his evening ablutions with great effort and crawled into bed.

He was too tired to fear what dreams might come, and none came at all.

Chapter Twenty

It was in a torrential downpour that Bradshaw arrived at the office of Seattle Salvage at ten the next morning, along with Professor Taylor, who was astounded to learn about Bradshaw's previous day's adventure and decision to dive that day.

"I'm simply flabbergasted. I'm speechless. I never in a million years would have gambled you'd make the attempt."

"When have you ever been speechless?"

"I am now. I don't know what to say." But he continued on saying, nonetheless, until Bradshaw introduced him to Captain Donovan.

"I appreciate your letting me come along, although I'm not sure I'm needed. Professor Bradshaw's ticking device sounds as if it will lead you directly to the spot. I've brought my own calculations, and I'm curious if they match up with the actual location. I used tide and current charts of two years past, so if there's any discrepancy, perhaps that will help find the treasure we seek."

The downpour continued, thundering on the roof and against the windows.

"If this keeps up, will we postpone the search?" Bradshaw asked.

Captain Donovan grinned. "Not lost your newly found nerve, have you, Professor? No, the rain will let up, and there's not much wind predicted. The search is still on."

The door opened and Troy Ruzauskas entered, draped in a dripping black slicker.

"Cats and dogs!" he said cheerfully. "Morning, Captain, Professor, and—"

Bradshaw said, "Professor Joseph Marion Taylor, this is Troy Ruzauskas, the window dresser from the Bon."

Troy hung his slicker on the coat rack with the others then shook Taylor's hand.

"You're the astronomer and mathematician?"

"Indeed, and you are the talented artist."

Troy shrugged but looked pleased. He turned to Bradshaw, "Professor, could I have a word?"

"Certainly."

Taylor politely invited the captain to look over his calculations, and Bradshaw stepped aside with Troy, who said in a low voice, "Professor, Jake Galloway lost his contract with Edison."

"When did you hear this?"

"Just now. Up on Jackson Street, at Gorham-Revere. They sell diving equipment. I wanted a pair of gloves for today. Charlie told me about them yesterday. Oh, say, I got you a pair, too." He fished in his pocket and pulled out a new pair of black rubber gloves with wrist straps. "They're felt-lined."

"Thank you." Bradshaw knew that the professionals preferred to go barehanded since so often they worked in the dark and found their way around wrecks by touch. But he was no professional and the gloves looked warm.

"Galloway was there. Edison is sending up a submarine from California. The outfit has its own expert divers, so they don't need him. There's a sunken ship in the strait that's got thirty thousand in copper ore no one's yet found that he's asked about, too. Edison, I mean. I think he figures he can pay for the hunt for Daulton's invention and make a big profit to boot."

"Jake must be none too happy."

"No, but he's feeling less angry than vengeful. Other than actual expenses, Maddock paid him nothing. He was supposed to get five grand for searching, and another five if he found the box."

"Sounds like Mr. Maddock is doing business as usual."

"Do you suppose Maddock has heard about you tossing the ticker box in the bay? He might be afraid we'll beat him to Daulton's box."

"That could be what motivated the change."

Troy bit his lip. "Now that Jake is free, Professor, you really should think about hiring him. He's the best around and you'll have better luck with him than with me. Charlie's experienced, but you could swap me out with Jake. You won't be hurting my feelings if you decide to go with him instead."

"I've hired the crew I want, and the divers. I trust you, Troy." As he spoke, he realized how very much he meant what he said. He did trust this young man. When he thought of abandoning him, and Captain Donovan, Berto and the others, for Jake Galloway, his gut gave a small clutch of protest. Jake did have the reputation and experience in his favor, but there was something calculating about him that Bradshaw didn't like. It was probably the fact that Galloway's search for Daulton's box was purely for profit, while Troy seemed to understand the true importance of the invention and the conflicting emotional connection Bradshaw had with it.

"Yes," he said, and repeated, because Troy looked doubtful, "You'll keep me safe, we'll find the treasure we seek, and then you'll paint a stunning depiction of our adventure."

Troy laughed and said he'd be sure of the first, pray for the second, and hope his artistic skills were up to the third. "But if we don't have luck, know my feelings won't be hurt if you later hire Galloway."

As suddenly as the downpour hit earlier, it now ceased, and a streak of sunlight pierced the windows, bringing dancing rainbows. Some might have interpreted the phenomenon as an omen. Bradshaw felt it as a kick to his belly for it meant the weather was clearing as the captain predicted and he would not be given a chance to delay.

They left the office and headed up the soaking pier to the *Beverlee B*, glistening in shifting sunlight. They were greeted by Berto and his cousins with hearty hails in two languages, and

Bradshaw hoped they didn't feel that yesterday had rid him entirely of his fears for he knew he'd need slow handling again today. With each step toward the ship, he recalled the feeling of being trapped in the helmet, and he imagined himself down not forty feet but sixty, or more, in a place not barren of life but teeming with it. What would he do if he saw a shark?

"Professor!" Bradshaw turned to find Jake Galloway sauntering down the dock, looking hale and hearty. Dressed in black from head to toe, a black wool cap and turtleneck sweater, his skin white in stark contrast. The cold had put color at the tip of his nose.

"Good morning, Mr. Galloway."

"It's Jake, Professor."

The crew on deck turned to look and to lift hands in greeting, calling out, "Hey, Jake!" Their admiration of Galloway was evident. He gave them a smiling wave, like a celebrity in their midst.

"Trying to steal our customer, Jake?" called out Captain Donovan. His tone was good-natured, but with an edge.

"No, no. I won't cheat you of a day's pay, Donovan. I'm simply letting the Professor know I'm available, if he has no luck today."

"We might not have your fancy new gear, but we'll get the job done, and we'll get the Professor to within an inch of his coordinates."

"The Professor? You're diving?"

"I am."

"I heard rumors you were here yesterday in diving gear. Has it got to you, too? The itch to find the missing invention?"

"Everyone else has looked. I thought I might give it a try, too."

"No offense, Professor, but you're hardly qualified to go as deep as will be needed after just one lesson."

"I'm not going alone. Troy, as you know, has much experience." He placed a hand on Troy's shoulder. "And Charlie is coming, too." He pointed at Charlie who stood with Berto on the diving scow.

Jake gave Charlie a wave, saying to Bradshaw, "He's good. Does a lot of repair and recovery work. But I'm better at treasure hunts, even he says so, and as I've told you, I know the bottom of Elliott Bay better than anyone. You've got a marker down below, I hear. Performed a reenactment of the famous event of two years ago? With special equipment?"

"That's right."

The captain and crew were silent, not a single one offering details of the special equipment that included a ticking box and underwater microphones.

Galloway said, "It was spring when the box first went overboard, time and tide and currents were different then."

"That's true."

"Your marker's likely too close to shore. The forces are greater this time of year, would have carried it in."

"Do you think so? Well, we'll see. Is it true you lost the Edison contract?"

"That I did, and hell if I'm going to let him find what's rightfully ours with that damned submarine he's bringing up. If you hire me, Professor, all I ask is for a fair share of the profits, when we find the box."

"There might not be a profit," Bradshaw said.

"How's that?"

"If it is found, I will examine it and determine what is to be done. I may choose to do nothing, in which case there will be no profit."

"Come now, that doesn't make any sense. We can sell it to Edison for a small fortune. Even if it turns out to be no good, it doesn't matter. Edison will buy whatever's found. He'll regret Maddock's tearing up my contract when he hears my asking price."

"But I'm not willing to sell it to him or anyone else unless I determine that to be the correct course after examination."

"You mean you might patent the thing yourself?"

"I might do nothing at all, as I've said. I appreciate your offer, but these men have worked hard preparing for today's dive. And I'll stick with them until the job is done. Thank you all the same."

"Well, it was worth a try. Remember I offered when you come up empty-handed. Tomorrow, I'll be back in the hunt.

Fair warning." He slapped his gloved palms together and rubbed them greedily. "Today I'm off to find some copper. I've got that new suit and compressors, and I'm feeling lucky." Jake gave a salute and sauntered away, whistling.

A hand touched Bradshaw's arm. It was Taylor. "Is he going to be trouble?"

"Only if he finds Daulton's box before us."

"What's that about copper?"

"Sunken ship in the strait." Bradshaw explained what Troy had told him about the submarine Edison was bringing up and the copper treasure he was rumored to be after. "Now *that* I hope Galloway finds. It would be considerable compensation for the lost contract."

"He's wrong about the current carrying your marker too close to shore this time of year. The conditions aren't that dissimilar, and I chose the time of day for tossing to match the tide as closely as possible. I'd say he's trying to weaken our confidence."

"He may also fear our damaging his reputation."

"If we find Daulton's box in water he claims to have thoroughly searched? Yes, I see what you mean. Maybe he's not as good as he claims to be."

Bradshaw watched Galloway's retreating figure. "No, I believe his reputation is deserved."

Then why hasn't he found Daulton's box? The thought ricocheted around Bradshaw's brain.

"Professor! Time to cast off!"

Bradshaw heard but didn't move. He felt his senses come alive. For the first time since he'd been summoned to the Bon Marché to investigate Vernon Doyle's death, his intuition kicked in. The hair on the back of his neck tingled. He turned to Taylor.

"Change of plans. I'm not diving today. You go on, and tell Troy and Charlie to concentrate on searching for the batteries."

"But, why? What did I miss?"

"I'll explain later."

Bradshaw hurried away, leaving Taylor to tell Captain Donovan the change in plans. By the time he reached his office in the Bailey Building, the *Beverlee B* and her diving scow were anchored in the bay, and Galloway's steamship was heading northward toward the strait.

When Bradshaw entered, he found that Henry had just gotten dressed and was pressing a ham sandwich with the electric iron.

"There you are," said Henry. "Where'd you disappear to yesterday? Even Mrs. Prouty didn't know where you were. You know, we ought to work out a system. You could be in trouble and I won't know where to begin to look."

"I was diving off the docks."

"And I was robbing a bank."

"Well, today you're robbing a diving company. Have you got any clothes here that will make you look like a longshoreman?" As he asked, Bradshaw strode into the storage room and opened Henry's trunk of clothes. Neatly folded inside were various pieces of clothing that could be assembled to resemble any number of professions, from priest to hobo. Bradshaw pulled out a pair of blue denim trousers and tossed them to Henry.

Henry grinned. "What are you going as?"

"Myself. Hurry. We only have a few hours. And iron me one of those, I'm starving."

Chapter Twenty-one

The secret to a daylight robbery, Bradshaw knew all too well, was in arriving when no one was paying much attention and looking as if one belonged. The waterfront was a hive of activity, and they simply looked like two more men doing business. When they arrived at Galloway's shanty of an office, they knocked and waited. This not only told them if any employee was within, but gave the impression to anyone paying attention that they were honest men paying a call. Behind the protection of Henry's bulk, Bradshaw tried the door and found it locked. Unlike his Capitol Hill neighborhood, theft was rampant on the waterfront.

On their way there, Bradshaw had caught Henry up on all that had happened, from his finding Daulton's hidden journal and the dry stack battery and what they portended, to his diving yesterday, to his instincts now finally working and telling him that Jake Galloway was their man.

"You're telling me Jake Galloway found Daulton's box years ago and has been capitalizing on the hunt for it all this time?"

"That's my belief."

"And you think Galloway was the man Vernon Doyle let into the Bon Marché the night he died?"

"I do."

Henry issued a string of comments worthy of a longshoreman.

"Why is he waiting so long to pretend to find it for Maddock? Son of a gun, now he's lost the contract!"

"He had his reputation to protect. He had to make it look like it was lack of the very latest equipment, the compressors that allow for deeper dives, that kept him from finding it all this time, not his skill."

Now, they went around the shack, to the bayside door. It was also locked, but not bolted, and the latch retreated easily into its casing when Bradshaw slid a slim metal card down the jam under the noise of the Great Northern, rumbling into town with a blast of her whistle.

Once inside, they began a systematic search.

An hour later, having searched every inch of the office, including storage space upstairs, they hadn't found Daulton's box, but they had located in a locked cabinet, which had yielded to Bradshaw's picks, the items missing when Tycoon Tommy was arrested—several of Vernon Doyle's better drawings, and the second cigar box stolen from Bradshaw's basement.

"Evidence!" Henry said.

"We'll leave it all here for Detective O'Brien." Bradshaw stood by the meager warmth of the woodstove, down to a few embers, and looked around.

"It's on his boat," said Henry. "He lives on the boat, makes sense he'd keep it there."

It was a very real possibility. Galloway could hide the box easily on his boat, and it would be convenient to slip into a diving sack when the day came for him to pretend to find it. But it would be much more difficult to search his boat, to somehow lure him off and keep him away. And where aboard would it be? Not where any of his crew could find it. In his bunk? Bradshaw pictured it, that big cigar box, wrapped in burlap, tucked under a pile of clothes, or wedged into a cubby.

The image didn't feel right. He began to pace. How long had Galloway had it? Over two years? Less? Bradshaw imagined he was Galloway, finding the box everyone wanted, making the decision to keep his find a secret because so many were willing to pay him to search for it. He'd already established a respected reputation as a treasure seeker. He could afford to pretend as if this one treasure eluded him, especially if he spread the rumor that it must be in difficult-to-search deep waters. In fact, time had turned Daulton's box into a much more treasured object, and when he did pretend to find it in deep water, his reputation would be that much more enhanced.

Had he intended on keeping it this long? Or had time gotten away from him, and then interest declined, and he figured the box had more value for him if it remained missing. Why not sell it? Had he not known until Maddock came to town that it could possibly be worth so much? And where did Vernon Doyle fit into it? And if he planned to someday claim to have found it, how could he present a box that was dry? That had clearly not spent over two years at the bottom of the bay?

Bradshaw stopped pacing.

Henry said, "What?"

"It's in water. It's underwater. Or it has been most of the time."

"Where?"

"Nearby. Where no one else would be looking. Easy for Galloway to get to. Hard for anyone else."

"For a diver, that could be a million places."

"On the day I met him, he'd been testing out his new suit, right here, off the pier."

"You don't think—under the dock?"

"Why not? It's the most ideal location. Why put it elsewhere? Here he could check on it. Here he could walk with that cocky self-assurance telling clients only he could find it."

"It's not still here, is it? You said he was about to claim to find it."

"Tomorrow, he is."

"Maybe he already brought it up. Maybe he was bringing it up the day you met him? Getting ready to find it for Edison."

"Maybe. Or it could still be down there." Bradshaw looked at the diving suit standing in the corner.

Henry guffawed. "You're not!"

"I am, and you're going to help me. And we need one more man. Someone strong and able to hold his tongue. Do you know anyone like that? In a hurry?"

"As a matter of fact, I do."

A quarter hour later, Henry was back with a toothless giant who mumbled in Russian and reeked of fish and tobacco.

"Meet my friend Gregor. Former lumberjack. We met in a bar in the Klondike."

Bradshaw was told no more, nor did he ask. If Henry trusted Gregor with this misadventure, then so did he.

With Gregor standing by watching with amusement, and Bradshaw giving instructions, Henry helped get him into the diving dress and lead boots. The weight belt wasn't on display, but they found one in the diving storage closet. With a minimal amount of cussing, Henry sorted out the straps and cinched the heavy belt snugly. The copper helmet was secured in place last of all, and Bradshaw stood before Henry and Gregor, unable to fully enjoy their awe at the sight of him because of his rising apprehension.

"Someone's going to see us," said Henry.

Through the small open window—which he still could not think of as a "light"—Bradshaw said, "Act like we belong, like we know what we're doing. This is a diving business, we're simply going for a dive. It happens all the time. But you should both put on one of those slickers with a hood so your faces can't be seen."

Henry donned the slicker, but Gregor was too large for any of them, so he pulled up his coat collar and pulled his hat low over his ears. They tromped out to Galloway's empty slip. A small orderly shed housed a pump, hoses, and ropes, ready for dive training and the testing of equipment. Too restricted in his cumbersome gear to move within the shed, Bradshaw pointed out what they needed and talked Henry and Gregor through the connections and operation. He hadn't been trained yesterday at the pump, but he'd operated similar machines over the years.

Once hooked up, Bradshaw gave Henry a quick lesson in tending and Gregor in pumping.

They practiced, Gregor spinning the wheel providing air, slowing down to provide less when Bradshaw tugged the lifeline and Henry relayed the order to Gregor.

"They usually have several men at the pump, Henry, and fresh men to give breaks at intervals. Once Gregor starts pumping, and I start descending, the resistance will rise and it will get harder and harder for him to turn the wheel, but he won't be able to stop for a rest. You may need to assist him. Pressure must be maintained the entire time. The air can't stop until I return to the surface. Can you do it? Is your back up to it? Be honest. Don't tell me what I want to hear, tell me the truth. My life depends on it."

Henry shook his head.

"You can't do it? It's too much?"

"My back can take it, I'm not sure about my heart. You sure this is a smart thing to do?"

"It's a ridiculous thing to do. But we're doing it. Now, let's review one more time. One tug means give me less air. Two means more. Three means pull me up. Got it?"

"One less. Two more. Three up. And you say if something goes wrong, that helmet holds five minutes' worth?"

"Yes. More than enough to get me back to the surface if you haul me up with the lifeline. The weight holds me down. I can't get up by myself."

"I'll get you back up, you don't worry about that."

"I'm trying not to."

"How much slack do I give you with the rope?"

"I'm not sure. Use your best judgment."

"I'll pretend I'm fishing, casting with weights. I'll lower you until I feel you bobbing up and down in the mud, then reel you in a notch."

It sounded like a fair method to Bradshaw, so he nodded. He donned the gloves Troy had given him. Then it was time. Henry held up the round faceplate.

"Ben, I'm telling you, I can't believe you're doing this."

"Say no more or I'll lose my nerve," he snapped. His heart thudded painfully, and his hands were beginning to shake. "Signal Gregor to begin."

Henry pointed skyward and shouted "Give him air!" Bradshaw heard air moving into the helmet. Down and up. That's all it was. Down and up. Quick. He could do this. He'd done it yesterday.

"Now screw on the plate and I'll start down. You must pay attention to both the air hose and the lifeline. Feed them out as I descend, and keep your hands on them to feel for tugs. Remember the signals?"

"One less, two more, three up."

Then the glass plate was in front of Bradshaw's face, and metal rasped as Henry twisted it on tight. Bradshaw moved to the ladder, turned around, and carefully began to climb down a few rungs. Henry's face appeared at the round window with a lopsided grin, then disappeared as he stood to man the lines. Bradshaw began his slow chant. Breathe, breathe, breathe.

And he began his descent down the ladder.

All went as before, only this time he didn't pause. The cold water enveloped him and bubbled over his helmeted head. He reached the last rung, and he let go. As before, the weights pulled him down while the air in his suit made the movement slow and gentle. But he didn't have Berto's guiding assistance. He had Henry's inexperienced feeding of the lifeline. In turns, the line would slacken then tighten, as Henry tried to get a feel for what it was like to have a diver floating at the other end.

Soon, Bradshaw's ears cracked, but his feet did not touch bottom. When he'd dived with Troy, he was certain his lead boots had touched down soon after his ears cracked, but now he was still descending.

Down, down, down. The water grew murkier and darker. He could see nothing. He heard himself whimper as he continued to drop. What if he never stopped? What if—and then his lead feet struck the bottom. He stood for a moment trembling and resisting the urge to tug frantically on the lifeline. He could breathe. He breathed.

As he stared out the little window into the darkness, the water pressure and bubbles roaring, he forced his thoughts to be analytical. He'd descended far lower than yesterday. Why? What was different here at Galloway Diving? It was an older pier, not one of the newly built. The pilings had not been bolstered with twenty to thirty feet of rocks and sand as the new ones had, and so the water was much deeper. When these piers had been built, sawdust and rocks had been poured around them, but that material had long since rotted and settled. He was down perhaps fifty feet. Or more. It felt like more. Captain Donovan said sixty feet was doable for some beginners. But was it so deep he should come up more slowly than yesterday? He'd not discussed timing at all with Henry, and there was no way he could communicate anything like that with the rope. He and Henry knew only the basic signals.

Pressure sickness was time related, he knew. If he did this quickly, then maybe the depth wouldn't cause a problem. But how was he to find anything in the dark? His eyes were beginning to adjust to the lack of light, but even so, the world beyond his faceplate was as dark as late evening. He could make out only a few shapes near him. A pile stood within arm's reach, looking like a giant black cylinder. He touched it with his gloved fingers, but he had very little sensation through the felted rubber. He removed a glove and tucked it under the weight belt but didn't reach yet for the pile. He dreaded what he might feel. He told himself he would spend ten minutes, no more. If he didn't find it, if Jake hadn't stashed it somewhere a blind novice like him could find, then so be it. Ten minutes, and this would be over.

The air came steadily and well into his helmet and he thanked heaven for Henry and his old Klondike pal Gregor.

He reached out to the pile, swallowing his repulsion at the crusty and slimy things his fingertips met. The old timber was riddled with sea life, with barnacles and seaweed. He moved his hands as high as he could reach, and down as far as he could

without bending over, but he felt nothing that indicated anything was tied or secured there. He could just make out the next
piling, two feet away. He hesitated. He could so easily get lost
down here, and he needed to stay near the ladder. He'd brought
nothing to mark his way.

He leaned back as far as he dared and looked up. The bubbles
from his helmet percolated up through darkness, to greenness,
and then light. The shining light of the world above. The sun
must have broken through the clouds, for the light suddenly
pierced the water, sending down shafts of glittering light that
faded long before reaching him. A small dark shape began to
descend toward him. A mere spot at first. As it dropped, the
shape became oval with stick legs, then it distinguished itself as a
crab. In the green section of water, it grabbed hold of Bradshaw's
lifeline with a big claw and scuttled down it expertly, like a huge
angular spider, until it disappeared in the darkness.

Was it still on the line? Would it soon be crawling over him?
He couldn't shake the line without sending confusing signals
to Henry.

Don't panic, he told himself. It's a crab. You like crab. They're
delicious with butter. No crab in the history of the world has
ever eaten a man.

A fish-shaped shadow zipped past Bradshaw's faceplate, and
his breath caught. He coughed, and gulped air, nearly choking
on the knowledge that should he truly gag, he was trapped
within the helmet.

So do not gag, he demanded. Stop gulping. Breathe through
your nose. He closed his eyes and replayed Troy's instructions and
thought of the young man's delight in being in this godforsaken
place. He wasn't sure how much time had passed, several minutes
at least, before he quelled his panic and was able to turn once
again to the task.

With iron determination, he studied the silhouette of the
pile before him, then turned to look at the next one. About ten
feet above the seabed, an irregular shape disrupted the straight
line of the timber.

He moved toward it, then realized he would need to rise to reach it. To rise, Troy and the others had taught him, he would need more air. He gave the lifeline two firm tugs, and almost immediately he felt the increase in air pressure and his suit puffed. He felt more buoyant, but not light enough yet to move up to inspect the shape on the pile.

He tugged twice again, and this time the increase lifted his lead feet from the seabed. He reached out as he rose, and his cold fingers clasped netting. He moved his hands over the netting, and when he felt the corner of a box, his elation overwhelmed his fear.

Quickly, he moved his fingers to the top of the netting and found where it was attached to the timber with a bolt hook, but it was tied fast. Why hadn't he thought to bring a knife? He put pressure on the bolt hook, pushed and pulled, back and forth, and he felt the bolt give ever so slightly. The timbers of Seattle's older piers, he'd once read, were being eaten by things called teredos and gribbles. He couldn't now recall their size, and he hoped they were too small to feel and that their appetite had sufficiently deteriorated this timber so that he could free the bolt. He grabbed hold of the neck of the netting and gave it swift pull. It didn't come free, but he felt it give, so he tugged again.

And he felt increased air pressure in his helmet. Henry must have interpreted his movement as a signal to send more air. He moved his hand carefully on his lifeline and gave it a single tug, telling Henry less air.

But more air came. Bradshaw's suit began to swell, and he felt himself rising. He signaled again, a single strong tug. But it was no use. Henry must have signaled Gregor to increase the air again, and Bradshaw was floating upward. He grabbed for the net with both hands, kicked his lead feet until he had them braced against the timber, then pulled with all his might. The net came free, and Bradshaw flew backwards in a torrent of bubbles.

From there, it was a blur. Before he'd stopped moving, before he could reach for his lifeline to signal Henry to haul him up, the air pressure increased again, bloating his suit, sending him upwards. He kicked his heavy feet and paddled with his free hand to get himself out from under the dock as the suit continued to fill. Just as he emerged into green water streaked with sunbeams, some magic number was reached, the air pressure in the suit overcame the pressure of the water, and he felt himself being shot upward like a torpedo, up out of the water, into the air, and for a moment he could see the sky, and the skyline of the city, and a tumbling red crab, through his little window. And then he crashed back down into the water, feet first, bobbing up and down like a cork. The relief valve in the helmet hissed like a steaming kettle.

As Henry reeled him in, Bradshaw wondered if he could have avoided his dramatic ascent if he'd simply adjusted the relief valve when he felt the pressure begin to build. Well. Nothing like a moment of insight a minute too late. Henry dragged him up onto the deck. He began to unscrew the faceplate, and the last of the air rushed out. Bradshaw now knew what it felt like to be inside a deflating balloon.

"Ben!" Henry shouted into the opening.

Bradshaw wondered if his own faced looked as pale and frightened as Henry's. He said, "I believe you mixed up the signals."

"I thought you were in trouble. You were down there so long, and you said five minutes was all the air you had if something went wrong, and then I couldn't tell if you were tugging once or twice, and I thought maybe the hose was pinched off."

"It wasn't."

"I can see that."

"Is my hand holding a net?"

"Huh?" Henry tore his gaze away to look at Bradshaw's side. Then he looked back at Bradshaw with a grin that returned color to his face.

Gregor's shadow moved over them. He said something in Russian, and Henry laughed, shaking his head. "He wants to know if he can see that again."

Chapter Twenty-two

Oscar Daulton's mysterious cigar box sat on an oilcloth covering Bradshaw's desk in his locked office in the Bailey Building. The once handsome wood was slimy with decay and exposure to oil, tar, and other pollutants in the seawater of the waterfront.

"Will it explode?" Henry asked.

"No."

"Then what're you waiting for? Open it."

An inspection of the exterior had revealed several cracks, and scars around the lid indicated it had been pried off at least once. With a small chisel, Bradshaw eased the lid up slowly. Small nails squeaked as they let go of the wet wood. Inside was a pile of yellow sulfur crystals. A putrid smell rose up to them.

"Well, you got that part right," said Henry, burying his nose in the crook of his elbow. Henry knew Bradshaw had guessed that Daulton had used sulfur to insulate his invention.

"It's shattered," said Bradshaw. Sulfur was insoluble in water, but it was brittle, and it had reacted chemically with the polluted seawater. The only way to see what the sulfur had insulated was to dump out the contents, so he did. With his letter opener, he carefully searched the foul yellow rubble. He found bits of glass, clumps of mushy paper, a few copper wires, and flecks of metallic paint. Were these remnants of a small Zamboni pile? Possibly. But the materials represented absolutely nothing out of the ordinary. Daulton had designed his invention cheaply, which made it ideal for anarchists. The materials would be fairly easy to come by, and the entire device very easily destroyed if it fell into enemy hands. Even without spending years underwater, the fragility of the sulfur meant attempts at examination would lead to internal damage and destruction.

Had this been the fearful ultimate weapon Daulton had written about? Or a piece of the weapon? A key component? Whatever it had been, it was no longer. Further examination would reveal no more. Still, he sat down and sketched what he'd found, listing materials, noting all he could think of.

Henry said, "So what now?"

Bradshaw rubbed his jaw.

Henry said, "Do we put it back so O'Brien can find it? Does it prove Galloway killed Doyle?"

"No, it doesn't. It proves he cheated a good many people, including Doyle, but it's not evidence of murder. I fear we will never have evidence of murder."

"We should still put it back so Galloway gets caught with it."

"No. We surely had witnesses. Galloway could say a pair of lunatics broke into his business today, used his equipment, and planted the box, then shot one of them into the air in celebration."

Henry laughed. "You should have seen yourself flying up like I don't know what. I thought my heart was going to give out from the shock."

"So did I."

"Someone might tell Galloway what they saw us doing today, Ben, but he can't come forward and claim we took the box from underneath the dock without admitting he had it in the first place."

"That's true."

"So O'Brien gets him for cheating his customers. How long will they lock him up for that? Can we just go to the police and tell them what we found? He doesn't own the underside of that dock."

"He'd probably just have to return his customers' money, maybe pay a fine. And there's a chance he can claim he's got rights to the box. He did find it, and he was under no obligation to report finding it. He could still sell it to Edison. I don't want him profiting from it."

"Then you keep it. He can't do a thing about it without admitting when he found it and how he's been hiding it."

"But if I keep it, then the madness will continue. The search will continue, even without Galloway. I want it to end. No, it must be brought to light. But in just the right way."

"Why not have that window dresser find it? He's a nice kid. You wouldn't have a problem with him making money selling it to Edison, would you? Now that you know no one can use what's left of it to make a weapon? It'd help him win that girl he's sweet on."

"That wouldn't be fair to the other diver or the crew. But you've given me an idea. I can sell the box to Mr. J. D. Maddock, and Captain Donovan and his crew and divers can split Edison's cash bonus."

"That's mighty noble of you."

"Not in the least. I will demand one more thing in exchange."

Henry frowned, then his eyes popped wide open. "Drop the lawsuits!" He got to his feet. "What's the plan?"

Bradshaw also rose and Henry helped him scoop the sulfurous mess into the box and secure the lid. "Now," Bradshaw said, "we smuggle this onto the *Beverlee B.*"

They headed for the waterfront where Henry knew a place at the King Street dock they could buy a ride out to the Seattle Salvage dive site. As they passed by a small drugstore, a gaily decorated window caught Bradshaw's eye, and he stopped. There beneath a glowing tree was a box of Edison's holiday lights. He thought of Galloway's old diving dress, which was now back on display in Galloway's office, dripping onto the wood floor. He thought of the shudder that had run through Galloway when he mentioned having once seen a ghost.

"Henry, wait. I've got something I need to do. You hire the boat and I'll meet up with you. Take this." He handed Henry the burlap sack that held Daulton's box.

Henry glanced at the window display, then back at Bradshaw.
"You're not."
"I am."

Chapter Twenty-three

A few hours later, Professor Bradshaw, Henry, Captain Donovan, Joseph Taylor, Troy, Charlie, and Berto and his five cousins pushed through Miss Finch's tiny office and into the presence of J. D. Maddock himself, who sat behind his desk with a look of annoyed astonishment. There was not an inch of free floor space remaining in the room. Miss Finch stood on tiptoe at the open door.

Captain Donovan set a small open crate on Maddock's desk, and Maddock half rose to peer inside, his nose crinkling. He sat down again, his eyes darting to Bradshaw, then back to the captain, who had been elected to speak.

"I am Captain Donovan of Seattle Salvage and approximately one hour ago, a diver under my command, Mr. Troy Ruzauskas—" Troy lifted a hand in acknowledgement, "—surfaced with this object in his possession." The captain then backtracked, explaining about Bradshaw's reenactment of the toss from the ferry, the white-painted ticking box and batteries, the microphones mounted to the *Beverlee B.* "We easily located the professor's ticking marker sitting at sixty-two feet, and his batteries very nearby. As this was an area previously searched, we speculated the original items must have been hidden or buried. We found Oscar Daulton's batteries buried in about eight inches of mud."

Charlie, near the window, held up the sea-scarred cylindrical batteries that were still strapped tightly together. He passed them forward, and Bradshaw set them on the desk.

"Later, the cigar box now before you was discovered, not sunk in mud, but in a bed of bull kelp, in the same general vicinity." He didn't say right beneath the boat, and Bradshaw knew that Captain Donovan and Professor Taylor were keeping quiet about their suspicions as to how the box suddenly appeared beneath the *Beverlee B* at the dive site. Henry stared at his feet, biting his lip to keep from smiling. As promised, Henry had easily found them a lift out to the dive site. He'd hidden Daulton's bulky cigar box under his jacket, giving him a rather rotund figure which hurt his ego but did the job. Bradshaw had instructed Henry to make his way to the stern, and when no one was looking, toss Daulton's box some distance away. But with so many on board, and being positioned so near the shore in the busy bay, such a moment had not availed itself. So Henry had simply stood at the stern rail, pulled the box from beneath his coat, and let it drop straight down.

Maddock steepled his fingers. "Am I to assume this foul-smelling item is something I want?"

"You've been advertising about it since you arrived in town. It's the invention Oscar Daulton threw overboard the ferry in the spring of '01."

"Do you have proof?"

Bradshaw spoke up. "You have my word. That is the box Oscar Daulton threw from the ferry, and the very one he demonstrated at the student exhibition, and the box which I discussed at length with your employer, Mr. Edison."

Maddock peered in the crate again. "Will somebody please open a window?"

Charlie obliged, letting cold air into the stuffy and increasingly malodorous office.

Bradshaw said, "In exchange for the box, we are asking for a monetary reward of ten thousand, and for the immediate withdrawal of all lawsuits you have pending against me and my patents."

Maddock chuckled. "You do have nerve, Professor. Five thousand, and nothing else."

Bradshaw reached for the crate. "Then we'll take our business elsewhere."

Maddock put a firm hand on the crate. "Now, now, don't be so hasty. This is called negotiation, Professor."

"I will not negotiate. There are plenty of others interested in this device. Mr. Westinghouse is but one."

"Has it been opened?" Maddock asked.

Although Bradshaw believed in justice, and he knew that at times a lesser evil prevented a greater one, up until now the sins he'd committed—deception, breaking into a locked office—had been minor and intended to expose a liar and catch a murderer. But knowingly selling a worthless box to Thomas Edison was pushing the boundaries of what he considered moral.

He said, "If you look closely at the box, you will see it has been cracked. You will also notice if you compare its condition to that of the batteries that it has weathered differently. There are no barnacles growing on it, and it has a slick feel, as if exposed to oil or other contaminants. The box was found where Captain Donovan stated, but its condition shows it has not been there for the entire two years and nearly seven months since it was tossed overboard. I myself opened the box and made an examination of the contents. I found nothing I wished to keep to myself, and it sits before you as complete as it was when found." He knew he lied through the sin of omission, but he couldn't say more without undermining the case. It was enough to ease his conscience.

"Are you absolutely certain this is Oscar Daulton's lost box?"

"I am." At last, a question he could answer in complete honesty.

"What proof have you?"

"None, other than my word."

"Given what you say, and I appreciate your candor, Professor, especially considering what's at stake for you, I would like to have twenty-four hours in which to examine the box and to speak with Mr. Edison."

"No, sir. I'll give you an hour to consult with Mr. Edison, but you will not examine the box until the agreement is made."

"You surprise me, Professor. That's the underhanded method of the thief that tried to sell me stolen goods. This could be worthless."

"Yes, it could. As I said, I found nothing that compelled me to keep it myself. And that's exactly why I'm sure you'll understand my insistence, and why this sale is not contingent on the contents leading to a patentable invention. I can assure you it is Oscar Daulton's lost invention. Its value has yet to be determined. If you decide against our offer, I will take the box elsewhere. Nikola Tesla, for instance, is likely to understand the value far better than I ever could."

"Excuse me a moment." Maddock squeezed through the crowd to get to his secretary's office.

"Miss Finch—" he said.

"Mr. Edison is on the line, sir," she said, a rare smile lighting her face.

Henry nudged Bradshaw. "Hey, she's not so bad when she smiles."

Maddock picked up the candlestick base and carried the telephone out the far door, dragging the cord behind him. His voice carried to them as an indistinct murmur. A moment later, he returned, handing Miss Finch the telephone. He squeezed his way back to his desk and stood, looking directly at Bradshaw.

"Mr. Edison has authorized me to comply with your offer." He held out his hand, but Bradshaw placed not his hand but a document into it. "My attorney has drawn up what we need. Let's get our signatures on paper, shall we?"

Henry let out a whoop and a holler, and the others followed with shouts of joy. A few minutes later, the straightforward document was signed by all parties, and Bradshaw waved toward the door, leading the rambunctious group out. When they got to the lobby he turned to them all, and for the first time in his life said, "Let's go get a drink. The first round's on me."

Chapter Twenty-four

The headline of the *Seattle Post-Intelligencer* the next morning said, DEEP-SEA DIVER HAUNTED BY GHOST OF CHRISTMAS! and the *Seattle Times* ran with DOYLE SPOOKS HIS KILLER!

Bradshaw sat at the kitchen table, reading the articles through squinted eyes and a throbbing headache. He'd lost count after the fourth round, and he couldn't clearly remember coming home, but he was fairly certain Henry was upstairs, feeling even worse. Or perhaps not. It could be that his rapid rise from the depths yesterday was adding to the pounding in his brain, but luckily, he manifested none of the warning signs of the bends.

The headlines came as a surprise and a relief. He'd hoped to put a good scare into Galloway, but he hadn't expected Galloway to confess.

A knock at the back door didn't wait for a reply. The door opened, and in came Detective O'Brien, chipper and alert. He poured himself a mug of coffee from the percolator then helped himself to a seat.

"You look like hell," he said.

"Whiskey."

"Celebrating, eh? Congratulations. I heard about the great find. Is it true Maddock paid ten thousand for it?"

"Yes. And he's dropping the lawsuits."

"You don't say? That is a bonus."

Bradshaw sipped his coffee and tried to open his eyes further. "Well, go on, spill."

"Spill?"

"I know you must have had something to do with Galloway's confession. That had to be you."

"It was a ghost, the papers say. Vernon Doyle's ghost."

"I can't figure out how you did it. Galloway said he kept Daulton's box under the dock where his boat is moored, so how did you get it? How did it get out to the dive site where you had your ticker locator?"

"That's a good question."

"Oh, come on. You must have arranged it. You hired someone to dive at Galloway's dock, right? Then you slipped the box out to the *Beverlee B*? Who'd you hire? Or did you get Henry to do it?"

"No, Henry didn't dive."

"Well, somebody did. I've been getting all sorts of reports of some diver near Galloway's dock yesterday, shooting up into the air like a rocket. Too much air, I'm told. But you can't tell me it wasn't your idea to pose that wet diving suit holding the Edison festoons. Pure genius, Ben. You should have seen Galloway when he came to my office last night to confess. It took me a half hour to get any sense out of him. He kept going on about Ebenezer Scrooge and Doyle's ghost of Christmas present. He kept saying Doyle's ghost had Daulton's box, and that he hadn't meant to kill him."

"What did happen the night Doyle died? The papers didn't have those details."

"Oh, it was an argument gone bad, like we speculated. After Edison came to town and Doyle started bragging he knew more than he actually did about Daulton's invention, Galloway heard about it, and they struck up a secret partnership. Doyle had Galloway convinced that if they found the box, he could figure out how it worked, and they'd get rich. So Galloway one day pretended he'd just found the box—he actually found it a few days after Daulton tossed it overboard—and he showed it to Doyle. They took the lid off and partially removed whatever was inside, but there wasn't anything to see. It had all crumbled and rotted. Doyle said it would simply take him more time. He'd get it figured out."

Had they removed anything from the box? Bradshaw wondered. Or had they dumped the crumbled contents back in as he had done? He thought of Doyle's inadequate drawings.

O'Brien continued. "A little time passed and Galloway got impatient. He began to fear Doyle was full of it. When Edison's man, Maddock, began offering a big reward to anyone who found Daulton's box, Galloway decided he'd go for a sure thing rather than wait for Doyle. He held out for a big offer, and when Doyle learned he'd signed a contract, he got mad. He threatened to tell Maddock that Galloway had already found the box. Galloway was scared he was going to lose the big contract as well as his good reputation. After fretting about it one night, and drinking too much, he went down to the Bon at two in the morning to try to convince Doyle to keep his trap shut. He tapped on the window, and Doyle let him in."

O'Brien didn't need to say more. They'd seen the evidence of what had happened. While they argued, Doyle bared the wire ends down to copper to join two festoons, and Galloway, in a fit of anger and frustration, threw the "Special" knife switch in the cabinet.

The front doorbell rang, and Mrs. Prouty's footsteps tromped down the stairs. A moment later, she came into the kitchen with a red-nosed telegram boy who handed Bradshaw a wire.

"A reply is requested, sir."

Bradshaw silently read the telegram.

WELL DONE. SHALL WE TALK? N. TESLA.

The youth handed Bradshaw an order pad, and he wrote:

THANK YOU. NOTHING TO SAY.

He paid and tipped the youth. When he'd gone, O'Brien said, "Does Mr. Tesla have spies in Seattle?"

"My guess is he knows someone who works for Edison." An image of Miss Finch briefly flickered through his mind.

The hall clock chimed the quarter hour, and O'Brien checked his pocket watch.

"Well, if you're not going to tell me what happened at Galloway diving, I'll be on my way. I'll go set Billy free. He was looking suitably contrite this morning."

Once released, the boy would be on a period of unofficial probation. Two days ago, his mother, Mr. Olafson, and Professor Taylor had met and discussed what was to be done. Apologies were to be made to those he'd maligned. Those who had lost their jobs on his account were to have their positions restored and financial retribution paid, over time, by Billy. His future at the Bon Marché was uncertain and depended on his willingness to accept demotion. They'd all agreed he stood a better chance of reforming as well as eventually succeeding if he were to openly and publicly admit his mistakes. Many men could not face such humiliation. But Billy would have the support and continued guidance of Olafson and Taylor and Bradshaw. There was hope.

"And say, I stopped by the photographer's on my way here. They have a glass plate negative of Mrs. Doyle's photograph of her boys."

"Oh? Did you ask them to develop a new one? I'll cover the cost."

"We'll split it. Make it a Christmas gift to her. After today, the chief has given me the rest of the week off. If no one gets murdered between now and Sunday, I will have a jolly holiday with my family. However you did it, Ben, I thank you for solving the case and saving my Christmas."

Chapter Twenty-five

He stood at the shadowed edge of the station platform where the bright rays of the arc lamps didn't penetrate. The whistle of the approaching train sounded, echoing in the blustery evening, and soon the bright eye of the engine appeared, and the platform under his feet thrummed from the great roaring rumble of the train's arrival.

Passengers emerged from several cars at once into the steam. He scanned the figures, his chest tight, searching. And then he saw her.

Carpet bag in hand, she hopped from the train with a lightness to her step in a sleek red wool jacket and a new slim gray suit that had none of the fashionable bumps and poufs that gave other women deformed figures. For a moment, he lost sight of her among the other passengers, and he rose on his toes to search, catching sight of her again as she slipped through the crowd. Heads turned her way, as they always did. As a would-be suitor had once said of her, she was compelling.

She was no classic beauty, he knew. Her nose was too long, her jaw too stubborn, her hair too short. And yet, the sight of her made him doubt the world's definition of beauty. After all these months apart, he'd known he'd feel anxious, but he'd not anticipated this overwhelming sense of awe. Her gaze swept the crowd as she moved, ignoring all the looks of male adoration, and at last found his. Her smile lit her eyes and quickened her breath and put a tinge of color in her cheeks.

He didn't know his own features were somber until she stepped up to him, her smile transitioning to puzzlement. She searched his eyes, and he heard her questions without her asking them.

He said, "No, no, everyone is fine. Justin is fine and eager to see you."

"And you?"

"Always," he said, but couldn't force a smile. The gravity of the moment enveloped him. "I've got a cab waiting. Do you have more luggage?"

"No, I'm traveling light. Penelope said I could borrow from her."

Penelope was the friend she'd be staying with over the holidays at the Rainier Grand Hotel where she'd once worked as a "hello girl."

He navigated her to the street where the brougham stood waiting. The cabbie took Missouri's bag, opened the door, and she climbed in. Bradshaw followed, sitting beside her in the small, plush space.

"Bit chilly," said the cabbie, handing them a wool blanket with an exaggerated wink. With a tip of his hat, he closed the door. His weight rocked the carriage as he climbed onto his seat, then he snapped the reins, and they were moving. Bradshaw had already given instructions.

Missouri spread the blanket across their laps, and he mumbled a thank-you. He turned, sitting slightly askew on the seat so that he could better see her. The lantern mounted just outside the glass window sent a meager light dancing across her features.

He was at a loss for words.

She shot him a glance then looked down at her gloved hands. "You're angry with me for going to North Carolina. Don't deny it."

"I wasn't about to."

"I am aware that my independent ways are not always agreeable with society, or you, but I am not as insensitive as you imagine. Sarah came with me, she's studying homeopathy, too, and always up for a lark. We roomed at a separate boarding house from Colin Ingersoll. It was all perfectly proper. I didn't include that in my wire because they charge per word and it would have cost a fortune. Besides, I felt you should trust me."

"Should or would?"

"Both."

"I do trust you, which is separate from feeling uncomfortable about your going, and disappointed about your delay coming home. Justin was especially disappointed."

"Oh, I am so sorry about that. I wish you both could have been there. It was so thrilling. They didn't get far with each flight, but just seeing it, knowing what it meant, was incredible."

"Tell me what you saw," he said, not truly wanting to hear just now, but needing time before he spoke. He listened, but it was the music of her familiar voice, so missed, that captured his imagination.

"The fellows from the lifesaving station at the beach helped out, and Colin said they'd been indispensable ever since the Wrights arrived at Kill Devil Hills. Orville Wright set up a camera to capture their attempts, and one of the lifesavers, a Mr. Daniels, was given the task of operating it. The Wrights were very secretive. Luckily, they respect and trust Colin, because I don't believe any other outsiders besides Sarah and me were allowed."

"It hasn't yet made the news here."

She looked at him, her mouth agape. "Are you telling me no one in Seattle yet knows?"

"Not unless they have friends or relatives elsewhere that have wired. I checked the *New York Times* as well, but so far, no mention."

"Well, they didn't invite any reporters. Colin said the Wrights hoped to sell rights to use their machine to the government, but they did intend to make it publicly known they were successful. They wanted it on record that they were the first."

"Go on, how did it happen?"

"You've seen photographs of the Wrights' gliders? The powered machine, which they call the *Flyer*, looks much the same, with the two sets of wings, only there's an engine and propellers." She gestured as she spoke, as if drawing him a moving picture in the air. "The machine was positioned on a flat truck on launch rails. They got the engine running, and the propellers spinning, and then Orville Wright climbed on. He lay flat in the center of the machine. They'd been taking turns, and on this day it was Orville's turn to be first at the controls. The machine was untied, and it launched forward on the rails, and then before we knew it, it was up in the air, sailing over the beach. Oh, it was something to see." She went on, describing the subsequent flights and the elation of all. Her words put him there, so much so, he could see her cheering, Colin Ingersoll beside her, and he found it impossible to believe they didn't turn to each other and embrace.

"Where was Ingersoll," he asked, without intending to, "when the flight occurred?"

"He was running down the beach after the *Flyer* so he could help if it crashed. Sarah and I were on the hill, watching it all. And I was thinking of you, I might add, and Justin, wishing you were there." She looked out the window suddenly and frowned. "We aren't moving. Our driver appears to have parked, but we're not at the hotel."

"I asked him to make a stop on our way so we could talk privately."

The atmosphere changed abruptly from her excited story-telling to silence. The moment had come and he didn't know how to begin. The silence grew and he feared he would make an absolute mess of it.

"You spoke to your priest," she said.

He nodded.

"Since you are not on bended knee nor smothering me in kisses, I'll assume the news is bad. I know how you abhor assumptions, but this one seems a safe bet. Please tell me, Ben. Do you truly believe the restrictions against us are right? Or are you afraid of being ostracized? Afraid of losing something that has always given you structure and comfort?" Her voice held a deep sadness but no condemnation. No plea. As with everything in her life, she wanted truth.

Truth was all he had to give her.

"You challenge everything about me, Missouri. I've never felt more alive, nor more confused, than I am when I'm with you. It's frightening, and exhilarating. Whether or not I can face the ostracism and loss of leaving the Church is something I don't know. We might drive each other mad with our differences. We might find blissful happiness. The point is, we don't know. We can't predict the outcome of our union. I could easily destroy what I love most about you."

"Your boulder and wildflower theory? You see yourself immobile yet crushing my spirit? I am more resilient than you give me credit for, and you are only stone on the outside."

"I fear chaos, Missouri. I fear the collapse of what I know."

"You taught me that nature abhors a vacuum. Something wonderful would move in to take the place of what you give up."

"So says the optimist. Vacuums can lead to explosive destruction before the void is filled."

She harrumphed. "So it's not just the Church putting you through such agonies?"

"I've had to admit to myself that there are tenets of the Church I disagree with. Opposition to marriage to you is just one of them. Still, to intentionally put myself in opposition—it's like jumping off a cliff." Or diving beneath the sea. "I fear most removing from my son's life the institution that has helped me guide him since his birth."

"And his schooling, his religious education, would be undermined by your exclusion from the Church? You would have to send him to another school?"

"No, they would not punish him for my actions, but if he stayed, he would, I fear, face ridicule and judgment." If given the choice, though, he knew Justin would choose ridicule if it meant having Missouri as his mother.

Her mouth trembled. "Well, I suppose I've been rather naive to think we could find a way, but I'm a big believer in trying, as you know." She sounded very near tears. "Look at the Wright brothers," she said, with a tremulous smile. "So many people said they were crazy to try, but they didn't give up, and now they've done it. It will go down in the history books that it was easier for mankind to at last achieve powered flight than it was for you and me to reconcile our differences."

"They had only gravity to overcome."

"And what is gravity compared to your fear of change? No, I'm sorry, that's not fair or even right." She wiped her eyes and took a deep breath. "You don't fear change, you fear discovery. If you were to explore all those things on which I challenge you, you would discover you don't truly believe in all the rules and habits you cling to. You've just admitted as much. But better to live the structured life you know, in sadness and darkness, than find yourself enlightened and lost."

"Yes. I mean, no. I mean I am more comfortable in the familiar, but you're misunderstanding—"

She sat forward and took his hands, and the feel of her touch silenced him. Her fingers were cold, but her palms warm. She brought his hands to her lips and kissed each one.

He said hoarsely, "I'm sorry it took me two years to understand this about myself."

"Please promise me one thing. Promise me you'll think about what you're teaching Justin. I know I'm not yet a parent and have no right to presume what you must feel about the choices you make on his behalf. But I do know you want what's best for him, you want to keep him safe. You want him to grow up to be a good and moral man. Do you also want him guided by his own curiosity and intelligence and moral compass? Or do you want him to always fear stepping away from socially accepted boundaries, even when he doesn't believe in those boundaries? Even when he believes them to be wrong? Life is about change. Humanity and civilization and even religions do change, Ben. But only when we have the courage to follow what we truly believe."

"I believe in you," he said, and he held her face in his palms. He put his lips to hers, and kissed her softly, tasting her warmth, the saltiness of her tears.

"I can't let you go," she whispered.

"Missouri," he said softly, reaching into his pocket and pulling forth the small velvet box. "You've misunderstood me. I'm telling you openly and honestly of my fear, not because I am running away from it, but because I am about to jump in with both feet. Missouri, I'm asking you to marry me."

Author's Note and Acknowledgments

One of the most wonderful things about being an author is meeting the most extraordinary people. I am not a historian, an electrical engineer, a chemist, nor a deep-sea diver. I'm a fiction writer, sitting at my laptop in the comfort of my home, vicariously partaking in exciting and dangerous adventures. Without the help and detail provided by other people, past and present, who lead much more courageous and interesting lives, I'd never be able to craft my stories. Thank you all for following your passions so that I can follow mine.

I am enormously grateful to three historical diving experts: Sid Macken, President, Historical Diving Society, USA; Dr. Sally E. Bauer, President, History of Diving Museum; and Neil Hansen, Diving Instructor, Divers Institute of Technology. For your boldness and generosity, you have my sincere admiration.

I found a wealth of information in historic magazines, my favorite being an in-depth investigative piece by journalist and detective novelist Cleveland Moffett, whose nonfiction book *Careers of Danger and Daring* was published in 1901.

Thanks also to Linda Perry, diver and member of my Monroe Wednesday Writers group. The Wednesday Writers sustain me each week with their amazing voices and emotional support. And, as a member of the Seattle7Writers.org, I am afforded the opportunity to be an active part of the "ecosystem of books" (as one of the founders, Garth Stein, coined it), supporting literacy efforts, libraries, and bookstores with some of the kindest, most talented writers in the Pacific Northwest.

Most of the time, I go in search of historical detail. Once in a while, it finds me. I was given the gift of the real historic figure of Joseph Marion Taylor, the University of Washington's first mathematician, astronomer, and Director of the Observatory, by none other than his great-great grandson, George Myers. I knew the instant I saw Taylor's photo that he was a friend and mentor to Professor Bradshaw. From all accounts, Taylor was a gregarious man and very well liked, as is George, a talented musician with the Nowhere Men and Acoustic Cadence. Taylor built the Observatory on the first university campus downtown and was responsible for purchasing the equipment. When the university moved in 1895 to its current location, and another Observatory was built near what is now known as Denny Hall, Taylor oversaw the transfer of equipment and the copper dome. They are still there today.

My thanks to Ana M. Larson, PhD, Senior Lecturer and Astronomy Director, for giving me a tour of the Observatory, now called the Theodor Jacobsen Observatory. While there, I met Albert Armstrong and Rod Ash of the Seattle Astronomical Society, and they shared insightful historical detail.

Throughout this series, I've kept a certain mysterious invention deliberately vague so that in my story-world it could become something of a legend, much like the death ray machine attributed to Nikola Tesla. The device in my series has never been built. It exists in the mind of my go-to science guy and research engineer Bill Beaty. I like to keep the science real and historically accurate in the Bradshaw books, and Bill's theoretical device, with its silent arc, ventures into science fiction. Besides imagining electrical devices for my villains, Bill also generously reads my manuscripts for me and advises on all the science. In a word, he's awesome.

John Jenkins, president and cofounder of the SPARK Museum of Electrical Invention in Bellingham, Washington, is another of my expert readers and sources of historical electrical detail. His museum remains one of my favorite places to visit, and John's book, *Where Discovery Sparks Imagination*, is always nearby as I write.

Thomas Edison didn't come to Seattle in 1903, but he did visit in 1908 with his wife and daughter, and they stayed at the Rainier Grand Hotel. They went sightseeing, and Edison was particularly curious about the sluice work at the Denny Hill regrade. He was interested in hydroelectric power, but his passion at the time was concrete housing. He was certain concrete would be the construction material of the future. Edison has been described by many as ruthless in his pursuit of dominating the field of electrical invention. While he was among those who propelled technology forward, his aggressive methods and callous disregard for his competitors prevented him from being the hero he's portrayed to be in many history books. It was the way of business in America then, and sadly now. Survival of the fittest, and merciless.

For historical details of the Bon Marché in Seattle, I give thanks to the Sophie Frye Bass Library and staff of the Museum of History and Industry. I did my best bring the Bon back to life as it was in 1903, although I took creative license with some details when digging failed to provide what I wanted to know. Thanks to Marv and Margaret Jahnke for helping me analyze old photos of the Bon Marché.

My gratitude to two early readers, U.S. Foreign Service Officer Michael Mates, a kind man with a brilliant eye for detail and a wealth of historical knowledge, and Anna Lyn Horky, who is blessed with the gift of spotting typos and the ability to turn a gangly sentence into one that flows smoothly. Special thanks to Torie Stratton for proofreading the ARC.

The hunt for a cover photo of early Christmas lights led me to Jerry Ehernberger, founder of the Golden Glow of Christmas Past, and his partner Bob; Thomas Carlisle, longtime member of Golden Glow; and Vicki Stapleton and her husband Tony Fracasso. They all generously spent time photographing their antique Christmas lights in various poses. Poisoned Pen Press' cover designer Rich Siegle considered all the photos and selected one by Vicki and Tony to feature. The lights date from approximately 1912-1920. They differ from the Edison GE outfits of 1903—the sockets are wood, they are battery-powered, and the lamps are round—but they are an excellent visual representation of the early days of Christmas lights.

I'm proud to belong to the family-team of Poisoned Pen Press, who all work hard to ensure that each book they publish is the very best it can be. Special thanks to my fabulous editors Barbara Peters and Annette Rogers.

I'm so very lucky to have the emotional support of family and friends, especially my mom and pop, sisters, and last but not least, my husband and son. I know I say this in every book, but it's true. You make everything in life worthwhile.

To receive a free catalog of Poisoned Pen Press titles, please contact us in one of the following ways:

Phone: 1-800-421-3976
Facsimile: 1-480-949-1707
Email: info@poisonedpenpress.com
Website: www.poisonedpenpress.com

Poisoned Pen Press
6962 E. First Ave. Ste 103
Scottsdale, AZ 85251